P9-CEC-027

CHILL OF FEAR

"Hooper's latest may offer her fans a few shivers on a hot beach." —*Publishers Weekly*

"Kay Hooper has conjured a fine thriller with appealing young ghosts and a suitably evil presence to provide a welcome chill on a hot summer's day."
—*Orlando Sentinel*

"The author draws the reader into the story line and, once there, they can't leave because they want to see what happens next in this thrill-a-minute, chilling, fantastic reading experience." —*Midwest Book Review*

HUNTING FEAR

"A well-told scary story." —*Toronto Sun*

"Hooper's unerring story sense and ability to keep the pages flying can't be denied."
—*Ellery Queen Mystery Magazine*

"Hooper has created another original—*Hunting Fear* sets an intense pace. . . . Work your way through the terror to the triumph . . . and you'll be looking for more Hooper tales to add to your bookshelf."
—Wichita Falls *Times Record News*

"It's vintage Hooper—a suspenseful page-turner."
—Brazosport *Facts*

"Expect plenty of twists and surprises as Kay Hooper gets her series off to a crackerjack start!" —*Aptos Times*

SENSE OF EVIL

"A well-written, entertaining police procedural...
loaded with suspense." —*Midwest Book Review*

"Filled with page-turning suspense."
—*The Sunday Oklahoman*

"*Sense of Evil* will knock your socks off."
—*Rendezvous*

"A master storyteller." —Tami Hoag

STEALING SHADOWS

"A fast-paced, suspenseful plot... The story's
complicated and intriguing twists and turns keep the
reader guessing until the chilling end."
—*Publishers Weekly*

"This definitely puts Ms. Hooper in a league with Tami
Hoag and Iris Johansen and Sandra Brown. Gold 5-star
rating." —*Heartland Critics*

HUNTING RACHEL

"A stirring and evocative thriller."
—*Palo Alto Daily News*

"The pace flies, the suspense never lets up. It's great
reading." —Baton Rouge *Advocate*

"An intriguing book with plenty of strange twists that
will please the reader." —*Rocky Mountain News*

"It passed the 'stay up late to finish it in one night' test." —*The Denver Post*

FINDING LAURA

"You always know you are in for an outstanding read when you pick up a Kay Hooper novel, but in *Finding Laura*, she has created something really special! Simply superb!" —*Romantic Times*

"Hooper keeps the intrigue pleasurably complicated, with gothic touches of suspense and satisfying resolution." —*Publishers Weekly*

"A first-class reading experience." —*Affaire de Coeur*

AFTER CAROLINE

"Harrowing good fun. Readers will shiver and shudder." —*Publishers Weekly*

"Kay Hooper has crafted another solid story to keep readers enthralled until the last page is turned." —*Booklist*

"Kay Hooper comes through with thrills, chills, and plenty of romance, this time with an energetic murder mystery with a clever twist. The suspense is sustained admirably right up to the very end." —*Kirkus Reviews*

BLOOD SINS

A BISHOP/SPECIAL CRIMES UNIT NOVEL

KAY HOOPER

BANTAM BOOKS
NEW YORK

2010 Bantam Books Mass Market Edition

Copyright © 2008 by Kay Hooper

Published in the United States by Bantam Books,
an imprint of The Random House Publishing Group,
a division of Random House, Inc., New York.

Bantam Books and the rooster colophon are registered trademarks
of Random House, Inc.

Originally published in hardcover in the United States by Bantam Books,
an imprint of The Random House Publishing Group,
a division of Random House, Inc., in 2008.

ISBN 978-0-553-58926-9

Cover design by Scott Biel
Cover art © Alan Ayers

Printed in the United States of America

www.bantamdell.com

2 4 6 8 9 7 5 3 1

BLOOD
SINS

Prologue

SENATOR ABE LEMOTT turned from the window and looked at the man in his visitor's chair. "So that's it?"

Bishop said, "The monster who killed your daughter will spend the remainder of his pathetic life screaming at the walls. Whatever was left of his mind got broken there at the end. Or maybe a long time before the end."

"And the monster who pulled his strings? The cold, calculating mind behind him?"

"We never saw him," Bishop answered. "Even though we believe he was close enough to watch. Close enough to affect some of us. Close enough to hunt and capture the... prey... for his pet killer."

LeMott's mouth twisted. "Like feeding a spider."

"Yes."

"So who spun the web?"

"So far we haven't found so much as a trace of evidence that he even exists. Except, of course, that we know he does."

"What else do you know?"

"I believe I know where to start looking for him."

Senator LeMott smiled. "That's good, Bishop. That's very good indeed."

One

SARAH KEPT to what little shadows the winter-bare trees provided as she worked her way through the forest that separated the Compound from the road. The full moon made this night an uneasy one for stealth, but she hadn't been given much choice in the matter. Waiting even another day was potentially far more dangerous than acting, so—

She sensed more than heard a sound and froze, her arms tightening around the sleeping child.

"It's just me." Bailey appeared to step literally out of the darkness not ten feet away.

"Are you early or am I late?" Sarah kept her voice as low as the other woman's had been.

"Six of one." Bailey shrugged and crossed the space between them. "Is she out?"

Nodding, Sarah relinquished the little girl, who was warmly dressed to protect her against the January chill. "She should sleep another couple of hours at least. Long enough."

"And you're sure about her? Because we can't keep doing this. It wasn't part of the plan, and it's too dangerous. Sooner or later, he's going to figure it out."

"That's what I'm trying to prevent. Or at least delay."

"It's not your job, Sarah. Not the reason you're here."

"Isn't it? He's getting better at choosing latents. Better at finding them and convincing them to join him. Better than we've been." Sarah was aware of a niggling unease that was growing rather than diminishing. "Speaking of, are we covered?"

"Of course. My shield's enclosing all three of us."

"What about more-conventional protection?"

"Galen's got my back. As usual. But once we leave, you're on your own again."

"I'm not worried about me."

"Sarah—"

"She could be the one, Bailey."

"She's six years old."

"All the more reason. Without the defenses we can teach her, she's vulnerable as hell, especially to someone bent on using her as a weapon."

Bailey shifted the slight weight of the child and sighed. "Look, are you sure you haven't been . . . influenced . . . by what this guy is preaching? All that prophecy stuff?"

"We believe in prophecy stuff," Sarah reminded her.

"Not the kind he preaches."

Sarah shook her head. "Don't worry, I'm not a convert. It's all I can do to keep up the facade of a loyal member of the flock."

"Many more defections and kids disappearing, and that's going to get a lot harder."

"Harder than this?" Sarah reached out a hand and lightly touched the child's long blond hair. "Her mother is gone. And I haven't seen her father in two days."

Bailey's mouth tightened. "You didn't include that in the report."

"I wasn't sure until today. But he's gone. I think he was beginning to ask too many questions. He didn't believe his wife would have just run away, not without their daughter."

"He was right about that."

Sarah had been expecting it, but the news was still an unwelcome shock. "She was found?"

"A few miles downriver. And she'd been in the water awhile, probably since the night she disappeared. No way to determine cause of death."

Bailey didn't have to explain that further.

"Are the police going to come around asking questions?" Sarah asked.

"They have to. Ellen Hodges was known to be a member of the church, and the last time she was seen it was in the company of other church members. Her parents know that, and they're more than willing to point the police in this direction. So if the good Reverend Samuel can't produce Ellen's husband or her child, he's going to have a lot of explaining to do."

Sarah managed a hollow laugh, even as the sense of unease she felt grew stronger. "You're assuming the cops who come here won't be church members or paid-off *friends* of the church."

"Shit. Are you sure?"

"From something I overheard, I'm convinced enough that I say it wouldn't be a good idea to take any local law enforcement into our confidence. Not unless somebody on our side can read them very, very well."

"Good enough for me. But Bishop is not going to be happy about it."

"I doubt he'll be surprised. We knew it was a possibility."

"Makes the job harder. Or at least a hell of a lot more tricky. Not that it wasn't already, with the town being so isolated and the church so insulated." Bailey shifted the child's weight again. "I need to get the kid out of here."

"Wendy. Her name's Wendy."

"Yes. I know. Don't worry, we'll take care of her. She has family who love her and will want her."

"She also has an ability she's barely aware of." Sarah reached out once more to gently touch the child's hair, then stepped back. "Protect her. Protect her gift."

"We will. And you watch your back, hear? You've got a dandy shield of your own, but if it's taking an effort to pretend you could belong here, Samuel or one of his so-called advisers could pick up on the fact that you're hiding more than a bit of doubt about the good reverend and his real agenda."

"Believe me, I know." Something cold was spreading through Sarah's body, and she took two more steps back, deliberately removing herself from the other woman's protective shield. "Tell Bishop and John that at least one of Samuel's closest advisers is a strong psychic. I've felt it. Not sure which one; there's nearly always a group of men around him."

"Maybe you were just picking up Samuel."

"No. With Samuel it's just the way it's always been, a . . . null field. As if he isn't even there, at least psychically. No sense of personality, no aura, no energy signature at all."

"That's more than a shield."

"I know. I'm just not sure what it is. I've never sensed anything like it before."

Bailey shook her head. "I was really hoping that had changed or you'd learned to read him somehow."

"I've tried, believe me, every chance I've had. But nothing. He's literally shut inside himself."

"All the time?"

"Whenever I've been close enough to try to pick up something. But I'm not part of the inner circle or one of his chosen women."

"No, we haven't been able to get anyone that close."

"And I don't know if we ever will. That inner circle is incredibly protective of him. And whoever the psychic is . . . he's got one hell of a shield, a readable one, so it's a given there's something powerful generating it. But I'm not sure what he can do, what his ability is. It could be anything. Tell them to be careful. Whoever else they send in needs to be careful."

"Sarah—"

"I'll report when I can." Sarah turned and hurried away, her slender form almost instantly swallowed up by the shadows of the forest.

Bailey hesitated, but only for an instant, before swearing under her breath and turning to retrace her own steps. She moved swiftly, even carrying the child, and covered at least thirty yards before she heard, from somewhere behind her, a sound that stopped her in her tracks and yanked her around.

The beginning of a scream, cut off with chilling abruptness, its echo bouncing around eerily in the otherwise silent woods.

"Bailey, move." For a big man, Galen himself moved with uncanny silence, but that wasn't the trait she was interested in right now.

"Sarah. Galen, you have to—"

"I know. Get to the car. If I'm not there in five minutes, leave." His weapon was in his hand, and he was already moving away, back toward the Compound.

"But—"

"*Do it.*"

Bailey wasn't a woman who accepted orders easily, but she obeyed that one without further question. Tightening her arms around the sleeping child and concentrating on intensifying the protective blanket of energy wrapping them both, she hurried through the woods toward the road and the car hidden there.

Galen had long ago perfected the art of moving through any type of terrain without making a sound, but he was all too aware that at least some of those who might hunt him in this forest could listen with more than their ears. Even so, he didn't allow the knowledge to slow him down, and he made good time.

Unfortunately, not good enough.

Then again, he acknowledged grimly, he had probably been too late at the first note of Sarah's scream.

She lay on her back in a small clearing, in a pool of moonlight so bright and stark it was like a spotlight. The agony contorting her features seemed an almost unreal Halloween mask of horror. Her wide eyes gazed directly up at him, terrified and accusing.

At least that was the way Galen saw it. He wasn't psychic in the accepted sense, but he could read people in his own way. Even dead people.

Maybe especially dead people.

He knelt beside her sprawled body, his free hand feeling for her carotid pulse even as he kept his weapon ready and visually scanned the woods all around them.

He didn't see or hear a thing

And Sarah was gone.

Still kneeling beside her body, he frowned down at her. There wasn't a mark on her that he could see, no visible cause of death. She had bundled the child well against the cold, but her own jeans and thin sweater had provided little protection, and the light color of her clothing allowed him to be fairly certain there was no blood to indicate any kind of wound.

He slipped his hand underneath her shoulder, intending to turn her over and check her back for any wounds, but paused as he realized just how she was positioned. She had been returning to the Compound, and unless she had somehow gotten turned around and changed direction, it looked as though she had been knocked backward from an attack she had run into head-on.

And yet the frozen ground around her, crystals of frost glittering in the moonlight, was very clearly undisturbed by any sort of struggle and unmarked by any footprints except for his own and Sarah's. Their footprints—arriving at this point. And Sarah's footprints continuing on. But not returning.

It was as if she had been lifted off her feet yards farther along and thrown back to the center of the clearing with incredible force.

Galen wondered suddenly if a medical examiner would find her bones so shattered they were virtually crushed, as Ellen Hodges's bones had been.

He hesitated a moment longer, weighing the pros and cons of taking her back with them. It wasn't in his nature or training to leave a fallen comrade behind, but the incredibly high stakes in this situation forced him to reconsider. Someone had killed her, and that someone would expect to find her body here. If she didn't remain where she was expected to be...

"Shit," he breathed almost without sound, the curse a small cloud of cold mist. "Sorry, kid. I—"

It was his instinct to look someone in the eye when delivering a hard truth, and so he looked into Sarah Warren's dead eyes when he began to tell her he would have to leave her body here to be recovered by her murderers.

Her eyes were changing. As he watched, they slowly fogged over, the irises and pupils at first dimmed and finally completely obscured by white. And in the bright moonlight the angles of her face seemed sharper, the planes becoming hollows, as if more than her life had been—was being—sucked out of her.

Galen had seen many dying and dead over the years, but he had never seen anything like this before. And for one of the very few times in his adult life, he felt suddenly vulnerable. Nakedly vulnerable.

His gun couldn't protect him here. Couldn't even help him.

Nothing could.

He found himself withdrawing his hand from under her shoulder and was conscious of an almost overwhelming urge to leave, now, to get as far away from this place as he could, as fast as he could.

But once again, he wasn't quite fast enough.

He was still rising, just beginning to turn, when he saw the three men only a few yards away, moving swiftly through the woods toward him with a silence that was uncanny.

The one in front, a tall man with wide shoulders and

a stone-cold expression, already had his weapon out and raised and offered neither warning nor any chance at all. The big silver gun bucked in his hand.

Galen felt the bullet slam into his chest before he heard the muffled report, felt the frozen ground hard beneath him, and was dimly aware of his own weapon falling from nerveless fingers. He couldn't seem to breathe without a choking sensation, and blood bubbled up into his mouth, sharp and coppery.

Christ, what a cliché. I can't think of something better?

Apparently he could not. He had a mouth full of warm liquid metal, and he could literally feel his life ebbing from his body. Not sucked out as Sarah's had been but just leaving him, the way his blood flowed from the gaping wound in his chest and soaked into the cold ground. For a few brief seconds he looked at the bright moon, then the light was blocked out as the three men stood over him.

He focused with an effort on the taller one, the one whose stone-cold killer's face he could not now make out. Just a silhouette with gleaming eyes, silent, watching him.

"Son of a bitch," Galen managed thickly. "You sorry son of a—"

The big silver gun bucked again, hardly more than an almost apologetic sneeze of sound escaping the silencer, and a train slammed into Galen, and everything went black and silent.

———

"**W**hat if he was a cop?"

"What if?" Reese DeMarco knelt briefly to pick up the automatic from the ground beside the outstretched arm of the man he had shot, adding in the same unemotional tone as he rose, "Search him. See if he's carrying I.D."

The man who had asked the question knelt down to gingerly but thoroughly search the body. "No I.D.," he reported. "No harness or holster for the gun. Not even a damn label in his shirt. Shit, you really nailed him. Two dead-center in the chest. I would've expected body armor and gone for the head shot."

"I doubt he expected armed opposition. Probably just a P.I. hired by one of the families with no idea what he was getting into." DeMarco thumbed the safety on the confiscated weapon and stuck it into his belt at the small of his back. "Amateurs."

The third man, who had stood silently scanning the woods, said, "I don't see any sign of the kid. Think she ran off?"

"I think she was carried off." The words had barely left DeMarco's lips when, faintly, they all heard the sound of a car's engine revving and then fading within seconds into silence.

"Amateurs," DeMarco repeated.

"And heartless, not to come back for their dead." It was said with absolutely no sense of irony, and the man still kneeling beside the bodies looked down at them sorrowfully for a moment before lifting his gaze again to

DeMarco. "I didn't hear Father say—does he want these two brought back?"

DeMarco shook his head. "Dump the bodies in the river, Brian. Fisk, help him. It's nearly dawn; we need to get back."

They obeyed the clear order, holstering their weapons and bending to the task of lifting the large, heavy man from the frozen ground.

"Over a shoulder would be easier," Carl Fisk panted as they struggled to manage the dead weight. "Fireman's carry."

"You can if you want to," Brian Seymour told him. "Not me. I go back covered in this guy's blood and my wife is gonna ask all *kinds* of questions."

"All right, all right. Just lift your share, will you? Shit, Brian—"

DeMarco looked after the two men for a long moment until they disappeared into the forest and he could measure their progress only by the continuing complaints and fading grunts of effort. Finally he returned his weapon to the shoulder holster he wore and knelt beside the body of Sarah Warren.

He didn't have to check for a pulse but did it anyway, then gently closed her eyes so the frosty whiteness was no longer visible. Only then did he methodically search her to make certain she wasn't carrying identification— or anything else that might cause problems.

It was a very thorough search, which was why he found the silver medallion hidden in her left shoe. It was small, nearly flat, and on its polished surface was carved a lightning bolt.

DeMarco held it in his palm, watching the moonlight shimmer off the talisman as he moved his hand. Finally, becoming aware of the not-exactly-silent return of his men, he replaced Sarah's shoe, got to his feet, and slipped the medallion into his pocket.

"That bastard weighed a ton," Brian informed DeMarco as they joined him in the clearing, still huffing from the effort.

"I doubt you'll have the same problem with her," DeMarco told him.

Fisk said, "We're lucky that the river's deep and the current's moving fast right now, but is it smart to keep using it for disposal?"

"No, the smart thing would be to make sure disposal isn't necessary," DeMarco told him, his tone not so much critical as it was icy.

Brian sent him a wary look, then said quickly to Fisk, "You get her legs and I'll get her shoulders."

Fisk, who had locked eyes with DeMarco, didn't respond for a moment. Then he said, "Just help me get her over my shoulder. She's not bloody and I can manage her alone."

Brian didn't argue. He didn't, in fact, say another word until Fisk was on his way back to the river, the small, limp body over his shoulder clearly not a burden.

"Reese, he's a good man," Brian said then.

"Is he? We lost Ellen under his watch. Now Sarah and the girl. And I don't believe in coincidence, Brian."

"Look, I'm sure Father doesn't blame Carl."

"Father has other things to occupy his mind these days. My job is to protect him and the congregation. My job is to worry about anomalies. And Fisk is a . . . worry."

Unhappily, Brian said, "Okay, I get you. I'll keep an eye on him, Reese."

"Do that. And report anything unusual. Anything, Brian."

"Right. Right. Copy that."

They waited in silence for Fisk to return, with De-Marco staring down at the dark glimmer of blood slowly freezing on the cold ground.

"Want me to cover that up?" Brian ventured finally.

"Not now. The weather service reports a front moving in, bringing rain by dawn. In a few hours there'll be nothing left here for anyone to see."

"And the questions we'll get? About Sarah and the kid?"

"When we get back to the Compound, go to Sarah's room and pack up all her things. Quietly. Bring them to me. I'll take care of the child's belongings. Refer any questions about either of them to me."

"Will it interfere with Father's plans? Losing the kid, I mean."

"I don't know."

"Oh. Well, I just thought if anybody would know, it'd be you."

DeMarco turned his head and looked at his companion. "If you have a question, ask it."

"I just . . . I wonder, that's all. About Father's plans.

He talks about the Prophecy, he talks about the End Times, says we're almost there. So why aren't we getting ready?"

"We are."

"Reese, we barely have enough guns to arm security for the Compound."

"Guns won't stop an apocalypse," DeMarco replied dryly.

"But . . . we survive. More than survive—we prosper. Father promised."

"Yes. And he's doing everything in his power to make sure that happens. You believe it, don't you?"

"Sure. Sure. I mean, he's never lied to us. All his visions have come true." Brian shivered unconsciously. "And the things he can do . . . The power he can tap in to whenever he wants . . . He's been touched by God, we all know that."

"Then why are you worried?"

Brian shifted in obvious uncertainty and discomfort. "It's just . . . the women, I guess. You aren't a married man, so I don't know if you could understand."

"Perhaps not."

Encouraged by that neutral response, Brian went on carefully. "I know it's important to strengthen Father's gifts. I get that, I do. And I understand—well, sort of understand—why he can draw what he needs from the women but not from us."

"Women were created to sustain men," DeMarco said, his voice still neutral, almost indifferent.

"Yes, of course. And I know it doesn't harm them—the opposite, if anything." He sounded faintly dissatisfied about that, even to himself, and hurried on before DeMarco could comment. "But not every woman is able or willing, Reese. Ellen, Sarah. The others. Should they be forced against their will?"

"Have you seen any force employed?"

Brian didn't look away, even though he could feel more than see those cold, cold eyes stabbing him through the moonlit night. "No. But I've heard things. And those who aren't willing, who aren't... flattered by serving Father's needs, they always seem to turn up missing, eventually. Or turn up the way Ellen and Sarah did."

DeMarco allowed the silence to stretch until Brian shifted again beneath his stare, then he said deliberately, "If you don't like the way Father runs things, Brian, if you aren't happy here, then perhaps you should talk to him about it."

Brian wavered for only a moment and then took a physical step back as he shook his head. "No. No, I've no complaint. Father's been nothing but good to me and mine. I believe in him."

"I'm glad to hear that." DeMarco turned his head as they both heard the noisy footsteps of their returning comrade. "Very glad. Remind me, will you, to have a talk with Fisk about maintaining quiet whether we're tracking or not, especially when we're outside the Compound."

"Sure." Brian was glad those cold hawk eyes were

focused on someone else. "But whoever took the kid is long gone, right? I mean, you don't suspect someone else is out there, listening? Watching?"

"Someone's always out there, Brian. Always. You'd be wise not to forget that."

TWO

Grace, North Carolina

TESSA GRAY looked at the two earnest women sitting in chairs on the other side of her coffee table and summoned a smile. "You're both very kind," she said. "But I really don't think—"

"It isn't easy for a woman left all alone," the younger one said. "People want to take advantage. You've had offers for this house, haven't you? Offers for the land?"

Tessa nodded slowly.

"And they were below fair market value," the older woman said.

It wasn't a question.

Again, Tessa nodded. "According to the appraisal. Even so, I've been tempted. This place is too much for me. And with land around here going for low prices—"

"That's what *they* say." The younger woman's eyes all but burned with righteous indignation. "What they want you to believe. But it isn't true. Land here is worth a lot, and even more when people who know what they're doing work it and handle crops and livestock as they should be handled."

"I don't know what I'm doing," Tessa confessed. "I mean, I'm glad the farm has a manager to run things for me just the way he did for—The land and business belonged to my husband's family, as I'm sure you know, and he wasn't interested in any of it himself. He hadn't even been back here in years, since high school, I believe. It's just a fluke that he inherited and . . . I was left with it all."

The older woman, who had introduced herself simply as Ruth, said, "The church can remove that burden, Tessa. Take over the running of this place for you, even the ranch in Florida. So you wouldn't have to worry about it anymore. It would all still be yours, of course; our laws forbid any member to turn over property to the church even if they want to. We're asked only to tithe, in money or in goods or services. If our properties and businesses make more than enough for us, for our needs, and we choose to donate the extra to the church, well, that's fine. It's a gift to help Father take care of us."

So the fourth visit is the charm, Tessa thought. Previous visits had offered the spiritual, emotional, and practical support of the church and its members, but no quid pro quo had been mentioned.

"I'm afraid I've never been very religious," she said.

The younger woman, improbably named Bambi, leaned forward in her eagerness to convince. "Oh, I wasn't either! The churches I went to growing up, they were all about punishment and sin and redemption and always promising a reward *someday* for being a good person."

Tessa allowed doubt to creep into her voice. "And the Church of the Everlasting Sin is different? I'm sorry, but it really doesn't sound—"

"Oh, so different." Bambi's voice softened, and her eyes began to glow with an expression of devotion so complete, Tessa wanted to look away, as though from something intensely private.

"Bambi," Ruth warned quietly.

"But she should *know*. Tessa, we believe that *the Everlasting Sin* is the one committed by those who believe that our lot in this life is punishment and atonement. We believe that denigrates Jesus and what He did for us. We were washed clean of sin when He died for us. This life we're given is ours to enjoy."

Tessa waited, and as she'd expected Bambi's expression clouded over. "There are people who want to punish us for that belief. People who are afraid."

"Afraid of what?"

"Afraid of Father. Afraid of his gifts. Afraid he knows the truth."

"Bambi." This time, Ruth's voice was firm, and this time the younger woman fell silent, her head bowed in submission.

With a slight smile and friendly eyes, Ruth told Tessa, "Obviously, Father inspires fierce loyalty in all of us. But, please—come and see for yourself. Visit our church. We hold services on Sunday, of course, and on Wednesday evenings, but the church is the physical cen-

ter of our community as well as the spiritual center, so
people are there most of the time, involved in one activ-
ity or another. Children as well as adults and young people. You're welcome to come anytime."

"Thank you," Tessa said. "I'll...think it over."

"Please do. We'd love to have you. Even more, Tessa,
we'd love to help you through this difficult time."

Tessa thanked them again and then saw them politely from the rather formal living room to the front
door of the sprawling house. She stood in the open doorway until the ladies' white van disappeared down the
long, winding driveway, then closed the door and leaned
back against it.

"Bishop was right," she said. "It's the Florida ranch
they're most interested in."

"Yeah, he has an annoying habit of being right."
Special Agent Hollis Templeton came out of another
room that adjoined the spacious foyer, adding in a
thoughtful tone, "I don't think Ruth meant to let that
slip, though. The way we set it up, that Florida property
isn't obviously yours; the fact that the Church of the
Everlasting Sin even knows about it smacks of the sort of
intrusive background check most people wouldn't be at
all comfortable with. Especially from a church."

"It also says something about the extent of their resources."

Hollis nodded. "One of the many things we're not
happy about. To get the kind of information the church
seems to be able to get so quickly and easily, the good

reverend's connections pretty much have to be national."

"Homeland Security?"

"Maybe, scary as that possibility is. But even though he hasn't said so in so many words, I think Bishop's worried it might be somebody in the Bureau."

"Which explains why Haven is out front on this one?"

"Well, only partly. It made more sense on several counts to have a civilian organization involved, especially given our ... dearth of evidence against Samuel or the church. Haven investigators can go places and ask questions we just can't, not legally. In a situation like this, that ability isn't only vital, it's critical."

"So John told me," Tessa said. She inclined her head slightly in invitation and walked out of the foyer.

Hollis followed the other woman into the big, sunny kitchen and nodded when Tessa gestured questioningly at the coffeemaker. "Please. I'm still jet-lagged."

Tessa hunted in a still-unfamiliar pantry for the coffee and didn't respond until she found it. "Eureka. Why jet-lagged? Don't you guys work out of Quantico?"

"Most of us, yeah, but I was out in California on another case. He didn't admit it, but I don't think Bishop expected the church to move so fast or to be so ... insistent once they made contact with you. You've only been here a couple of weeks, after all. From our research and experience, it usually takes a couple of months for them to even begin to gather a potential new convert into the fold."

Measuring out coffee without looking at Hollis, Tessa said, "It took months for Sarah, didn't it?"

Hollis slid onto a bar stool at the kitchen's island and clasped her hands together on the granite surface, frowning down at a chewed thumbnail. "It did. But her cover wasn't quite as enticing as yours is."

"Is that why I was placed here even before anything happened to her?"

"Well, the plan was to have...multiple fronts, as it were. To use every avenue possible to find information and, hopefully, evidence. We couldn't be entirely sure, from the outside, just what sort of background or situation would prove to be the most attractive to the church and Samuel. And not every agent or operative is going to be working the same way or be able to gain access to certain levels of the church hierarchy. Sarah wasn't able to get near any of Samuel's closest advisers in any meaningful sense, but she was still able to gather valuable intelligence. And able to get a couple of the kids out."

"Have they found her?" Tessa asked quietly.

"No." Hollis waited until Tessa got the coffee going and faced her before she added deliberately, "The bodies always turn up downstream. Sooner or later."

Tessa looked at her for a moment, then said, "It takes a while, I'm told. To build that shell around your emotions."

Unoffended, Hollis smiled slightly. "Sometimes. But it's usually all smoke and mirrors. None of us would be in this line of work if we didn't care deeply. If we didn't believe we were making a difference."

"Is that why you got in?"

"I was dragged in. More or less." Hollis's smile twisted a bit. "When your entire life changes, you build a new one. But when that change happened to me, I was lucky to have kindred spirits around me, people who understood what I was going through. Just like you were lucky when they crossed your path."

"It was easier for me," Tessa said, adding, "My abilities weren't triggered by trauma."

"Adolescence is trauma," Hollis pointed out.

"Of a kind, sure. But nothing like what happened to you."

Musing rather than revealing much of herself—or, perhaps, revealing a great deal—Hollis said, "In the SCU, my experience isn't so unusual. Not even the degree, really. The majority of the team went through some kind of personal hell, coming out the other side with abilities we're still trying to figure out."

Tessa recognized the courteous warning and shifted the subject back to answer Hollis's implicit question. "I didn't find kindred spirits because I went looking for them; Bishop found me. Years ago. But I didn't want to be any kind of cop, he left, and I thought that was the end of it. Until John and Maggie got in touch."

"And you decided to be a cop without a badge?"

"Mostly, I haven't been. Investigating, but not in any sort of dangerous situation. Not like this one. Not with people dying. There've been eight bodies found in this general area, right? So far. Eight people killed the same way. The same very unnatural way."

Hollis nodded. "Over the past five years, yeah. That we know about, anyway. If we knew for sure . . . probably more."

Tessa didn't move from her position but leaned back against the counter and crossed her arms in a gesture that wasn't quite defensive. Hollis took due note of that and asked herself for at least the third time since she'd arrived here hours ago if John Garrett, the director and co-founder of Haven, had made a wise choice in sending Tessa Gray on this particular assignment.

She was a little above medium height and slender, almost ethereal, an impression emphasized by her pale skin, fair hair, and delicate features dominated by large gray eyes. Her voice was soft, almost childlike, and when she spoke it was with the absolute courtesy of someone who had been raised to be polite no matter the circumstances.

Which made her sound as vulnerable as she looked.

She was *supposed* to look vulnerable, of course; that was part of the bait for the church. Without family, lost and alone after the sudden and unexpected death of her young husband only a few months previously, burdened by business concerns she had inadequate knowledge to handle on her own, she was just the sort of potential convert the church had a history of aggressively pursuing.

Although never before this aggressively, Hollis mused, at least as far as they knew. And the question was why.

What was it about Tessa that Reverend Samuel and

his flock considered so important? Was it only the property in Florida, highly valuable to Samuel for a reason that had nothing to do with the value of the land? Or was it because he had, somehow, sensed or otherwise discovered Tessa's unique abilities?

Now, there was an unnerving thought. The idea that your ace might be in plain view for all to see—and other players to use—pushed the possible stakes much, much higher.

Given what they were reasonably sure Samuel could do, it made the stakes potentially deadly.

"I've never been sent in undercover," Tessa said. "Not like this, with a whole other life to remember."

Hollis cast the useless speculation aside. "Second thoughts?"

A little laugh escaped Tessa. "More like first thoughts. I mean, John explained the situation, and Bishop filled me in on what happened last summer in Boston and a few months ago in Venture, Georgia. They both told me how dangerous it could be—would probably be."

Not a big believer in sugarcoating, Hollis said, "Yeah, if Samuel is who and what we believe he is, there's a pretty good chance a few more of us won't be left standing when it's all done. Even assuming we win."

"Do you doubt we will?"

"Honestly? Having some idea of what he can do, I have more than a few doubts."

Tessa frowned. "Because you've already faced him, fought him?"

"Not exactly. Not even by proxy, really. He just wanted me out of the way. Bishop believes he's afraid of mediums and that's why he sicced his pet killer on me in Georgia."

"Why would Samuel be afraid of mediums?"

"Well, think about it. If you were responsible for dozens of brutal deaths, would you be all that anxious to have someone around who could open up a door and allow your victims to pay you an extremely unsettling visit?"

"Probably not."

"No. In Samuel's shoes, neither would I. We figure that's the reason, though more because it makes sense than because we have any kind of solid proof."

"But that's the one ability we're pretty sure he doesn't want. If he is who and what we believe he is."

"Safe bet. In fact, my semieducated guess as a profiler-in-training is that the reverend's terrified of finding out for certain that with the reality of spirits come all the other traditional trappings of an afterlife many of us are raised to believe in. Accountability. Judgment. Punishment."

"Is there?" Tessa asked, figuring a medium would know if anyone would.

"Yes," Hollis answered simply.

"Hell?"

"Some version of it. At least for monsters like him. And isn't it ironic? The only thing Reverend Samuel could preach with complete conviction and total honesty from his pulpit is the truth of Judgment Day. And that's the one thing he's spent twenty years making very, very sure his church denies."

Washington, D.C.

"So that's his Achilles' heel?" Senator Abe LeMott sat utterly still at his desk, hands clasped atop his neat blotter, and studied the man in one of his visitor's chairs. "The one thing he fears?"

"We believe so." Special Agent Noah Bishop matched the older man in stillness, though his steady gaze was, if anything, more watchful. "He had every chance to take the abilities of one of our strongest mediums. Instead, he tried to have her killed."

"She was also bait for a trap, was she not? Bait for you?"

"Bait. We're not entirely sure what his ultimate aim was. We can't be. All we can know is what happened. Dani was the one he attacked, the one whose abilities he tried to take, most likely because he knew those abilities could be used as offensive weapons. Maybe he didn't go after the rest of us because he believed we weren't so vulnerable. Maybe he can only take one ability at a time— or that was his limitation then. Maybe it was all a test of our strengths. And weaknesses. Maybe our abilities weren't important to him because he already has his own version of them."

"That's a lot of maybes."

"Yes, I know. I did warn you, Senator, that there'd be

no quick or easy answers, not if we want the whole truth. But we did get the man who murdered your daughter with his own hands."

"And do you believe, Agent Bishop, that the man who commands or wills another to act for him is any less guilty of the act committed?"

"You know I don't." *If anything, more guilty.*

"Then you know why I can't be satisfied by the capture of that evil creature clawing the walls of his cell as we speak."

Bishop nodded. "Believe it or not, Senator, I want the man behind that killer as badly as you do."

"Oh, I do believe that." LeMott's smile was hardly worth the effort. "He's the first real threat you've faced, isn't he?"

"The Special Crimes Unit—"

"Has withstood many threats over the past few years, yes. I don't mean to detract from that in any way or demean your considerable accomplishments. The SCU has faced evil in most of its incarnations, including many killers, and usually defeated them. We both know that. But this is a different kind of threat. A far, far more dangerous threat to you and your people. From all the evidence available, this killer means to use your own tools, your own weapons, your own advantage against you. And though you certainly have him outnumbered, *his* advantage is that it hardly matters how many agents you send after him."

"It's not the number, Senator, it's their training and skills versus his."

"And their abilities versus his? Abilities he wants? Abilities he can apparently take from them by force without even laying a finger on them—and then use those abilities against them?"

"We don't know what he's capable of. But what happened in Georgia may have taught him at the very least that he lacks the ability, the strength, to take *anything* he wants. He has limits just like the rest of us. Weaknesses. Vulnerabilities. He's certainly not all-powerful. Not invincible."

"We can both certainly hope not. But it does seem clear, Agent Bishop, that your enemy knows you at least as well as you know him and quite probably better, especially if he tracked and watched Agent Templeton as long as the photographic evidence you discovered in Venture suggests."

"We don't know that he tracked any other member of the unit."

"You don't know that he didn't."

"No. If it comes right down to it, there's no way for us to be absolutely certain that he was the one doing the surveillance. Those photographs could have been taken by a private investigator hired for the purpose."

"A private investigator too dim to realize his target or targets were FBI agents?"

"Maybe that's why we only found shots of Hollis. Maybe whoever it was decided that it was just too risky to follow and photograph agents of the federal government."

"More maybes."

Bishop was keenly aware that he was, as he had been for many months now, dealing with a powerful man who had nothing left in his life except a raging grief and an obsession for revenge.

Not justice for his murdered daughter, not anymore. Abe LeMott wanted revenge. For the loss of his daughter. The loss of his wife. For the destruction of his life.

Which made him hardly less dangerous than the man they both wanted.

So Bishop chose his next words carefully. "Whatever he may or may not know about members of the SCU, what *we* know is that he does have at least one weakness, one vulnerability. Where there's one, there's more. That's been true of every criminal, every evil, we've ever fought. It's true of Samuel as well. We'll find those weaknesses. And we'll find a way to exploit them."

"Before you lose any more of your people?"

"I don't know. I hope so."

LeMott's eyes narrowed. "You haven't seen the end of this, have you? No vision of how it all turns out? You and your wife?"

"No. We haven't."

"But you won't let that stop you."

"No."

The senator conjured another smile, just as faint as before, and this time there was a hard, flat shine to his eyes. "I could hardly ask for more than that, could I?"

Bishop was silent.

"I trust you'll keep me advised, Agent Bishop. I do appreciate that courtesy." LeMott didn't rise or offer his hand, but it was clear nevertheless that the meeting was over.

"Of course, Senator."

Bishop didn't wait to be shown out; after so many months, he knew his way and as always took the less-public exit that bypassed both the senator's secretary and his assistant. The door led to a short, infrequently traveled hallway, which in turn led to a wider, brighter, much busier space. People passed in both directions, some carrying briefcases or folders, many talking on cell phones, and all wearing preoccupied expressions.

A tall, gorgeous brunette with electric-blue eyes stood half screened from many of those passing her by a big plant on a pedestal, and as Bishop emerged into the busy hallway he saw her open the I.D. folder she was holding in one hand and flash her badge in the face of an obviously crestfallen young man. The admirer took two steps back, saw Bishop approaching, and managed a weak smile before continuing hastily on his way.

"I never know if it's the badge or the wedding ring," Miranda said thoughtfully as Bishop joined her.

"Combo," Bishop told her. "You always hold the badge in your left hand, so they see both."

"Ah. Well, as long as it discourages them. Do you have any idea just how many married men in this building are looking for a little action?"

"I think I'd rather not know." Bishop took her hand, and they joined the flow of traffic moving toward one of the main exits. "I take comfort in the sure knowledge that my very hot wife is not only disinterested and able to read minds but is also a black belt and a sharpshooter."

"That would probably give them pause."

"If they're thinking with any body part north of their belts, yes."

"One can only hope. This is a government building."

Both their voices had been a little amused and wholly casual, and anyone not also telepathic couldn't have imagined that a much more important and far more grim conversation had also just taken place.

How far do you think he's gone?

God knows.

You couldn't read him?

I couldn't read him quite well enough to get details—and it's getting more difficult to read him at all. He avoids even shaking hands with me now, and I don't think it's because he's pissed at the lack of progress. But given his history, his background, and the emotions driving him right now, my guess is that the senator's gone as far as money and connections could take him. It's a sure bet he has someone inside law enforcement in North Carolina.

What about the church?

He's known about Samuel since October. God-dammit, I should never have given him a name.

You had to. No choice.

Maybe. Not that it matters now. LeMott's had almost as much time as we have to get someone inside. If he's succeeded . . .

If he had, wouldn't Samuel be dead?

Not necessarily. Whoever it is could be under orders to gather information before anything more permanent is done. LeMott wants revenge, and he wants it to hurt. Know your enemy if you want to inflict the maximum possible amount of pain.

Does he even give a shit that we have people on the inside? People risking their lives to get the man responsible for his daughter's murder?

I think he's beyond caring.

Then we don't have the luxury of time, not any longer.

No. We don't.

Bishop's fingers tightened on his wife's hand, and the two of them hurried from the building.

Three

THE BODY HAD SNAGGED on a half-submerged tree blasted by lightning back in the summer. It bobbed a little as the current continued to snatch at it, rolling sluggishly back and forth a few inches. Long brown hair flowed out around the partially submerged face, obscenely graceful in the water, a solitary sign of what might once have been beauty.

There was nothing beautiful about her now.

It was fortunate, given the fast-moving river, that there had been something to catch the body before it wound up miles downstream where the water was more shallow and campers were wont to vacation on the picturesque banks.

Not that many did in January, Sawyer Cavenaugh acknowledged absently to himself as he studied the dead woman. Still, there were usually a hardy few, seeking nature when it was a bit less crowded, and most towed their kids along.

Thankfully, a child had not found this body.

Bloated and showing gashes and other postmortem injuries from the rough downstream journey of at least a couple of miles, she was a sight horrifying enough to give even a veteran cop and chief of police the promise of nightmares to come.

As if he didn't already have more than his share.

Sawyer rose from his crouch and walked a few feet to where one of his officers stood with the unhappy citizen who *had* made the grisly find.

"This is the second one for you, isn't it, Pel?"

"I swear to God, I'm never walking Jake along here again," Pel Brackin said with considerable feeling, one hand on the head of the calm chocolate Lab sitting at his side. "Much more of this and he could be one of them cadaver dogs. Jesus, Sawyer—what the hell is going on up there?" He jerked his head in the general direction of upstream.

"Up there?"

"Up at the Compound. Don't treat me like an idiot— I chased you out of my apple orchard when you were just a snot-nosed kid."

Sawyer sighed, not bothering to ask for an explanation of the parallel. "Is there anything you can tell me that might help me to find out what happened to this woman?"

"All I know is what I found, and we can all see that."

"You didn't see or hear anything else out of the ordinary?"

"Nah, nothing I don't usually see around here. Though..."

Sawyer waited a moment, then prompted, "Though what?"

With his free hand, Brackin rubbed the nape of his neck. "I don't know what it'd have to do with her. Or with that other poor woman last week."

"Let me be the judge of that. What is it, Pel?"

"It's . . . the wildlife."

Sawyer felt his brows rising. "The wildlife?"

"The lack of it, really. Jake and me, we usually see a lot of critters on our morning rambles. These last weeks, since back before the holidays, really not so many."

Thinking out loud, Sawyer said, "A mild winter, so far. Not very cold, almost no snow."

Brackin nodded. "This sort of winter, there's usually plenty of wildlife visible. Deer, foxes, rabbits, squirrels. Plenty of raccoon and possum. Even some wild boar coming down out of the mountains. And lots of birds. But . . . now that I think about it, my wife's bird feeders haven't been very popular. Not even doves or cardinals, and we generally have dozens of them about the place all winter." He shrugged, suddenly uncomfortable. "Like I said, probably nothing to do with these killings. Just something weird, is all."

"Okay. Anything else you can think of?"

"Nah. I'll call if I think of anything, but I told Robin here—"

"Officer Keever, Pel. Come on," she protested.

"Well, then, *Officer* Keever, I'll be *Mister* Brackin to you."

She rolled her eyes but then caught Sawyer's and subsided. "Right. Sorry, Mr. Brackin."

Satisfied, he finished: "I told her everything I remembered from the time Jake started barking and I saw the body."

"Not an easy question, but I suppose you don't recognize her?" Sawyer asked.

"Shit, Sawyer, her own mother wouldn't recognize her."

"I had to ask."

"Yeah, yeah. If I've ever seen her before, I can't tell by looking at her now. Look, can I go? It's not like you don't know where I've lived for the last sixty years of my life, and I'm not going anywhere except home. My feet are freezing, I want my coffee, and Jake wants his breakfast."

Sawyer nodded. "Yeah, go ahead. Sorry to keep you."

With a grunt that might have been meant as thanks, Brackin headed downstream toward his place, avoiding so much as a glance at the corpse in the river.

"Wildlife," Sawyer murmured, more to himself than anything else.

"Chief?"

"Nothing." Mildly, he added, "Robin, when you're fighting an uphill battle to be taken seriously, it helps to act like a professional."

"I know. Sorry, Chief."

"Just don't make me sorry I cleared you for fieldwork, that's all I'm saying."

She nodded, now wearing a slightly anxious expression.

Her face was an open book, Sawyer reflected, betraying her thoughts and her emotions equally. Which certainly gave the lie to the whole inscrutable Asian stereotype, since Robin had been born in China. But, adopted by the Keevers at the age of three, she had been brought up in traditions a long way from Asian. That Southern rural background had left her, twenty years later, with an accent that was pure Carolina Mountain, an occasional turn of phrase that would have astonished and possibly horrified her ancestors, and a slight chip on her shoulder that came from being different from most everyone around her.

Sawyer could relate.

But all he said was "I gather Pel didn't see anything helpful."

"He claims he never went within twelve feet of the body, and the lack of footprints on the bank there bears him out," the young deputy reported crisply. "Ely had a look around while I waited with Mr. Brackin, but he didn't see anything out of the ordinary."

Sawyer glanced past her, up the shallow bank to where their cars were parked just off the road, and noted that Robin's sometimes partner, Officer Ely Avery, was leaning a hip against their cruiser, obviously trying not to look bored.

There was a second cruiser parked up there, possibly intended to fend off curious onlookers who had not appeared, and the two officers in it, Dale Brown and

Donald Brown (no relation, they always explained), appeared just as bored and/or equally detached from the situation.

No taste for or even interest in homicide investigation there. Sawyer made the mental note, then returned his gaze to Robin Keever's earnest young face. She was smart, more than capable, and she was ambitious; he'd known that for a while now.

But more important at the moment, she's fully engaged and intensely curious. Good.

Because he damn sure needed all the help he could get. Nothing in his years as a small-town cop had prepared him for anything even remotely like this.

"I checked with the station as soon as I got here," Robin went on, "and we have no reports of missing persons fitting—well, no women reported missing from anywhere in the county."

"Yeah, I checked too." But the last female missing person had turned up in this same stretch of river barely a week before, looking an awful lot the way this one looked, so Sawyer was inclined to start searching for a connection between them.

More than inclined. In his experience, there really was no such thing as a coincidence.

Robin was thinking along the same lines. "Do you think she could be from the Compound, like Mr. Brackin suggested? From the church?"

"I think she's been in the river long enough that somebody should have noticed she was missing."

"And since no report was filed..."

"Well, Reverend Samuel and his flock never look for help outside the Compound. Maybe they've got trouble of the nasty kind and believe they can handle it themselves."

"A killer inside the church?"

"Maybe."

"Or?" Robin was watching him intently.

"Or maybe the church has an enemy out here. A very, very pissed-off enemy."

"And he's taking it out on the women?"

"We have a couple of men unaccounted for, remember? Just because we haven't found bodies doesn't mean they didn't wind up the same way these women wound up."

Robin shifted her weight from one foot to the other. "Chief, is it true what I heard about the woman last week? That Ellen Hodges was . . . that somebody beat her to death?"

"The state M.E. hasn't completed the autopsy. Their office currently has a six-week backlog."

Characteristically, Robin wasn't deterred. "Okay, but Doc Macy examined the body before she was shipped to Chapel Hill, right?"

Sawyer nodded, wondering just where in hell their county M.E. was at the moment, since he should have arrived by now.

"What was in his report?" Robin persisted.

"Sure you want to know?" He waited for her decided nod, then replied, "Doc's report recommended we ship the body to the state chief medical examiner, where the facilities are a lot better than any in this area. Because his X-rays showed that virtually every bone in her body had been broken, almost pulverized—and there wasn't a mark on her anywhere to indicate how that happened."

Tessa Gray had put off actually visiting the Church of the Everlasting Sin's Compound as long as she dared, a reluctance that had, according to the more experienced Hollis, worked for her so far.

So far.

"But you need to get out there," Hollis said, early on the afternoon that Sarah Warren's body was found in the river.

Tessa was still grappling with that, and it wasn't easy. It was the first time she'd ever been on assignment when a fellow Haven operative had lost her life—though not the first time it had happened.

The stakes were high.

And Tessa accepted that, got that. No operative joined the organization without being warned repeatedly, by John and Maggie Garrett, cofounders and codirectors of Haven, and by Bishop, another cofounder as well as Chief of the FBI's Special Crimes Unit and someone who certainly knew better than most what price could be demanded of the soldiers in this war.

That was the most unsettling part of the death of a fellow operative, the stark reminder that this *was* war, that people could and did die fighting what they all believed were necessary battles. They were none of them superheroes; being psychic hardly made them invulnerable. In fact, it was often the opposite.

Depending on the ability and its individual quirks, being psychic could be a weakness at best, and an active liability at worst—especially some of the least common and even unique abilities, and most especially when those abilities were held by operatives or agents with erratic control.

Unfortunately, those with erratic control far outnumbered those with a better mastery over their capabilities.

Tessa was uncertain of where she fell on that score, since her own ability had not really been tested under fire. She knew she was considered to possess excellent control, but who knew what might happen under extreme and dangerous circumstances? She was trained to handle a gun and was licensed to carry a concealed firearm. But she wouldn't be going into the Church of the Everlasting Sin's Compound carrying a weapon of that sort. Worse, she had to appear and act like an extremely vulnerable woman who was ripe to be dominated by stronger people, stronger minds.

A terrifying prospect, especially since they weren't at all sure how Reverend Samuel achieved his seemingly absolute domination over his flock. If he *was* using psychic ability to control them, Tessa had no way of knowing whether that same control would work on her.

Until she put her shields to the test by exposing them to the church Compound. And Samuel.

"The police will probably be there," she objected finally.

"Not necessarily. They haven't identified the body yet."

"But we have."

"Yeah. It's Sarah, no question."

"Did you see . . . ?"

"Her spirit? No." Hollis frowned. "I seldom see the spirits of team members—or people I know, for that matter. I wonder why." It wasn't a question so much as it was an acknowledgment that the universe was arbitrary in its choices.

Tessa waited a moment, then asked, "How can we be sure it was Sarah's body?"

Hollis pushed aside her musing with an almost physical gesture. "Hoping for a mistake in identification? Don't. We have someone else in the area, and the I.D. of her body is confirmed."

"By someone I'm not supposed to know about, I gather."

Patiently, Hollis said, "What you don't know, you can't communicate—on any level—to anyone else. Tessa, *I* don't even know for certain how many of our agents and Haven operatives are working this case. And right now, I don't care. *Someone* is killing people, about as viciously as I've ever seen. As inexplicably as I've ever seen. And everything we know or think we know suggests Reverend Samuel is the one responsible. We believe he's doing that killing using no weapon or tool except for the power of his mind, using paranormal abilities we haven't been able to count, far less define and understand. I don't know about you, but that scares the hell out of me."

"I just . . . I never knew psychic ability could be like that. Could be used as a weapon."

"It's rare, but we have at least one agent who can channel and focus energy well enough to make it a destructive force. And Haven has at least one operative who can do it."

"And if there are two on our side . . ."

"There are likely to be at least a couple on the other side, yeah. We've had evidence in the past of psychic abilities in some really evil and twisted bad guys who could do some scarily remarkable things psychically. Look, we haven't discovered our own limits yet. But it only makes sense that in the wrong hands, driven by the wrong intentions, at least some psychic abilities could be corrupted. Dark energy channeled in ways more powerful than anything we've experienced so far."

"And used to kill. But why?"

"The question we desperately need answered, Tessa, especially since we have no direct evidence so far pointing to either Samuel or his church, not evidence that would stand up in court. We know precious little, but what we *do* know from interviewing the very few defectors we've found tells us that Samuel built himself a church because something very seriously traumatic happened to him more than twenty years ago, something so mysterious or terrifying even the defectors wouldn't or couldn't talk about it, and whatever it was, it changed him forever.

"Problem is, we don't believe he was all that stable to begin with. It's difficult to know for certain, because the early background info we have on him is sketchy, to say the least. Can't even find a reliable birth certificate on him, though we've found half a dozen phony ones. In any case, he had a few early run-ins with the law, so he's on record as having a troubled childhood. His mother was apparently a prostitute, and not of the high-class variety."

"I'd call that a troubled childhood," Tessa said.

"Yeah. We can't find attendance records, so if he even went to school it was rare and sporadic. We haven't been able to find any evidence that he started fires or tortured animals or displayed other signs of a budding sociopath, but there's so little solid information on him that we can't rule anything out."

"Except that he grew up to become a cult leader."

"Except that," Hollis agreed.

Tessa shook her head. "I read up on cults and cult leaders when I got this assignment, and just the regular, run-of-the-mill leaders without psychic abilities are more than scary. The patterns of behavior they follow, the power trips and growing paranoia, the isolation, the need to dominate and control their followers—*and* the means they use to impose that control—is all so..."

"Deadly, in many cases. Certainly in this one. We know women, men, and even a few children have gone missing from that compound in the last year, all van-

ished without a trace—and that none of them was reported missing by the church or any of its members.
What we don't know is why. Why his own have been tar-
geted, and why these people in particular."

Tessa frowned. "Maybe he's culling. Weeding out
those of his people he can't trust."

"That could very well be. Except that it doesn't really
explain the kids, does it?"

"No. We're sure kids have gone missing?"

"We're sure. No reports to the local police, but we're
sure."

"And we're not talking about the kids Sarah got
out?"

Hollis shook her head. "No. Creepy thing is, one or
both of the parents of at least two of the missing kids are
still church members. Not only did they not report the
kids missing, but they don't seem to miss the kids."

"What?"

"Either they don't remember or don't care. I'm
guessing it's the former. And we have no idea how that's
even possible. If Samuel can affect people's memories, especially the sort as deeply rooted and emotional as the
memory of a child..."

She really didn't have to finish that.

Tessa drew a breath and let it out slowly, trying to
fight off a chill that was seeping into her very bones.
"The missing people, kids included, weren't all psychics,
I assume?"

"We have no way of knowing for certain, but as far
as we've been able to determine, among the known

missing and murder victims only Sarah was psychic. If he found out who and what she was, then chances are he's even stronger than we believed. Which means he's even more deadly than we believed. "

Officially, the children of the Church of the Everlasting Sin were home-schooled. Unofficially, they were often involved in church-supervised activities throughout the day. And like the adults who had chosen this refuge from the world, the children had a unique inner life that outsiders would have found odd.

Some of the adult church members would have found it odd as well. And not a little alarming.

Because not all of the children believed.

And some of them were afraid.

"Do you think Wendy got away?" Brooke kept her voice low, audible only to the small group at the playground's covered picnic table. The group was busily collecting numerous toys left by some of the younger children now being shepherded toward the church.

"I think so." Ruby's voice was equally low. She held open a cloth bag so that Cody could pile in all the alphabet blocks.

As he did so, he said, "Yeah, but I don't think Sarah made it."

Ruby and Brooke exchanged looks, and then both stared at the dark, solemn-eyed boy.

Replying to their silent question, he said simply, "I don't feel her anymore."

"Are you sure?" Hunter was the fourth member of the little group and the accepted leader, despite being the youngest at eleven. "Just because we haven't seen her doesn't mean she's gone. I mean *really* gone. She has a shell. We've all felt it."

"I don't even feel that now. Do you?" Cody said.

Hunter frowned, concentrating on collecting all the small plastic pieces of a miniature dairy farm. "No. But I thought it might just be me. Because I hardly feel anything at all."

Blinking back tears, Brooke said, "I was going to ask Sarah if she could get me out next."

Ruby said, "We aren't supposed to know she got anybody out, Brooke. We aren't supposed to know she was here to snoop around."

"I didn't tell anybody. I wouldn't have."

Cody muttered, "Just because you don't tell doesn't mean somebody doesn't *know*."

"I was careful. I'm always careful. But it's getting harder and harder. I can't stay here anymore, I just can't. My aunt Judy lives in Texas, and she doesn't like the church. I know she'd let me live with her."

"What about your mom and dad?" Hunter asked.

"What about them?" Brooke fixed her gaze on the crayons she was gathering into a plastic container. "They believe in the church. They believe in Father. They're never going to leave here."

After a moment, Cody said, "My mom isn't so sure anymore. She's beginning to be afraid."

"Does she know you feel that?" Ruby asked him.

"No. She pretends everything is just the same."

"Don't tell her," Hunter warned. "We can't tell any of our parents. Not what we know, and not what we feel. We have to keep hiding it. Because we all know what'll happen if we don't."

"Then what *do* we do?" Cody spoke more quickly, his gaze on the two adult church members coming toward them.

"We keep our mouths shut."

"Until?"

"Until we figure out something better."

"Like what?"

"I don't know, Cody. But I do know we're safer doing nothing until we figure out *what* to do."

Ruby said, "That's easy for you. You two aren't girls."

"No," Brooke agreed, also aware of the approach of two of their...keepers. "It's different for us. Once the Ceremonies begin. Once Father notices we're growing up." Her last few words were whispered, "Once Father starts watching us...."

Tessa hadn't known Sarah very well; Haven was a growing organization whose members were spread out all over the country, most living quiet, seemingly normal lives—at least until they were called into service—and many of them had never even met one another. But not knowing a fallen comrade, she had discovered, did nothing to lessen the feeling of loss.

One of their own was gone.

That knowledge was too painful to think about unless Tessa could make something meaningful of it. And right now that was all but impossible for her, especially when she was going into the same situation that had cost Sarah her life.

Hollis said, "Your shield is stronger than Sarah's."

"You're a telepath now?"

"No. You wouldn't be human if you weren't thinking about it."

Tessa didn't want to think about it. Instead, she thought about the young church member Bambi's expression of adoration, and that of others she had met. She said slowly, "They don't seem to be afraid of him. His followers."

Hollis didn't push it. "Well, not the ones he sends out in public, anyway." She shook her head. "Given the typical profile of a cult leader, there's often some kind of sexual domination and control, but we aren't sure about that with Samuel. For one thing, the church has existed long enough that I would have expected him to have offspring by more than one woman if he was using sex. But as far as we can determine, he's childless."

"Sterile, maybe?"

"Maybe. Or maybe he genuinely sees himself as a more traditional prophet in the sense of being a holy man, above the needs of the flesh. He's a bit older, somewhere in his mid-forties, and they do call him Father, after all."

A cold memory stirred in Tessa. "Didn't Jim Jones's followers call him Father?"

"Yes, as I recall. It's the rule rather than an exception for a cult leader to portray himself as a patriarchal or messianic head of his church. An absolute power structure with a single figure at the top."

"I think some of the younger church members I've talked to so far would respond strongly to that idea of a protective father image. But the older ones? The ones closer to his own age? How does he hold them? How does he convince them to follow him?"

"More questions we don't have answers for. And we need them. If we have any hope of stopping Samuel, we need information."

"I know." Tessa drew a breath and let it out slowly. "I know."

It was that sense of urgency rather than any confidence on her part that finally sent Tessa, later on that Wednesday afternoon, several miles outside the very small town of Grace to a nice if deceptively ordinary wrought-iron gate at the end of a short lane off the area's main two-lane highway.

There was what appeared to be a small farmhouse to the left and just inside the surprisingly pretty brick and wrought-iron fencing. Tessa had only a moment or two to wonder if the clearly very sturdy and certainly very expensive fence ran around the entire two-hundred-acre Compound, before she saw a tall man in jeans and a flannel shirt come out of the house and approach the other side of the gate.

The two sides of the gate opened inward as he neared them, giving Tessa an unsettling feeling that wasn't lessened a bit by his casual air *or* by the fact that he addressed her by name as soon as she put the car window down—and she had never met him before in her life.

"Good afternoon, Mrs. Gray. Come for a visit?"

Tessa managed to avoid even a glance at the plain gold band on her left hand, its weight still an unfamiliar, slightly uncomfortable sensation. "Yes. Ruth said—" She broke off when he nodded.

"Of course. She'll be waiting for you at the Square. Just continue along the drive all the way to the end. And welcome."

"Thank you." Tessa hoped he couldn't see that her fingers were white-knuckled with tension on the steering wheel as she drove through the gates and followed the long asphalt drive that disappeared into a dense-looking forest.

She glanced into the rearview mirror in time to see the big gates slowly closing behind her, and her feeling of being trapped owed nothing to any sense except the very primitive one of self-preservation.

Sawyer Cavenaugh didn't think he'd ever get used to it. In the ten years since the Church of the Everlasting Sin had set up its main parish in Grace, and most especially in the past two years since he'd been chief of police, he had never seen any church member away from the others alone. They always traveled in pairs, or groups of three or four, but never alone.

Except for the guy at the gate, who was always seen alone.

Unless you were a cop, of course, and were perfectly aware of being closely observed from that innocuous little "farmhouse" a few yards away just inside the fence.

There might be video security. There was certainly someone watching from behind at least one of those mirrorlike windows. Maybe armed—though Sawyer had never once seen any evidence, any sign whatsoever, of guns anywhere in the Compound.

And he had looked. Hard.

"Good afternoon, Chief Cavenaugh. What can we do for you today?"

"Afternoon, Carl." Sawyer smiled a smile every bit as polite and false as the one being smiled at him. "I called ahead and spoke to DeMarco. We're expected." He knew damn well that Carl Fisk *knew* they were expected.

He always knew, and they always played this little game anyway.

"Ah, of course. Officer Keever."

"Mr. Fisk." Robin's voice was entirely formal and professional; she wasn't one to make the same mistake twice.

Fisk kept his meaningless smile in place as he stepped back and gestured. "I'm sure you know the way. Mr. DeMarco will meet you at the church, as usual."

Sawyer nodded and drove the Jeep through the open gate.

"I don't like that guy," Robin announced in a decided tone. "He smiles too much."

"You read Shakespeare?"

"That one may smile and be a villain? Yeah."

"Smart guy, that Shakespeare. And a gifted observer."

"You don't like Fisk either."

Sawyer smiled faintly. "Now, did I say that?"

"Yes." Robin followed up that defiant statement with a far more hesitant "Didn't you?"

"As a matter of fact, I did." He didn't wait for her response but slowed the Jeep slightly as it entered the forest and disappeared from the view of anyone near the front gate. Then he said, "I don't want to stop, because they time you from the gate, but take a look around and tell me if you notice anything out of the ordinary."

Robin obediently looked out the Jeep's window at the forest through which they passed. "They time you from the gate?"

"Always. See anything?"

"Well . . . no. Just woods."

"They've planted a lot of holly bushes all through here," Sawyer told her. "Big ones. Good natural barriers if you don't want visitors. This time of year, plenty of birds count on the holly berries for food. See the bushes?"

"Yeah."

"See any birds?"

"No," she replied slowly.

"There were birds in town," he said. "I took special notice of them. But the farther out we came, the closer we got to the Compound, the fewer birds I saw."

Robin turned her head and stared at him. "What on earth does that mean?"

"I wish to hell I knew."

She was silent as the Jeep picked up a little speed, then said, "What Pel said. No wildlife on his morning walks. Why do I get the creepy feeling that when we get to the main part of the Compound, we aren't going to see any dogs or cats?"

Even though she had never formally been inside the Compound, Robin, like most residents of Grace, was undoubtedly familiar with the physical layout of the place.

It got discussed in town. A lot.

The church was sited pretty much dead-center on the two-hundred-acre parcel of land it owned. Around the large and impressive central building that was the church proper was a formal square, with neat little houses lining three sides of the square and set out with equal neatness along the four half-mile-long roads that stretched out from the corners of the square and ended in cul-de-sacs.

Sawyer could have drawn it out on a map. In fact, he had, bothered by the neatness and exactitude of the Compound. But if there was a pattern there, it meant nothing to him.

"They used to have animals," he told his officer. "Most every house had a dog in the backyard, a cat on the front porch. There were always a couple of dogs tagging along after the kids, and a cat or two in every barn to help control mice. Plus livestock in the pastures. Ponies for the kids, some trail horses, milk and beef cattle."

"But not now?"

"No. I wanted to warn you, in case you noticed, not to say anything."

"No pets at all? No livestock?"

"Not visible. I suppose there might be dogs or cats inside, but they used to be easy to spot."

"When did you notice they weren't?"

"Last week, when I came up here to talk about Ellen Hodges. Before then I hadn't been up here since, probably, back in the fall sometime. I remember dogs barking then and seeing cattle and horses in the pastures around the Compound. Last week, nothing but people."

Robin cleared her throat. "You know, the first thing that popped into my head when you said that was—"

"Some kind of devil worship. Animal sacrifice. Yeah, I figured."

"You don't think?"

As the Jeep emerged from the woods and into a wide valley where the church and its score of small, neat houses lay just ahead, Sawyer answered, "I have a hunch the truth's a lot more complicated." He knew that Robin was looking around at the houses as they neared the Square, that she was looking for dogs or cats or signs of livestock, but Sawyer's gaze was fixed on the tall, wide-shouldered man waiting for them on the steps of the church.

The man who checked his watch as the Jeep entered the Square.

"A hell of a lot more complicated," Sawyer repeated.

Four

GIVEN WHAT she'd been told and what she'd learned on her own about cults, Tessa had expected to be disturbed on any number of levels while she was among the congregation of the Church of the Everlasting Sin, but what she hadn't expected to feel was a sensation of sheer unreality.

It was, she decided, a surface place.

The surface was pretty, ordered, calm, peaceful. The people Ruth introduced her to were smiling and seemingly content and greeted her with courteous welcome. The neat little houses boasted neat little well-manicured lawns and pruned shrubbery. The children—all home-schooled, she was told—laughed and ran around the very nicely designed playground off to the right of the main square, pausing in their play only long enough to run up, when summoned by Ruth, to be introduced en masse to Tessa.

"Children, say hello to Mrs. Gray. She's visiting us today."

"Good afternoon, Mrs. Gray. Welcome." It was a chorus, bright and cheerful, accompanied by big smiles.

Tessa wasn't all that familiar with children, but this bunch struck her as exceptionally polite. And rather eerily similar in that they were all impeccably dressed—especially for playtime—without so much as a smudge of dirt or visible wrinkle in their neat white shirts, light-weight blue jackets, dark pants (the boys), and dark skirts (the girls).

"Hi," Tessa responded, wondering how many of these kids Sarah had known, if there were any she had been close to. By all accounts, she had taken a special interest in the children. "No school today?"

"Our children are home-schooled," Ruth reminded her.

"And it's our playground time," a dark, solemn-eyed boy told Tessa. "Not as cold as yesterday, so we can be outside longer."

"I see."

Ruth shooed them away before Tessa really had time to pick out any more individual faces; she wasn't even certain whose small hand touched hers briefly before the group ran back to their playground.

"They're all fine children," Ruth said to her.

"I'm sure they are." What else could she say?

"Perhaps you can visit with them longer another time. I didn't want you to be overwhelmed, Tessa. So many faces, so many names. I do want you to meet some of our members, even though we have plenty of time for you to get to know everybody."

"Yes. Yes, of course."

Ruth continued the tour, pointing out this or that as they walked slowly around the Square.

As scrubbed and neat as the children, all the buildings were beautifully maintained, as though they had been freshly painted only this morning.

Especially the big, gleaming white three-story church itself, which was very churchlike, with rows of stained-glass windows (though generic abstract patterns, with no biblical scenes Tessa could identify) and a tall steeple with a simple cross atop a bell tower.

She could see the bells gleaming even from ground level.

The church was surrounded, like all the houses in the little neighborhood, with a neat lawn. Wide steps led from the front walkway that was pretty and cobbled up to the gleaming wooden doors that were wide and welcoming.

But there was something just a little bit off in all the Norman Rockwell Americana perfection, and it wouldn't take a psychic, Tessa decided, to pick up on it. There was an eerie sameness to the faces, the smiles, the simple clothing, even the gestures. From the children to the adults, they all looked . . . almost indistinguishable.

Interchangeable.

I wonder if the missing people were just replaced by fresh ones, new recruits. And nobody noticed. Or cared.

That was a horrifying thought and one Tessa shoved grimly from her mind as Ruth continued to introduce her around.

"Welcome, Mrs. Gray. We're happy to have you here."

"Thank you." Tessa shook hands with a couple who looked a lot like the previous six couples she had met since her arrival: somewhere in their thirties, a faint scent of soap clinging to them, a kind of bedrock serenity in their smiles—and an odd, shiny flatness in their eyes.

Stepford. I'm in Stepford.

"Everyone would love to meet you on this visit, of course, but we know that would be too much," Ruth told her as she led the way, finally, back toward the church. "Plus, many of our members work in town and haven't gotten home yet today."

The church, peaceful and perfect in appearance, was now marred slightly by a dirty Jeep parked nearby, the logo on its side the seal of the Grace Police Department.

Cops. Cops she could trust?

Or cops who would prove to be one more layer of deceptive normality in this place?

"I had no idea the Compound was so large," Tessa lied, ignoring the Jeep. "How many families live here?"

"We have twenty-one cottages, plus the gatehouse," Ruth answered. "I believe all of them are currently occupied. And, of course, we have rooms and dormitories for our single members in the church itself."

"Really? Isn't that unusual?"

"Not for our church."

Since she wasn't offered any opening to probe that further, Tessa shifted the subject a bit. "No members live outside the Compound?"

"A few, though not many. We're a community," Ruth told her, smiling. "We don't require all our members to live here, but so far most have chosen to. Eventually."

That last word was oddly chilling, and Tessa did her best not to shiver visibly; it was a very mild day for January, after all. "I already have a home in Grace," she pointed out.

"Your husband's family home. Forgive me, but can it really feel like home to you?"

Tessa allowed the silence to stretch as she walked beside the other woman up the wide steps to the open front doors of the church, not answering until they stepped over the threshold. "It doesn't," she admitted after a moment, being more honest than Ruth could know. "The house is too big and . . . I ramble around in there. Sometimes it almost echoes it's so empty." She allowed her voice to wobble a bit, her eyes to tear.

"I'm sorry, Tessa—I didn't mean to upset you."

"No, it's just . . . The happy families out there . . . The way I feel in Jared's family home—"

"There's a restroom off the vestibule where you can have a few moments alone. It's as safe a place as you'll find in there. The stalls are tiled from the floor almost to the ceiling, and the doors are big. The recreation area where people tend to congregate at odd hours is downstairs, so the main-floor restroom isn't used much except around the times of services."

Tessa managed to squeeze out a tear. "If you don't mind—a restroom?"

"Of course, of course. It's just over there, ladies' room on the left side." Ruth's voice was warmly sympathetic. "I'll be here. Take your time."

The restroom was fairly large and brightly lit, with six stalls and three sinks, and like everything else she had seen was exceptionally neat, to the point of appearing to be newly scrubbed. Tessa looked around briefly but wasted little time in locking herself into the stall farthest from the door.

Hollis's information had been right: These stalls were designed for a great deal more privacy than those usually found in a public facility. In fact, the stall struck Tessa as a bit claustrophobic, and she had to take a deep breath as she closed the toilet lid and sat down on it.

Focus. Concentrate.

She was wary of opening herself up completely in a place where she felt so uneasy and even trapped, but she wasn't at all sure control was a luxury she could afford. Still, as she closed her eyes and concentrated, she did her best not to drop her shields completely.

Pain.

It was immediate and intense, fire burning along her nerve endings, exploding in her mind, and it took everything Tessa had not to cry out. Her hands reached out to the tile walls on either side of her, and she instinctively braced herself, or tried to, pushing against the cold tile, against the hot, shimmering pain, against the incredibly strong presence she was instantly aware of.

I see you.

He'd been given at birth the triple-barrel name that sounded so biblical and had served him so well: Adam Deacon Samuel. His mother's mocking joke.

There was certainly nothing biblical about being the bastard son of a whore.

Samuel frowned and shifted in his chair, keeping his eyes closed. It was his custom to meditate every day at this time, and every day God tested him by beginning the ritual with forcing him to remember where he came from and who he had once been.

It was ... difficult. But there was no relief, no peace to be found until he forced his way through the memories.

The first few years were fuzzy; by the time he was old enough to wonder why she hadn't just aborted him, he knew the answer. Because she wanted someone to endure a more tormented existence than she did herself.

And she made sure he did.

He doubted most of the johns had even noticed, much less cared, that a usually filthy and often hungry boy had crouched in the corner of some seedy motel room and watched, eyes wide and fixed, the fornication that was always hurried and furtive, and often abusive.

She'd taught him to smoke, both cigarettes and pot, by the time he was four, burning his body with the glowing embers until he could inhale without coughing. Taught him how to steal by the time he was six and how to defend himself with a knife before he was seven — though she could always take the weapon away from him on those rare occasions when he found the guts to try to defend himself from her.

"Stupid little bastard. I could have let them scrape you out of my belly when I knew his seed had taken root. But that don't mean I can't scrape you out of my life now. Understand, Sammy? Or do I have to show you just what I can do to you?"

It never made any difference if he answered, because she always "showed" him. Sometimes he was locked in a closet for a day or longer. Sometimes she beat him. Other times she…played with him. Like a cat with a mouse, mangling and torturing its prey until the pathetic little creature just stopped trying to escape and waited dumbly for the end to come.

He'd believed he was numb to all of it, enduring his lot in stoic silence, until she began bringing in johns with…special tastes.

It amused her to watch them use him. And then there was the money. She was able to charge a premium for his virginity. After that…well, he was still small. Young. As good as a virgin, she told them. She developed a skill for finding those men who enjoyed using him no matter how many had used him before.

Samuel gripped the arms of his chair and forced himself to breathe deeply and evenly.

Memories.

Just memories.

They couldn't hurt him anymore.

Except, of course, that they did. Always. But less and less as time had passed. As if holding a burning coal in his mind, in his soul, and blowing on it from time to time, like this, he could feel layers of himself being seared away. Cauterized.

It was a good thing.

He hadn't been able to do that then. Not in the beginning. Hadn't been able to stop the pain in any way at all. Hadn't been able to stop the mother who abused him or the johns who did even more unspeakable things to him.

Looking back now, in the light of God's pure certainty, he understood what had finally happened to him. He understood that God had tested him. And tested him. He understood that those early years had begun to shape the steel of God's holy sword.

He hadn't seen those miserable, dark, dank motel rooms as a series of crucibles, or those faceless men, brutish and cruel, as anointed by God to destroy the base metal he had been in order to make of it something great.

But he saw now. He understood.

The first destruction of who and what he had been took place in one of those desolate rooms, late one night when it was cold and stormy outside. Maybe it had been winter. Or maybe it had just been one of those perpetually cold cities along his mother's long, wandering life. He couldn't remember.

He remembered only that he'd been vaguely surprised that she had found a john at all on such a night, far less one looking for a boy. But his stoic resignation had turned to quivering terror when a hulk of a man filled the doorway, almost forced to turn sideways in order to come into the room.

Samuel remembered few details of the next few hours, but he remembered a broad, coarse-featured face in which small eyes burned cruelly. And he remembered his mother's glee, her laughing encouragement, as the john held him in one giant paw and literally ripped the worn, too-small clothing from his body.

He could hear her laughter even now, echoing in his mind. Hear the john's hoarse grunts of sadistic pleasure. And he could feel his body ripping, tearing, feel the warm blood and the white-hot shimmering blaze of pure agony that had crackled across every nerve ending his small body possessed.

And then... nothing.

A darkness unlike anything he had ever known or imagined surrounded him, enfolded him in warmth. He felt strong. He felt calm. He felt cherished. He felt safe.

Samuel had no idea how long that had lasted, though judging by what he found when he woke up, it was hours at least.

The room was warm when he woke, which surprised him because the sort of motels his mother chose invariably had heaters and air conditioners that hadn't worked in years, and this particular hovel was no exception.

The room was warm, and he was warm, and at some point he must have braved the stained and moldy bathtub, because he was clean and dressed. He wasn't even sore, which surprised him a lot because he was always sore and that john had been so big—

Samuel saw him then. The john. Pinned to one wall of the room like a giant, ugly-ass butterfly in somebody's collection. He was bloody. Very bloody. He looked surprised.

The knife his mother always carried was buried to the hilt in the john's left wrist, and the knife Samuel had stolen for himself months before was likewise buried in the john's right wrist.

Neither would have supported the huge man's weight if not for the thick piece of wood protruding from the center of his chest, clearly driven into the wall behind him. It was a table leg, Samuel realized, from the rickety old table that had sat near the door.

He turned his head just far enough to see that the tabletop lay on the floor, upside down. With all four legs missing.

The room was utterly silent, except for his own suddenly audible breathing.

Slowly, Samuel turned to look at the wall across from where the john hung and saw his mother. Like him, she hung suspended, spread-eagled and pinned in place.

She looked surprised too.

One of the table legs, split neatly in half, pinned each of her wrists to the wall. Another table leg, also halved, had been driven through her legs just above her ankles.

The fourth and final table leg, whole, was driven into her body between her breasts, buried so deeply that only a few inches were visible enough to identify what it had been.

It looked like she had bled a lot; thick reddish stains

coated the peeling wallpaper below her wrists and legs, and the short skirt she wore was no longer pale pink.

Samuel stared at her for a long, long time. He thought he should probably feel something, even if only relief, but all he felt was a kind of indifferent curiosity.

It must have taken a lot of strength, he thought, to have pinned the huge john to the wall. And he knew his mother, knew how ferociously she'd fight to defend herself. So it would have taken somebody strong to do that to her. Somebody really strong.

Her eyes were open, he realized.

Open—and white. No color at all.

When he looked at the john, he saw the same. Eyes open. But totally without color.

Weird.

He still didn't feel anything and for a long time just sat there looking back and forth between the two dead bodies. Eventually he got up and dragged his mother's old duffel bag from inside the closet. Since they never unpacked, his few bits of clothing and her things were still in it. He dumped all the contents on the bed, then picked out his own things and put them back in the duffel.

He raided the bathroom of its meager supplies of threadbare towels and tiny shrink-wrapped soaps and put those in his bag. He found on the floor the man's pants and emptied the pockets, finding a big switchblade, a few coins, a couple of crumpled receipts, and a wallet. The wallet had several credit cards and a surprisingly thick wad of cash.

Samuel hadn't spent more than a week at any one time in school, but when it came to money, he could count. Twenty-seven hundred dollars.

It was a fortune. It was enough.

He put the money and the knife in the duffel, then added to it the far-less-princely sum he found in his mother's secret hiding place. Less than two hundred dollars.

He put the last of her cigarettes in the duffel, weighed her lighter in one hand for a moment, then set it aside and zipped the bag closed. It was heavy even with so little in it, but he was strong for his size and lifted it easily. He picked up his mother's lighter and went to the door, pausing only then to look back at the bodies.

He wondered idly what had happened to their eyes, because that was just weird. Really weird.

Then he shrugged it off, life so far having taught him that if the answer wasn't obvious, it was probably best left alone.

The lighter was the kind you didn't throw away, the kind with a lid that opened and a wheel that turned and sparked off a flint. He opened the lid and turned the wheel with his thumb, and for a moment he just watched the small flame. Then he tossed the lighter to land on the floor near the bed, where an ugly, stained bedspread lay crumpled.

Immediately, it began to burn.

Adam Deacon Samuel unlocked the door and left the motel room, closing the door behind him. He turned right, because it seemed as good a direction as any other, and started walking. He never looked back at the burning building.

He was ten years old.

Tessa struggled to breathe.

Pain. Awful, soul-rending pain that wasn't only physical but emotional as well. Pain that washed over her in waves, each one greater than the last.

And darkness. A darkness so black it was almost beyond comprehension, so black it swallowed all the light and reached hungrily for life. Reaching...grasping...

She could hear herself trying to breathe, hear the jerky little pants, but every other sense was turned inward as she grappled with the pain, tried to dull it.

Hurt...

Mute it.

Hurt...

Deflect it.

Hurt...

She tried to feel her way through the horrible darkness, beyond it.

It seemed impossibly difficult for the longest time, for what seemed eons, until finally, faintly, she became aware of other things besides the continual burning pain.

Sensations. Emotions. Fragmented thoughts.

...the poor thing...

...must get away...

...should it feel so good?

...have to get away...

...joy...utter joy...
...why did he kill them?
...it won't happen...
...why them?
...have to get Lexie out of here...
...it can't happen...
...if that's what heaven is...
...escape...
...he takes...
...takes...
I'm hungry.

Her eyes snapped open, and Tessa stared fixedly at the stall door. That last bald statement, stark in the darkness, gnawing in its hollow desperation, echoed inside her mind. For no more than a heartbeat or two, she had the sense of an emptiness so great it was almost beyond her ability to grasp.

And then it was gone. All the other emotions, gone. The bits and pieces of thoughts, gone. The overwhelming pain was gone.

She was safely protected, once again, behind her shields.

Tessa drew a breath and felt her hands slide down the cold tile, felt the ache in her arms that told her she had been literally pushing against the walls of the trap she had felt in her mind.

I see you.

Hard as she tried, Tessa couldn't decide if that clear statement, that amazingly strong presence, had been positive or negative. She thought it was not the same "voice" that had declared its hunger, because that voice had definitely come out of the darkness.

I see you.

Who saw her? Who was able to reach her like that? Able to reach her mind, semiguarded though it had been, and deliver that simple, clear statement?

She got to her feet, shaky, and automatically flushed the toilet before leaving the stall. She went to one of the sinks and stared at her reflection in the mirror, only then aware that her cheeks were wet with tears, her eyes red-rimmed.

It might, she supposed, look like grief.

But the trickle of blood from one nostril would not.

Tessa got some tissue and wiped away the blood, conscious now that her head was throbbing and she was chilled to the bone. Neither of those things was something she had ever experienced before while using her abilities.

Had her own efforts caused it, leaving her vulnerable to damage from the sheer force of the energies in this place? Could it be that simple, that—relatively—unthreatening?

Or had it been a specific attack, force directed at her?

She didn't know.

But either possibility was frightening.

When she was sure the bleeding had stopped, she splashed water on her face, then dried it with a paper towel, wondering how long she had been in here. Not as long as it seemed, surely, or else Ruth would have been knocking at the door.

Right on cue, a soft knock fell.

Tessa gave her reflection one last look, squared her shoulders, and then went to open the restroom door.

"I'm sorry—I didn't mean to be so long."

"Oh, no, child, no need to apologize." Ruth's sharp face softened, and she reached out to pat Tessa's shoulder. "I should be the one to say I'm sorry, to have upset you."

"It wasn't you, honestly. Just...I just felt overwhelmed for a few minutes. It happens sometimes."

"But less and less often. I know, child. I'm a widow myself."

"Then you understand." She managed a smile, wondering if it ever got any easier, pretending to be something she wasn't.

"Of course I understand. Everyone here understands, believe me. We've all faced loss of some kind. Grief. Pain. And we've all found solace here."

As the older woman took a step back, Tessa came out of the restroom and joined her in the vestibule. She was just about to say something about still being unsure, knowing it would be viewed with suspicion if she seemed to give way and give in too suddenly, when three other people appeared from inside the church, paused near the front doors, then came toward them.

"Oh, dear," Ruth murmured beneath her breath.

The obvious cop was the young woman, hardly more than a girl, really, who wore her crisp uniform with an entirely visible pride. But the man on her right was also a cop, if Tessa was any judge, even though he didn't wear a uniform. At least a decade older than the young woman, he was casual in dark slacks and a leather jacket worn over an open-collar shirt. No tie. In fact, the shirt looked somewhat rumpled.

He looked somewhat rumpled.

His square jaw was shadowed by a faint beard that probably needed shaving more than once a day, and his dark hair looked as though fingers or wind had ruffled it in the very recent past. But there was nothing untidy or careless about that level, dark-eyed gaze.

Oh, yeah. Definitely a cop.

Tessa looked at the third person, a tall man with wide shoulders and the most coldly handsome face she had ever seen on something not made of actual stone. He had thick fair hair and pale blue eyes, and even though he was expressionless and without the pleasant, eerily serene smile worn by practically every other person she had seen here, he unquestionably belonged.

With an effort, Tessa pulled her gaze away from that hard face.

"Hello, Mrs. Gray," the male cop greeted her. His tone was probably meant to be polite, but nature had given him a rough, gruff voice that rumbled slightly and made his words somewhat abrupt.

"I'm sorry," she said. "Have we met?"

"Not officially. I'm Chief Cavenaugh. Sawyer Cavenaugh. I knew your husband."

Oh, great. That's just great. Because I never met the man.

Five

SAWYER WASN'T all that surprised to find Tessa Gray here in the Compound and within the church. A woman in her situation—newly widowed, alone in a strange town, and quite wealthy in terms of property and business—was just the sort of potential church member who would have been on their radar from the day she arrived in Grace.

Possibly even before she arrived.

He had intended to warn her but had wanted to give her a week or so to settle in here. And then people had begun going missing, anxious relatives had been calling him, and bodies had turned up. Warning Tessa Gray about the aggressive recruiting practices of the Church of the Everlasting Sin had simply fallen down his list of priorities.

He was sorry about that now.

She'd been pointed out to him in town, from a distance; up close, she looked even more vulnerable, more fragile. And also very attractive.

With a slight, strained smile, she extended her hand, saying, "I'm sorry, Chief Cavenaugh. Jared didn't say much to me about Grace or the people he knew growing up here. He told me he left for college and never came back."

"No, as far as I know, he never did. We weren't close," he felt compelled to add, "so we didn't keep in touch."

Extremely attractive.

Don't be a jerk and hit on your dead childhood friend's widow when he's barely in the ground, Sawyer chided himself, holding that delicate hand as gently as he could manage—and very aware of DeMarco's silent attention. *And don't provide the ghoul with his amusement for the day.*

Even so, he heard himself saying, "Call me Sawyer, please."

"Thank you. I'm Tessa."

Sawyer forced himself to release her hand, very reluctantly. "If there's anything I can do to make things easier for you, Tessa, I hope you'll let me know." *Idiot. Could you sound any more awkward?*

"I appreciate that," she responded, grave now.

Belatedly, Sawyer introduced Robin Keever to the others, and then Ruth Hardin introduced Reese DeMarco to Tessa.

So now we all know who we are.

Sawyer didn't know why, but he couldn't seem to shut up the sarcastic voice in his head. It was, actually, a bit unnerving.

"The chief had some questions," DeMarco told Ruth. "What we heard was true. There was another body found in the river this morning."

"Oh, how awful." Ruth shook her head. "Do they know who it was?"

"The chief seemed to feel we might know that."

"That we might know? Why?"

"Because of Ellen, I gather."

"I don't understand."

"Neither do I," DeMarco said dryly.

The chief sounds like a moron.

Ruth looked at Sawyer. "Poor Ellen. We do feel that we failed her, Chief Cavenaugh." She sounded genuinely troubled. "If we had only known how upset she was—"

"Mrs. Hardin, no one here even reported Ellen Hodges missing, something I find surprising since she was clearly in the river at least a few days before her body was discovered. Nor has her husband or daughter been reported missing, despite the fact that neither can be found."

"Chief, our church is hardly a prison. We told you—showed you—that Ken and Wendy's clothing and other things are gone. That the family car is gone. Obviously, whatever caused Ellen to take her life—"

"She did not commit suicide," Sawyer said.

Ruth's chin jutted stubbornly. "I know what I believe, Chief. I'm very, very sorry Ellen couldn't find what she needed in our church, in us, but I am absolutely convinced that no one here had anything to do with this tragedy."

"Yes," Sawyer said. "I know you are." *But not all of you are convinced. At least one of you knows otherwise.*

He glanced at Tessa, a little surprised that she was so still and silent, and even more surprised when he caught her gaze for only an instant and saw an unexpected sharpness lurking in those big gray eyes.

Huh. Maybe not so vulnerable, after all?

"In any case," DeMarco said, his tone still dry, "excepting the Hodges, we're all present and accounted for, as I told the chief."

Ruth nodded. "Absolutely. Everyone was at morning prayers today."

"As I'm sure you'll all swear," Sawyer muttered.

"Of course. It's the truth."

I wish I could see something unexpected in her eyes. But, no. She believes what she's saying. She always does.

"I'd still like to talk to Reverend Samuel."

"The reverend is at his afternoon prayers, Chief. A very important private time of quiet and meditation for him, especially before evening services. And you don't, after all, have any evidence connecting the unfortunate person found today in the river with any of us or our church." DeMarco's smile was hardly worth the effort and never came close to warming his eyes.

Robin cleared her throat and shifted her slight weight just a bit.

She could stand a little inscrutable right about now.

"I have plenty of evidence," Sawyer said stubbornly, "connecting Ellen Hodges to all of you and this church.

And while I'm sure Mrs. Hardin is completely sincere in her beliefs, my job requires me to explore that evidence."

"Which you have done," DeMarco countered.

"It's an open case. A death under mysterious circumstances."

"Mysterious?"

"She didn't drown," Sawyer said. "She didn't die of a heart attack or a stroke. She wasn't shot or stabbed or hit over the head. But she is dead. And I will find out what happened to her."

Yeah, toss a gauntlet at his feet. That'll probably work out just great.

"I'm sure you will, Chief."

Arrogant bastard.

"I think," Tessa said a bit hesitantly, "I should probably be going."

"Oh, no," Ruth protested. "I haven't even had time to show you around inside the church."

Under normal circumstances, Sawyer would have apologized for keeping them and got out of the way. But not this time. This time he merely waited silently. Because he wasn't about to do anything to help them get their claws deeper into Tessa Gray.

Yeah, you're purely unselfish, you are.

"I can always see the rest of the church another day," Tessa was saying with a polite but clearly strained smile.

Ruth shot Sawyer a look that didn't hold a lot of Christian forgiveness, then said to Tessa, "Of course you can, child. I'll walk you back to your car. Chief. Officer Keever."

"Ladies." Sawyer watched the two women until they passed through the main doors and out of the church, then shifted his gaze to find DeMarco watching him with a little smile.

Irritated, Sawyer said, "I could stick around for Wednesday evening services, just in case Reverend Samuel has a few minutes afterward to talk to me."

"Yes. You could. Though Reverend Samuel is always very tired after services and retires to his apartment for the night. Still, you're more than welcome to stay. Is that what you'd like to do, Chief?"

You don't need to chase after Tessa now; she'll think you're a stalker. Or something worse. Take advantage of this offer and do your damn job.

Sawyer told the sarcastic inner voice to shut the hell up and said, "Yes, as a matter of fact, I would like to stay."

Reese DeMarco smiled that smile that never softened his stone face or warmed his icy eyes and said, "Our doors are always open, Chief."

Bambi Devenny had been christened Barbara, but her delicate, doe-eyed beauty as an infant had led to the nickname, and she had really never answered to anything else. It had gotten her teased in school, her situation not helped by the fact that she had matured much faster than the girls around her, skipping the training bra entirely and going straight to a C-cup.

After that, only the other girls teased her.

The boys liked her. A lot.

Or, at least, so Bambi had believed. It hadn't been until the school guidance counselor had talked to her about her skimpy tops and too-tight jeans and baldly asked if she was using birth control and protection against STDs that it had slowly dawned on Bambi that all the muttered I-love-yous in the backseats of cars and under the bleachers at football games meant a lot less than she had believed.

She didn't think she would ever forget the mixture of compassion and distaste on the counselor's face as she explained that Bambi's mother should have warned her about boys and how they would take advantage of girls who slept around.

Had taken advantage.

Bambi had gone home that day nearly in tears to find yet another "uncle" laughing and drinking with her mother, and when the man had turned his hot-eyed gaze on the daughter as soon as the mother passed out, the lesson had been reinforced.

Bambi fended him off with an empty whiskey bottle, then packed her few things and left. She hadn't seen her mother since.

How she had wound up, finally, at the Church of the Everlasting Sin was a tale of a rough and sinful life on the streets, doing what she had to do in order to survive.

"We understand, child," Father told her, his voice deep and warm and inexpressibly comforting. "You had no choice."

"Yes, Father. I hated myself, but it was the only way I knew to make enough money to eat." She kept her gaze on his kind face, oblivious, as she always was when giving Testimony, to the other church members watching and listening from the pews.

As long as Father heard, as long as he understood, she didn't care about anyone else.

"Go on, child." He put his hand on her shoulder, and Bambi could feel the warmth of that touch spreading all through her body.

"It was harder to earn money sometimes," she said obediently. "No matter what I—I was willing to do. So sometimes I got a meal and a cot at some mission or soup kitchen or church. I'm sure plenty of the people there tried to help me. To talk to me. But I wasn't ready to listen."

"Until?" Father prompted gently.

"Until I met someone at a soup kitchen in Asheville back around Thanksgiving. Someone who told me about the Church of the Everlasting Sin. She said I'd be welcome here. She said I'd find peace here. She said I'd find God here."

"And have you, child?"

"Oh, yes, Father. I've found *everything* here." Bambi sank to her knees before him, her head bowed. "Bless me, Father."

"God blesses you, child." He lay both his hands, one over the other, on her bowed head and began to pray out loud.

The church was dim, the lights down low, except for the very bright spotlight focused on the two who were on the—Sawyer could only think of it as a stage. The whole thing struck him as a kind of performance, as it had the other dozen or so times he had "visited" here during services.

As he watched intently, paying little attention to the prayers Reverend Samuel was intoning, he saw the man change, saw his rather ordinary face grow pale for a few seconds—and then regain its former color and more, becoming flushed in the cheeks. He lifted his face toward the heaven to which he was praying, and there was an expression of exaltation on his regular features.

That look transformed him from any man—every man—to a man touched by a divine presence.

Or so it seemed.

As for Bambi, when the prayer concluded, to an echoed "Amen" from the congregation, and she was helped to her feet by Reverend Samuel, her legs appeared wobbly and her face, like his, was transformed. It glowed. Her cheeks were flushed, her mouth half open, lips glistening, and her breasts rose and fell visibly as she breathed in jerky little pants.

For all the world as though she had just had an orgasm—or at the very least soared right to the brink.

Even from where they were standing at the rear of the church, Sawyer could see all that, and it creeped him out as it had every time he had seen it happen. Which was every time he had watched and listened to one of the female members of the church give their "Testimony."

"Is it just me," Robin whispered from the corner of her mouth, "or do you feel like we've been looking into somebody's bedroom?"

Sawyer indicated the door with a jerk of his head, and they both slipped out of the church. He didn't speak until they were at the top of the steps with the doors closed behind them. From inside they could hear the congregation singing a hymn with a fervor and volume that made it sound as if they numbered several hundred voices rather than barely one hundred.

"*Was* it just me?" Robin demanded.

Sawyer zipped his jacket against the cold of the evening and jammed his hands in the pockets. His sigh misted in the air. "No, it wasn't just you. That's the way it always looks."

"Always?"

"Always when the women give Testimony."

"But not the men?"

"No."

"So there is something...sexual about it?"

"You saw what I saw," Sawyer reminded her. "He touched her shoulder and her head, nothing more until he helped her to her feet after it was all over with. He prayed over her for about a minute. He called on God to bless her. Whatever happened to her then...Hell, I don't know. I've never been able to figure it out."

Though it does keep his female followers completely devoted to him, doesn't it? Blindly devoted.

"Doesn't look like any church I've ever been to," Robin said. "And in addition to the more traditional versions, my parents tried out every Bible-thumping, singing-for-salvation, speaking-in-tongues, snake-handling, out-of-the-mainstream church you could name."

Sawyer frowned. "Aren't they Baptists?"

"Yeah. But they wanted me to experience religion in every possible form so I could make up my own mind. We even drove to Asheville to try out Catholic churches and Jewish synagogues. I'm sure if they could have found a Buddhist temple or an Islamic mosque, we would have gone there too."

He shook off various peculiar mental images with an effort and said, "Well, then you know that offering testimony isn't that uncommon, though it's not a regular thing with most of the churches I know of. Here, it is. At every service, at least one member goes forward to tell their story."

"Is it always that depressing? I mean, I had no idea what all Bambi had been through."

"Well, that's the thing about this church. Everybody has a sad story. Everybody was lost, alone, and at the end of their respective ropes when they found the church— or the church found them. Very convenient, isn't it?"

"So it's true. They do target vulnerable people."

"I believe so."

"What's in it for the church?" Robin asked, always practical. "I mean, collecting lost souls should be enough for any religion, but a church usually needs stuff in return. Like money."

"Members are expected to tithe."

"That's it?"

"Well, the church doesn't officially accept land or the titles to businesses or other properties directly from their members. But they do have a habit of offering up help to members' businesses, they do gain goods and services from members, and they do buy up, with their surplus funds, parcels of land all over the place."

"Why?"

"I have no idea. Useless land, mostly, often with abandoned buildings falling to ruin."

"They hoping for a real estate boom?"

"Beats the hell out of me."

Robin turned her head to look out on the peaceful, well-lit square, the neat little houses all around, each with lighted windows even though virtually every soul in the Compound was inside the church. She shivered visibly and zipped her own jacket closed.

"Spooked?" Sawyer asked.

"I have to say I am. I'd heard stuff—plenty of stuff. But actually being inside there and watching... I dunno. Nothing obviously weird happened in there, and yet..."

"And yet it felt wrong."

"Totally wrong. Can we leave now, please?"

"Might as well." *Because you know damn well De-Marco will make sure you don't see Samuel tonight. Not after services. Not when he's drained and possibly less guarded. Dammit.* "If tonight is like every other night they hold services, they'll be in there singing and praying another hour or more."

"How often do they hold services?" Robin asked as they headed down the steps and across the Square to the parked Jeep.

"Officially, Sunday and Sunday night, and again on Wednesday night."

"And unofficially?"

"I have no idea. Every time I've been here, there've been people inside the church. Some sitting in the pews, I guess praying or meditating. A lot more down in the recreation area."

"Playing instead of praying?"

"Playing sedately. Reading, sewing, playing Ping-Pong or cards or air hockey, putting together jigsaw puzzles, watching TV or movies."

They both climbed into the Jeep, and Sawyer hastily got it started so the cold interior could begin to warm up.

"Maybe I'm being paranoid," Robin said, "but I half-expected DeMarco to be sticking to us like glue. Especially once we left the building. I mean, we could go anywhere. Unsupervised."

"If we'd done anything but walk straight to the Jeep and get in, we would have had company immediately. I gather you didn't notice all the cameras?"

Robin looked out the window toward the now very brightly lit church. "Honestly, no. There was so much else to look at." She sounded apologetic and a little annoyed at herself.

"Don't beat yourself up about it. The cameras aren't obvious. If you didn't know what to look for, you'd never see them. And even if you did, I doubt you'd be able to tell that they're infrared and motion-activated."

"Monitored?"

"Oh, yeah. From somewhere inside the main building, I imagine, though I've never seen the actual control room of this place. I doubt many people have."

"So the whole time we've been here—"

"We've been watched. Less likely that there are microphones, outside at least, but I've never been sure."

"Jesus. Can we go? Please?"

Since he'd had his fill of the place himself, at least for today, Sawyer merely nodded and put the Jeep in gear.

"**S**he couldn't tell where the pain was coming from?" Bishop asked.

"Not really." Hollis propped the phone between her ear and shoulder as she rinsed her coffee cup. "Seemed to come from all around her, or was just…unfocused. Maybe impossible for her to get a fix on at the best of times, far less during her first visit to the Compound. She did say it was overwhelming, and she certainly looked like she'd been through the wringer. It's barely ten, and she's already gone up to bed."

Bishop was silent for a moment, then said, "She sensed at least two extremely strong personalities."

"Yeah. A lot of fragmented stuff, but those two 'voices' were perfectly clear. One said, 'I see you,' and the other said, 'I'm hungry.' And if Tessa wasn't sure about the former, she's damn positive that the latter voice was dark as hell. She was absolutely adamant about that."

"But no real sense of identity."

"No. She met a lot of people up there, but Ruth Hardin was the only one she really spent time with. Probably too much to expect her to connect a voice in her head with anybody she might have met fleetingly."

"When she returned, was she just tired? Or spooked?"

"Tired *and* spooked. Didn't want it to show, I think, but it did. I didn't ask too many questions, but I gather she's never felt a physical sensation during a vision. This time, she did. Whether someone was out to physically hurt her or it was simply the intensity of the experience, this is the first time her abilities have been painful."

"Evolving? Or affected by whatever energies Samuel is using up there?"

"I don't know. Either. Both. I felt something odd about this place the minute I hit town."

"Odd how?"

"It's nothing I can really pinpoint. Small town, a bit isolated, quiet. Almost too quiet, though. Almost too . . . placid. It's sort of eerie, really. Have we tested the water here?" She was joking. Mostly.

"We've tested just about everything," Bishop told her. "So far, nothing suspicious has turned up."

"Maybe I'm wrong. But it strikes me as more than a little strange that not even the local newspaper has given much space to inexplicably dead bodies found in the river."

"The owner is a church member. So is the senior news editor and at least one of the reporters."

"Okay, then probably not so strange. But no less creepy. It means Samuel's influence extends outside the Compound."

"Yes."

"And we don't know whether that influence is *only* emotional and psychological—or psychic as well."

"No, we don't know. Yet. But the Compound is the center, and that's where the answers have to be. Samuel hasn't left the property in weeks."

"So whatever the weirdness is, it's in all probability caused by Samuel and would be most intense up there. Maybe he's getting stronger, just naturally evolving. Or maybe he's about to blow. Either way, it could affect *our* abilities, especially when any of us are in or near the Compound. Cause them to change, to fluctuate. To evolve. Sarah had been having problems, right?"

"Yeah." Bishop's voice flattened slightly. "Difficulty in concentration, in focusing. And she felt her shield had become weaker over time."

"Felt correctly, I'd say." Hollis kept her own voice even. "For whatever reason, her shield couldn't protect her. The question is, can Tessa's shield protect her?"

"I have to believe it will."

The choice of words struck Hollis, in particular his slight emphasis on the second word, but before she could probe, Bishop asked another calm question.

"She's sure about Chief Cavenaugh?"

"Seemed to be."

"And the others?"

"She couldn't get a fix on either Officer Keever or DeMarco but said Ruth Hardin is an open book."

"What was the reading?"

"What Sarah reported weeks ago. That Ruth, like virtually all the women in the Compound, believes in the church and Samuel utterly and completely. They'd step between him and a bullet without a second thought."

"Devotion indeed," Bishop said slowly.

"Uh-huh."

"You aren't convinced."

"That they're devoted to him, absolutely. That they'd take a bullet for him. But I'd sure like at least one of us to be able to get inside their heads and find out exactly *why* that's true."

"Any other visits from Ellen Hodges?"

"Not so far. It might have taken all the energy she could muster, so soon after dying, to reach me in California. It's a long way from where she died, and that seems to make a difference."

"They do always seem to find you, don't they?"

Hollis returned to the island bar stool where she'd been attempting to work and looked down at maps of the area spread out on the granite surface. "Yeah, I'm definitely supposed to be part of this. But you already knew that."

"Hollis—"

"Bishop, I swear to God, if you don't come clean with me this time—totally clean—then I'm walking." Her voice was very, very calm.

"All right," her boss said finally. "But you aren't going to like it."

Six

SAWYER TOLD ROBIN to go home once they reached the station, but he had a mountain of paperwork and a lot to think about. Added to the fact that he didn't have anyone to go home to, working well into the night and possibly even sleeping on the couch in his office was preferable to returning to a dark apartment with only the TV for company.

Pathetic choice for a grown man to have. Work or an empty apartment. What the hell have you been doing all these years?

It was a good question. He only wished he had a good answer. What did any man do when he hadn't found a woman he wanted to share his life with by the time he was eyeing forty as his next milestone? He worked. If he was lucky, he had a job that occupied most of his time and energy.

And if he was very lucky, that job meant something, counted for something in the sense of attempting to make the world a better place.

Or attempting to just make sense of it.

Not that he was having much luck at the moment.

The station was quiet, the second shift beginning to think about going home at midnight, desk conversation and radio chatter dealing mostly with that and plans for the following day. If he hadn't known a woman's body had been found in the river only that morning, he sure as hell wouldn't have been able to tell it from the relaxed behavior of his officers.

Maybe they have lives.

No, he thought, it was something else. Something more. And it bugged him more than a little. They had always seemed to him curiously detached, most of them. He thought it was undoubtedly a characteristic of officers in any big-city police department, where getting too emotionally involved in stubborn homicide investigations could lead swiftly to burnout, but not so much in small towns where murder was still rare.

Or had been.

They should have been more agitated about these murders. Or at least, by God, interested in them.

"Coffee, Chief?"

He looked at the smiling and slightly quizzical face of Dale Brown and frowned. "You were on duty this morning. Why're you still here, Dale?"

"Picked up an extra shift on account of Terry needing to visit his mom in the hospital up to Asheville. I don't have much overtime in this month, and you said now was the time to get it if we wanted it, what with these bodies turning up in the river."

Sawyer had indeed told his people that, but when he glanced past Dale toward his desk, all he saw was an open magazine.

Dale followed his gaze and said, "My turn to answer the phones, Chief. Only call that's come in tonight was somebody complaining that a neighbor's stereo was turned up too loud."

Sawyer accepted a cup of coffee from his officer. "Check missing persons again. A hundred-mile radius. I need to know if there's any chance that woman might *not* be from the Compound."

"Sure thing, Chief." He sounded almost cheerful.

Why doesn't he *have a sick feeling in the pit of his stomach?*

But Sawyer couldn't really criticize anyone for not being as visibly upset about the situation as he thought they should be, so he merely stopped by another desk for his messages and then went back to his office.

"Tom? What're you doing here? And get the hell out of my chair."

Dr. Tom Macy, the medical examiner for Unity County, took his feet off the desk and unfolded his tall length from Sawyer's chair, yawning. "Almost asleep," he confessed as he moved around the desk to the far less comfortable visitor's chair.

"Is that why you weren't at my crime scene first thing this morning? Pull a double shift at the hospital yesterday?"

He doesn't have anybody to go home to either.

"I did. And it wasn't a crime scene, we both know

that. It wasn't even a dump site, not as far as forensic evidence is concerned. Her body just happened to catch on that fallen tree."

"You should have been there, Tom."

"I got there as soon as I could. And I can't tell you anything much anyway, same as before."

"Nothing more than you told me this morning? That she could have died anything up to a week ago?"

"Yeah, about that." Macy shrugged bony shoulders. He was tall, and thin enough to be familiar with cadaver jokes, especially given his position as county M.E. "Hard to know for sure. Nights have been cold and that mountain river is icy this time of year, so it probably slowed decomp—always assuming she was dumped in pretty soon after she was killed. Not many predators in and around that water as a rule, it moves too fast, but from what I saw, there were enough postmortem injuries that she could have been caught on fallen trees or half-submerged rocks a dozen times while the body worked its way downstream."

"Downstream from the Compound?"

"You know I can't tell you that. Not for sure. She could have been dumped in the river twenty miles away."

"Or two miles away?"

Macy nodded. "Or two miles."

"Which means she could have come from the Compound."

"I can't rule it out," Tom Macy said.

————

Hunter threw a pebble against her window around ten-thirty, and Ruby slipped easily out of her bedroom window to join him outside. "It's early," she whispered. "My parents are still up."

Up and arguing, even if it was so quietly she wasn't supposed to know about it. Arguing about the church.

"They won't be for long," he whispered back. "Besides, I waited until they tucked you in."

Ruby remembered with a pang the days of endless bedtime stories and of being sleepily aware that her mother always checked on her a final time before she and her father went to bed. The girl pushed those painful memories aside.

Things were different now.

Things had been different for a long time.

She followed Hunter as they slipped from her yard and across the next two backyards, heading for the accustomed meeting place at the barn over the hill in the west pasture. They kept well away from the church—and the cameras.

"I can't stay out long," Hunter whispered as they worked their way cautiously toward the barn. "My parents still do a bed check, but it's never before eleven-thirty."

"Why're we meeting at all? It's dangerous, Hunter."

"Because Cody says Brooke's going to make a run for it, and we have to talk her out of it."

"Run for it? Where would she go? All the way to Texas by herself? She's only twelve."

"Yeah, that's why we've got to talk her out of trying."

Ruby didn't speak again until they reached the barn and found their friends had already arrived. The barn had housed three ponies and half a dozen milk cows at one time; now it held only a few small pieces of farm machinery that wouldn't be needed until spring.

It smelled mostly of machine oil and metal.

Not like a barn at all, Ruby decided. But her mind shied away from thinking about that, as it always did. And she simply said to Brooke, "Are you crazy?"

Her friend's strained expression was obvious even in the dim light provided by Cody's small Cub Scout lantern. "Ruby, you're one of the Chosen too. And we're not like the other girls—we know what's happening. What it's doing to us. Don't tell me you aren't scared."

"We have shells." Ruby was trying her best to pretend she wasn't scared.

"And how long are those shells going to protect us? Sarah had a shell, and she's gone. How many others have there been?"

"Brooke—"

"How many? People who just go away—or at least that's what Father and the others tell us. And people who don't go away, except that they *do* because they're different. Because they change."

"We won't change."

"How do you know?"

Before Ruby could respond, Cody spoke up for the first time. Gravely, he said, "I know Brooke can't get all the way to Texas, not without help. But I know something else too. Whatever it is Father's been waiting for, it's nearly here."

They looked at one another in the dim light, and none of them pretended to not be scared. Not even Ruby.

"**S**he didn't drown?" Sawyer asked his medical examiner.

"No. No water in the lungs. No sign of a gunshot wound, or a knife wound, or any blunt-force trauma to the skin or muscle that wasn't postmortem."

"And her bones?"

"Just like it was with Ellen Hodges."

"But you can't tell me how it happened."

"Jesus, Sawyer, in my wildest imagination I can't think of any way it *could* have happened. I mean, it should be an impossibility. How do you pulverize bones without damaging the skin and other tissue those bones are surrounded by? I don't know. I don't believe the chief medical examiner in Chapel Hill is going to know."

"That's not a whole hell of a lot of help, Tom."

"Sorry."

"I don't suppose you were able to establish an I.D.?"

"On my end? No. There were no tattoos, no birthmarks, nothing especially distinctive. She was five-seven, probably slender, early thirties, brunette. My report's there on your desk."

Sawyer opened the folder and scanned the forms it contained. "You don't have eye color noted." He didn't exactly ask, because he knew what the answer would be. Knew with a queasy certainty.

"Couldn't tell what that was before she died. Right now her eyes are white."

Sawyer drew a breath and let it out slowly. He put a hand to the nape of his neck, realizing only as he did so that he was trying to ease the crawling sensation of his body to something beyond his understanding.

He hadn't wanted to be right.

"Like Ellen Hodges," he said.

Macy nodded. "Another thing that beats the hell out of me, because there's no medical explanation. No sign chemicals were used, no signs of trauma, just no color. Like the bones: Something that shouldn't be, is."

"You have any theories?"

"About the eyes? No. In all the years I've been in medicine, I've never seen anything like it. And I hope I never see it again."

"Amen to that." Sawyer leaned back in his chair, scowling. "I've managed to keep the...oddities of the deaths quiet, but I don't know how much longer I'll be able to keep a lid on that. Once it gets out—"

"Once it gets out," Macy interrupted, "most of the town will believe what you believe. That these deaths are connected to the church. Somehow."

"Ellen Hodges was one of their members."

"Yeah. Do we know the same about this woman?"

"According to them, nobody's missing."

"And you're not buying it."

"No. Not that it matters what I believe on that

count—unless you can give me something, some bit of evidence, to tie that woman to the church."

"Wish I could. Sorry."

"Goddammit."

Macy frowned. "Are you still getting pressure from Ellen's family?"

Sawyer reached over and tapped a stack of messages to the left of his blotter. "Of this dozen messages, ten are from her father. Today."

"But they aren't coming to Grace?"

"Pretty sure I talked him out of that."

"What about their granddaughter?"

With a shrug, Sawyer said, "I gather they buy the church's story there. That Kenley Hodges took Wendy and left the church, the Compound—and Grace. For all I know, he's been in touch with them; they've certainly stopped pushing for more searches of the Compound."

"I'm a little surprised the judge granted you a warrant to search it in the first place."

"Because he's a church member? Probably *why* he signed the warrant. Didn't want to be seen openly protecting the church or Samuel."

"Yeah, you're probably right." Macy shrugged. "It also gave them the chance to publicly clear the good name of the church. You didn't find Hodges or his daughter, didn't find any evidence that Ellen was killed there, and everybody was extremely cooperative."

"Oh, yeah," Sawyer said. "They were just cooperative as hell. They always are."

"You know, it's just barely possible that they cooperate because they have nothing to hide."

"You believe that if you want to, Tom."

Almost apologetically, Macy said, "It's just that I can't think of a reason why. Why kill these women? What would Samuel or his church have to gain by it?"

"I don't know," Sawyer replied bluntly. "And that's what's driving me nuts. Because every instinct I have is telling me that all the answers are inside that Compound. I just don't know where to look for them. And I'm not at all sure I'd recognize them if I found them."

For Samuel, meditation after services was even more necessary than it was before services; as well as becoming centered and calm, he needed the time to focus his mind, to assess his condition. And, of course, God required of him this self-examination.

It was never easy, reliving those early years, but he did so, again and again, because God commanded him to.

Reliving the hell of abuse, experiencing the pain as though it were happening all over again. And, always, the blackout he could never penetrate, that lost time during which horrible things had happened. Horrible things he never wanted to believe himself responsible for.

But you are, God insisted. *You know what you did. You know what happened. You know you punished them.*

In my name. With my strength, you punished them. You were my justice.

You were my sword.

He accepted that, because God told him it was so. But no matter how many times he tried, he could never remember just what precisely had happened.

His life entered a new and in many ways equally painful phase after he turned his back on that burning motel and walked away. He had to keep moving, for one thing; a child with no adult guardian within sight drew attention, and remaining too long in one place guaranteed that would become a problem. Likewise, he soon found that hitchhiking was risky and more than once escaped by the skin of his teeth from both predatory truck drivers and those good Samaritans who wondered why a little boy was all alone.

He would realize later that God had, clearly, watched over him during those early years, but at the time he saw nothing especially remarkable in his ability to take care of himself. He had taken care of himself for most of his life. If he had depended on his mother to feed and clothe him he would have gone hungry and worn rags more often than not.

He kept moving. He didn't really have an ultimate destination other than Survival and remained in any one place only until his instincts—or some event—told him it was time to move on. The money that had seemed a fortune didn't last very long, even though he was careful, but he was able to pick up a day's work here and there by skillfully convincing this shopkeeper or that farmer that his mother was sick, the baby needed diapers, and his father had disappeared on them.

He developed a sure eye and ear for the more gullible or, some would say, more compassionate souls he encountered. And he managed to get what he needed, what was necessary for life—even if that life was hardscrabble and lonely.

He wandered. He managed, somehow, to mostly stay out of trouble so that the law was never interested in him. It was a matter of self-preservation; he knew records existed of petty thievery charges incurred while he was still with his mother, and despite the lack of convictions (because they'd always skipped town), he knew those charges would surface if he were to be picked up.

So he was careful. Very careful. Not that he never committed an illegal act, but he took pains to make sure to not get caught.

Samuel shifted uneasily in his chair, disturbed as always by the unpleasant memories. Because there had been times, when decent work was impossible to come by and thievery untenable, that he had resorted to using the only commodity he knew he could sell. His body.

Soul shriveling, those times.

And maybe that was why he had so often paused during his wanderings at this or that church. Sometimes they offered a meal and a cot, but even if they didn't, they were at least warm and dry inside. He would find a dim corner and settle there, sometimes dozing and sometimes listening if there was an especially passionate preacher delivering an interesting sermon.

Somewhere along the way, he was given a Bible, and though his first inclination was to sell it, he tucked it inside the increasingly worn duffel bag instead. He had taught himself to read, and eventually he began to read the Bible.

There was a lot he thought was good.

There was a lot he didn't understand.

But, somehow, it spoke to him, that book. He read it and reread it. He spent hours and hours thinking about it. And he began to spend more time in churches of all denominations, listening to sermons. Watching how the congregation did—or did not—respond. Making mental note of what obviously worked and what failed to move people.

Within a few years, he was preaching himself, in small churches and on street corners and in bus stations.

He found God.

Or, more accurately, God found him. On a scorching hot July day when he was thirteen years old, God reached down and touched him.

And his whole life changed.

He was very good at eluding electronic security. Any kind of security, really, but especially the electronic kind. He called it his own personal stealth technology, and as far as he knew it was unique to him.

Part of what made him special.

Getting past the fence and into the Compound would be easy. They did not, after all, want to look like they were an armed camp bristling with weaponry or technology. They did not want to appear threatening or even especially unwelcoming. The surface had to be peaceful and calm.

Simple folk, that's what they were supposed to be.

What most of them were, probably.

At any rate, they didn't electrify the pretty wrought-iron and brick fence, they merely set up an electronic detection zone just inside it, so they knew who was coming into the Compound.

Usually.

He made certain he was far enough away from the gatehouse that no guard with infrared binoculars might be able to pick up what the security cameras would never see, but otherwise he didn't worry about being detected. It was late, and he was reasonably sure that most of them were tucked safe and sound in their beds.

It helped that there were no longer any dogs acting as alert and faithful guards in the night. He wondered if they had thought of that. If they might have regretted that. If they had even guessed it might happen.

Ah, well. Hardly his fault if they were unable to think like soldiers.

It was what happened when amateurs tried to make war.

Things got sloppy.

With a shrug, he slipped over the fence and into the Compound. There was virtually no moonlight tonight, with the full moon ten days in the past and overcast skies to boot. He didn't mind. He adapted easily to the night and preferred darkness. He worked his way across the fields and through the woods and the undergrowth that also provided something of a barrier, at least for a casual intruder: big, prickly holly bushes.

Not fun, but also not unbreachable.

Within minutes, he was through the woods and into the clear fields on the other side, in the central area of the Compound.

Where all the homes lay.

Where the church lay.

He had a set pattern in mind, a definite plan, and followed it methodically, moving from house to house in utter silence. At each small, neat cottage, he probed the exterior of the building, pinpointing every piece of electronic security and then tagging it with a very tiny electronic device of his own. An electronics expert would have been hard-pressed to spot it; he didn't expect any of these amateurs to.

No one would discover his handiwork.

He began at the outer edges of the Compound and circled his way in, moving house to house, toward the church itself, keeping an eye to that direction all the way. But the church was still and silent. No one came or went; only a few lights on the upper floors illuminated two or three of the stained-glass windows.

There was an almost eerie quiet out here, he acknowledged. In January there weren't even crickets, or bullfrogs calling from the river, and without summer sounds or dogs barking, it was . . . silent.

Strange and uncomfortable, that realization. He who

enjoyed silence had finally found a place where it screamed at him.

Shaking off the decidedly unpleasant sensation, he went on, keeping to his schedule. By the time he reached the main building, even the few lights on the upper floors had gone out, and the interior was dark and silent. It would have been a peaceful sight, if not for the security lights casting pools of bright, harsh light around each entrance.

He didn't worry about those.

It took him more than half an hour to slowly work his way around the very large church. He was more careful now, efficient, less inclined to assume he was dealing with amateurs.

Because not all of them were.

He found and tagged more than two dozen cameras and an equal number of motion detectors, and by the time he reached that point, he was grimly certain there were experts involved in protecting at least this building. And they were very, very good.

Almost too good.

But he was good himself, and though it required that he spend at least two more hours than he'd planned in the Compound, he was reasonably sure he had found everything of interest. Not absolutely positive but reasonably sure, which was all he had been aiming for on this trip.

He glanced toward the eastern sky and saw the first gray beginnings of dawn but lingered another few minutes to check some of the locked doors. Then he planted just a few more of his own devices and retreated toward the fence, leaving as silently unobserved as he had come.

Or so he thought.

Tessa didn't sleep well, which was hardly surprising. It took a lot out of her to open herself up like that, especially in a place that literally radiated negative energy.

Negative energy in a church.

A giant red warning flag from the universe, that.

She had gone over everything with Hollis but hadn't been able to offer a decent interpretation to the federal agent. Because the truth was, Tessa had never experienced anything quite like that.

"Cases almost always affect our abilities, usually in unexpected and unpredictable ways," Hollis had told her, more resigned than anything else. "Considering what we know about Samuel, that he's probably one of the most powerful psychics we've ever encountered, it stands to reason the energy there is going to be... supercharged, for want of a better word."

"You mean not just more but more powerful?"

"Negative energy tends to be."

Tessa frowned. "I can't say I like the sound of that."

"None of us does. The problem is, most of us deal with positive energy—literally—in our own abilities. We don't know why, but that's what all the science we have to depend on is telling us."

"Good guys equal positive? And bad guys equal negative?"

"Weird, isn't it? Like I said, we don't know why that would be true. Maybe it's just a chemical thing in our brains; the same hardwiring that makes us inclined to be cops or investigators also makes our psychic abilities work from the positive pole. And whatever wiring gets crossed to produce a sociopath also causes any psychic energy to be negative in those particular brains."

"Because it's all about balance."

"That's the theory."

"Mmm. So in this case my own abilities aren't going to work the way they always have?"

"If I had to guess, especially after your experience today, I'd say probably not. Energy affects us. And negative energy can affect us in some really bad, really painful ways. I speak from bitter experience."

"But there's no way for me to know just how my abilities may have changed—until the change becomes obvious?"

"Yeah, pretty much. The good news is, it's seldom a drastically *different* ability but an expansion or enhancement of the ability or abilities you already possessed."

Tessa *had* been warned about that, but as with so many things about being psychic, experience was really the only teacher. Up until now, she had never experienced any drastic change in her abilities—until she sat in that bathroom stall inside the Church of the Everlasting Sin and deliberately opened up her mind, expecting the usual jumble of thoughts and emotions.

She had not expected actual physical sensations.

Her body still felt sore from the waves of pain it had endured inside the church.

And no use telling herself it had all been in her mind. Like most psychics, she had long ago discovered the often unpleasant truth that what happened in the mind could be and, in fact, usually was far more "real" than anything the outer five senses could claim.

She tossed and turned for what seemed like hours, her mind replaying what she had seen and heard and sensed in that place, all the disjointed emotions and fragmented thoughts. Always circling back to that final, oddly chilling statement.

I'm hungry.

Who was hungry? Hungry for what? Everyone had certainly looked well-fed and, besides, every instinct told her it was not food that voice, that presence, hungered for. So what was it?

And who was it that had offered the simple *I see you*?

A friend, or at least a potential ally? Someone trying to tell her that another mind up there was capable of communicating in silence and secret?

Or bait on a hook?

Tessa pulled her pillow around so that she was as much hugging it as resting her head on it, conscious of a strange, unsettling feeling. She kept wanting to look over her shoulder, though every time she did there was only her bedroom in the Gray family home, illuminated for her by the light she left on in her bathroom. It was, admittedly, a space that was still strange to her, but until this night she had not felt uneasy here.

Not felt as though someone was watching her. Almost as though someone was, even now and very lightly, touching her back.

Ridiculous. There's nobody watching. Nobody touching you. You're just tired and you need to sleep. So sleep. Get some rest, and tomorrow everything will be clearer. Tomorrow you'll have a better handle on what's going on here.

Tessa wasn't at all sure she believed that, because a certainty inside her—deeper than instinct—insisted that during or after her trip to the Compound, something was different, changed, maybe even her. And it was a difference she didn't understand.

She needed to understand, but her thoughts chased themselves in circles uselessly until finally, exhausted, she slept.

And dreamed.

Seven

"YOU SENT for me, Father?"

"Yes, child. How do you feel?"

Bambi smiled. "Oh, I feel wonderful, Father. I always do, after Testifying."

"I'm glad to hear that, child." He positively beamed as he came around his desk and took her hand. But even with the smile, he looked pale and weary, and his eyes were darkened and held a curiously flat, almost empty shine. "I want you to sit here and talk to me for a little while."

"Of course, Father." She sat down in the single low-backed visitor's chair in front of his big mahogany desk.

He perched on the edge of the desk, still holding one of her hands. "You've been happy here with us, haven't you, Bambi?"

"So happy, Father. It's just like I said in my Testimony. I found peace here. I found God here."

"And God is happy you found Him. He loves you very, very much."

Bambi began to tear up. "I feel that. Thanks to you and the church, I really do feel that, Father."

"I know you do, child. And God knows. But it never hurts to pray to Him and give thanks for your happiness." He slipped off the desk and went around her chair, releasing her hand so that both of his could rest on the top of her head, just as they had earlier in the church.

And just as in the church, she bowed her head and squeezed her eyes shut.

"Pray with me," Reverend Samuel said, half-closing his eyes as his voice thickened. "Give thanks with me, child."

"Yes, Father. I give thanks to God—" She jerked suddenly and moaned, her head tipping back.

He cradled her head in his hands, his fingers moving gently as though massaging her scalp, his own head moving side to side like some creature searching blindly. "Give thanks to God," he said hoarsely. "Give thanks to me. Give yourself to me, child."

Bambi moaned again. Her hands, resting on the arms of the chair, twitched spasmodically and then curled over the wood, fingers tightening until they turned white with the force.

"Give to me, child. Give me all that you are, all you have."

"Yes, Father…yes…oh, God…it feels…so good…"

Her breasts rose and fell jerkily and her body shuddered. Again and again, as though shaken by wave after wave of sensation. Long minutes passed. Her face paled, then flushed, then paled again. Her moans grew quieter, weaker. Her hands relaxed their grip on the chair, fingers loosening and finally letting go.

Reverend Samuel lifted his head, his eyes opening. He looked down at her for a moment, then took his hands off her and walked around behind his desk.

He was . . . changed. His face showed a healthy color, his eyes were bright, and his every movement showed a dynamic energy. Even his hair looked more silver than gray. He seemed almost to glow.

"Thank you, child," he said softly. He settled into his chair, then pressed a button on a very elaborate-looking phone system.

The door opened, and Reese DeMarco stepped into the room.

"Bambi and I are done," Samuel said.

"Of course, Father." DeMarco went to the visitor's chair and picked Bambi up, holding her limp body easily. His face was completely without expression. "Will there be anything else tonight?" he added, waiting there with the young woman cradled in his arms.

"No, I think not. Good night, Reese."

"Good night, Father." DeMarco carried Bambi from the room, closing the door quietly behind them.

Samuel leaned back in his chair and chuckled. "It's good not to be hungry," he said.

Tessa sat up in bed with a gasp, her heart pounding.

Oh, my God.

He was feeding off them.

"He's a—a goddamn psychic *vampire*."

"Sounds like it," Hollis agreed.

Tessa turned to face the other woman, cradling her cup in both hands as she took a cautious sip of the hot coffee. "You don't seem surprised," she said finally, slowly.

"Well, we had the suspicion it would work like that. Or that it could, at least. A brain apparently hardwired to steal psychic abilities is already stealing energy. Somewhere along the way, he must have realized he could steal enough to replenish whatever he expended."

Hollis sounded and looked wide awake, despite the fact that it was half past four in the morning and she was in a nightgown and robe, just as Tessa was.

Tessa stared at her. "Most people just rest when they've used up energy reserves."

Hollis shook her head. "Most people don't use energy the way psychics do. Even so, the majority of psychics probably do just rest, sleep. Hell, after one case, I slept for four days straight."

"Samuel can't do that?"

"Maybe he can. Maybe he can't. Maybe he can't afford the luxury of being that weak and vulnerable for that long."

"Because he has enemies?"

"Because he has to hold on to his flock."

Tessa thought about that for a moment. "If he weakens too much, or for too long, then his grip loosens. And they—what? Wake up? Realize they've been held captive by a kind of power most of them would consider witch-craft?"

"If I were him, that's what I'd be afraid of. Especially if I'd risked a lot of power once, maybe even nearly all I had—and came home, weakened, to find my followers in the middle of a minor revolt."

"Did he?"

"According to some information Sarah found, it happened last October. A number of weird things happened last October. Just about the time we thought we were wrapping up a serial murder case in a little town outside Atlanta."

"Venture."

"Venture."

Tessa frowned. "You didn't mention that before."

"I didn't know." Hollis grimaced. "I talked to Bishop last night. He told me then. Apparently, Samuel was able to reestablish control over his people fairly quickly, but we're not really sure how he managed that."

"Psychically?"

"If that's the hold he has over them."

"You sound doubtful."

"Well . . . I am. Controlling the mind and will of just one other person is an incredibly complex thing, beyond the limits of any psychic we've yet to encounter, no matter how powerful he or she was. The closest we've seen to any kind of mind control was between blood siblings, and even then the control was extremely erratic and uncertain. To control over a hundred people? All at once? All the time? Some of them outside the Compound, miles away in town? No. Samuel's not that powerful. He can't be."

Tessa accepted that, but more because she didn't want it to be true than because she was absolutely convinced. And she wasn't entirely sure that Hollis didn't feel exactly the same way. "Okay. If he isn't controlling them psychically, then how?"

"I think he's using his abilities but in a far more limited and precise way. You read up on cult leaders; they all use a combination of techniques, from strictly controlled schedules and structures to sleep deprivation, social isolation, sexual or emotional domination, public confession of sins and supposed sins, and flat-out brainwashing. Indoctrination through hours and hours of sermons, the central theme of which is always a variation of Us Against Them. Us being the chosen ones, of course. Them being everybody else, all outsiders, who are collectively and individually a dire threat to Us."

"Yeah, I remember reading all that. But none of the cult leaders I read about was psychic."

"I imagine they would have loved to be, though. For one thing, the hours of sermons wouldn't be as necessary if you could make every single one pack a supercharged punch."

"Is that what Samuel does?"

"We think so. From Sarah's reports, 'services' aren't an everyday thing, much less an all-night thing. But he does appear to speak to and touch every one of his followers every single day, and they do appear to be, for want of a better word, mesmerized." Hollis shrugged. "Plus, just think about all the nice, convincing...miracles you might be able to pull off in front of a highly suggestible audience more than willing to believe you're God's messenger on earth. We humans have a long and storied history of following prophets and messiahs."

"No matter where they lead us."

"No matter where they lead us," Hollis agreed.

Brooke knew her friends were right. She knew she couldn't get all the way to Texas all by herself. But knowing that didn't help. Knowing that she *had* friends who knew what she knew, who understood, didn't help.

She was afraid.

She didn't doubt Cody when he said something bad was going to happen, something even worse than the things that had already happened. She didn't doubt him because Cody was never wrong about stuff like that, and because she felt it too.

It was like a weight she couldn't escape, that feeling. She lay in her bed for hours feeling it on her, heavy and dark. She tried hard to make her shell even stronger, even thicker, but that didn't seem to make any difference at all. The weight remained. And it was getting heavier by the minute.

She wanted to cry out, to run to her parents' bedroom, as she had once done when a nightmare woke her, seeking comfort. And seeking reassurance that nothing was going to hurt her, that nothing lurked in the darkness of night that she need be afraid of.

Once, that had been true. But not anymore.

In the darkness of her bedroom, lying very still in her bed, Brooke began to cry.

On the other side of the Compound, in her own bed, Ruby lay awake. She, too, had been working to strengthen her shell, but even as she did so she had the guilty awareness of hiding at least one truth from her friends. Not because she didn't trust them, of course, it was just . . . It was just that she had only one thing left in the whole world that truly belonged to her, one thing Father hadn't been able to take away.

One thing she had to protect.

Ruby turned on her side in bed and cuddled Lexie close.

"It's all right," she whispered. "I won't let anything hurt you. No matter what."

Tessa frowned. "So . . . Samuel could be precognitive, with a history of visions that came true. Telekinetic, with the ability to move things, maybe even levitate his own body. Telepathic, with the ability to read minds."

Hollis was nodding. "Any of which could get their attention, convince them to listen to him, believe him. Follow him—even off a cliff. Maybe help keep the men in line by convincing them he's the alpha, the natural leader chosen by God, that they're destined to follow him. Especially if he added his own unique twist to the whole control issue."

Tessa was still struggling with the idea that left her more than a little queasy. "The women. He found a way to give them . . . something better than a drug."

Grim, Hollis said, "They don't call it 'the little death' for nothing. An orgasm can produce an extraordinary amount of sheer energy. If he's found a way to psychically trigger that, and then . . ."

"Steal the energy for himself?"

"Why not? As long as he has the control to stop pulling energy before he takes too much, it's pretty much a renewable energy source. Especially if it affects them like a drug and makes them more than willing to submit to him again and again. It could affect him like a drug. Hell, they could all be addicted to it."

Tessa set her coffee cup down on the kitchen island and crossed her arms beneath her breasts. "I might be sick," she muttered.

"Yeah, me too. A kind of sexual domination for the books, that's for sure."

"And the men, the husbands? They just allow it?"

"Probably aren't quite willing to believe what they may suspect. Maybe can't believe it. From all accounts, he's not causing women to climax in public, in the church during services, at least not fully. Though Sarah said there were at least a few women who seemed to go right to the brink. But a total orgasm, what you saw in your dream? If what you saw is true, he's keeping that part of it very private. A little one-on-one with Father, the results of which are known only by a handful of his retinue. Maybe just the guy you saw."

"DeMarco? Chief Cavenaugh thinks of him as a ghoul."

"He sounds like one. Especially if he's carrying Samuel's drained victims back to their beds in the dead of night. No way to know what his motivation is; maybe he genuinely believes in Samuel. Or maybe he's just a hired gun."

Tessa's frown deepened. "I didn't get anything from him. And his face sure as hell didn't give his thoughts or emotions away."

"If he's Samuel's closest . . . adviser, bodyguard, lieutenant, whatever the hell he calls himself, he may be the only one who knows the truth, knows what goes on in private. In public, during services, the other men may well see in the women what a lot of true believers see and feel in church—a kind of rapture. Not quite orgasmic, but close to it. A *spiritual* experience tying them with even stronger bonds to their father."

Sawyer woke so abruptly he was already sitting up on the couch when his eyes opened. He looked around his dim office for a moment, his heartbeat thudding in his chest, then swung his feet to the floor and ran his fingers through his hair.

Just a dream.

Yeah, you keep telling yourself that.

Ignoring that sarcastic inner voice, he checked his watch and grimaced when he saw that it was barely five A.M. He had slept four hours, if that. And, tired as he was, he knew it would be useless to try to go back to sleep.

Because he never could. And because the dream nagged at him.

It always did.

But even more now. Especially now. And you know why. You just won't admit it.

Still ignoring the inner voice, he rose from the leather couch, stretching to ease the kinks and stiffness, and crossed the small room to his desk. He had left the work lamp on, and in the pool of light the folders and maps and other papers covering the blotter looked like chaos.

But Sawyer knew where everything was, and when he sat down, his fingers reached unerringly for a folder underneath two others. It contained summarized reports of half a dozen suspected homicides, all bodies found in the river—but all so far downstream they were well out of his jurisdiction.

Hell, two of them had washed up in a different state.

The victims had been and continued to be unidentified, so were listed as John and Jane Does. Four women, two men.

Sawyer had not requested autopsy photos, but attached to each report was a single photo of each victim as he or she had been found. Stark black-and-white, cold, clinical, ugly.

As were the reports themselves, just clinical facts

couched in unemotional medical terms. All the victims had been young, in their twenties or thirties. None had shown signs of disease or conventional antemortem injuries, and no cause of death had been determined.

No *conventional* antemortem injuries. No bullet wounds, or stab wounds, no strangulation or blunt-force trauma, and no signs of drowning. No evidence of poison, and the toxicology screen on each victim had come back negative for drugs or alcohol.

The only thing these victims had in common was that they should not have died.

According to all the reports, at least. But when Ellen Hodges's body turned up in his own bailiwick, Sawyer looked more closely at what had, until then, been a nagging but unofficial worry. He had requested and studied all the reports, and then he had personally called each of the M.E.s or coroners involved and asked a few direct questions.

People in the investigative fields, he had found, did not in general have lively imaginations. They dealt in facts, usually ugly facts, and if something fit outside the box of an individual's knowledge and experience, it was usually given short shrift, overlooked at best and actively ignored at worst. So it hadn't been easy to get the answers he sought without also tainting the information by asking leading questions.

But patience and tenacity served him well, and he had eventually learned details that were not included in these reports.

Such as the fact that the bodies of every single one of

these victims had possessed at least one internal oddity the investigating officers and medical personnel had not been able to explain.

Bruised and even burst organs. Crushed bones.

White eyes.

"Jesus, what's going on up there," he muttered, rubbing the nape of his neck with one hand as he sifted through the reports, reading again and again what he had already memorized. And recalling conversations that had, in the end, sounded eerily the same.

"I wish I could help you, Chief. Wish I had an explanation for how that man's heart was bruised and damaged with no external injury to account for it. I don't know how it happened. I don't know how it could have happened. It's almost as if . . . as if an incredibly powerful hand reached inside his body and—But that's nonsense, of course."

Of course. Of course it was.

Nonsense. Impossible.

Sawyer leaned back in his chair until it creaked in protest, his gaze fixed across the room but focused on something much, much farther away. Focused on another brief and seemingly casual conversation on a downtown street corner five years in the past, a conversation that had baffled and unsettled him then and disturbed him deeply now.

"You'll make a good police chief, Sawyer."

"What? Reverend Samuel, I have no intention of—"

"I only hope that, when the time comes, you'll know who your friends are. Who you can trust."

"*Reverend—*"

"*I know you aren't a member of my church, but people like us...we should stick together. Don't you agree, Sawyer?*"

"*I don't know what you're talking about, Reverend.*"

"*No? Well, perhaps not.*" He smiled, nodded politely, and continued on his way, leaving Sawyer staring after him.

Sawyer pulled his thoughts from the past with an effort and realized he was looking at the television set on the other side of the room. He didn't intend to focus on it but found himself thinking that it was still too early to watch what passed for "local" news on the Asheville station—

The lamp on his desk flickered, and then the TV came to life, muted as he had left it the day before and showing an infomercial.

"Shit." He checked quickly to make sure the blinds were still closed, relaxing only a little when he was certain none of the third-shift officers in the bullpen could see into his office.

Good.

He looked down to see that his watch had stopped, and he swore again, this time half under his breath.

Not good. But not at all unusual.

You should have bought stock in a major watch company years ago. Or just give it up and buy yourself a sundial....

A sundial. And a cell phone that lasted more than a

week before dying. And he should have bought stock in whoever sold lightbulbs, because he tended to blow those completely when he was very tired and very worried and not paying attention.

He closed his eyes briefly, making the necessary mental effort to gather in straying thoughts and energies. It wasn't difficult, after all these years of determined concentration and practice, but it was a control that tended to slip when he was weary or distracted.

And that was not good.

"...*people like us...*"

That was really not good.

Tessa was shaking her head in response to Hollis's theory about physical pleasure being taken for spiritual rapture. "Okay, explain the women. Tell me how a woman—a grown, sexually active woman—could not know she's having an orgasm. And how any woman could explain that away as a religious experience."

"Some do, I'm told."

"Hollis."

"Okay, okay. I'm betting it's another aspect of Samuel's abilities. He can't *control* their minds psychically, but I'll bet he can plant the certainty—like a posthypnotic suggestion—that what they're experiencing is a spiritual rather than a physical rapture. I even bet that those he calls into the inner sanctum most likely wake up the next morning convinced they only had an erotic dream."

Tessa shivered. "That's ... twisted."

"And then some."

"But he can't be drawing all the energy he needs just from the women, can he?"

"Doubtful. Now and then for a fix or in an emergency, yeah, but they can't be his primary source. Not if he's expending an unusual amount of energy."

"Do we know he's doing that?"

"No. We know he has in the past, but we have no idea how much of his energy he has to expend—in controlling his flock and in order to reach his other goals. Whatever those are."

"We don't know a whole hell of a lot," Tessa observed.

"Yeah, welcome to our world. That's par for the course."

Tessa picked up her cup and took a swallow of her cooling coffee, giving herself a moment to think. "So, if we're assuming he's using more energy than he possesses—for whatever reason—we also have to assume he has to replenish that energy somehow."

"Every psychic I know has to. And while rest is the most natural way, it isn't the quickest; quite a few of us also can draw energy from external sources. Electrical storms and strong magnetic fields, for instance. Don't storms bother you? They make me feel like one giant exposed nerve."

"They make me feel edgy," Tessa acknowledged, and then stopped, frowning. "Wait. When I was reading up on Grace, on the area, one of the things I remember reading is that the weather here from spring to fall is unusually violent. Something about the granite in the mountains, the shape of this valley, and the way weather fronts move through. Lots of storms, especially electrical ones. Is *that* why Samuel based his church here?"

"We think so. Also why he's so interested in the Florida property you supposedly own. Last time I checked, Florida held the record in the US for most lightning strikes within a given period. Summer storms can be vicious. Just like here."

"But almost always spring to fall here. Winter storms are really rare."

Hollis nodded. "Which means that during the winter months, like now, there's rarely a handy supercharged electrical or magnetic field available from which to draw or replenish his energy. But he's using energy, and probably at a high rate. The negative vibes you picked up, possibly even the pain, are probably no more than a discharge: unfocused remnants of energy left over after he's used his abilities."

"Which means..."

"Which means he has to need something a lot more powerful to recharge, to restore his own energy balance. Assuming there's anything balanced about him, which I take leave to doubt."

Tessa ignored the muttered aside. "Then what does he do? You said the women couldn't be his primary source. For part of the year, neither can the weather. So?"

Reluctant, Hollis said, "The body produces a great

deal of energy during orgasm. It also produces an extreme amount of energy during the dying process—especially a terrifying or agonizing traumatic death. Believe me, I know."

"Are you saying he's *killing* in order to *feed*?"

"I'm saying it's possible. It could explain those...inexplicable deaths. And it's that possibility, that suspicion, that brought us here."

"Doesn't the FBI have to wait to be invited?"

"In a conventional homicide investigation, sure. We're very careful to respect state and local jurisdictions. But for some crimes, FBI involvement is automatic—and that includes a serial killer who's crossed state lines in his rampage."

"But didn't that part of the official investigation end in Venture? I thought there was no solid proof linking Reverend Samuel with that killer."

"The evidence was...tentative," Hollis admitted.

"Meaning it was gained through psychic abilities?"

"Let's just say we have more than one reason to keep a low profile here in Grace."

"I see. And we have no hard evidence linking the reverend to the bodies pulled out of that river either."

"Tessa—"

"Do we?"

After a long moment, Hollis said, "No. We don't. We have no hard evidence against him at all."

Eight

"**U**P EARLY?" Bailey asked as she walked into the room. "Or up late?"

Bishop looked at her, frowned for an instant, then replied, "I'll catch a nap later."

"Up late, then." She shook her head. "You'll be no good to us if you don't get some rest. This thing could go on for weeks, even months."

"No. It couldn't. It won't."

Rather than take a chair, Bailey perched on the conference table, crossing her ankles and swinging her feet idly. She was, by nature, a very serene woman, not easily rattled and very patient. As the SCU's strongest guardian, she tended to take a less active role than most of the other agents in ongoing investigations, spending much of her time on the clock sitting at bedsides or otherwise sticking close to someone under threat of attack. And not an attack using conventional weapons.

Looking at her, Bishop thought, as he so often had, that she didn't wear her toughness on the outside where ordinary eyes could see it. She was unexpectedly fragile-looking, a tall, slender brunette with large dark eyes so calm and deep they were almost hypnotic. Perhaps her serenity came from a thorough understanding of human nature; like most of the guardians in the unit, she was a trained counselor and, in fact, held a doctorate in psychology.

She didn't look tough.

She was.

Her particular psychic talents hadn't been something he expected to need, back in the beginning. But it wasn't long before he realized how valuable a psychic able to shield others could be. It wasn't long before he saw the need for one.

"Penny," Bailey offered.

"For my thoughts?" Bishop shook his head. "Don't waste your money."

"So you're still grappling, then? Still trying to figure out how Samuel is doing it?"

"That isn't the question that worries me."

"What his limits are."

Bishop nodded. "Do you know what the lead in today's *Grace Gazette* is going to be? It's already posted online. The town council met and considered a minute raise in property taxes." He paused, then added, "The corpse found in the river yesterday barely rated a mention on the back page."

"Well, with the owner and editor being church members, to say nothing of at least one reporter . . ."

"I honestly wish I believed that's all it is," Bishop

said. "That Samuel's influence extends outside the Compound only through his followers. But it's more than that. The whole town *feels* wrong, and virtually every one of us has been aware of it and has commented on it. The place is off somehow. Placid. Incurious. Hollis asked me, rather jokingly, if we'd tested the water."

"Which we did. And found absolutely nothing out of the ordinary." It was Bailey's turn to frown. "Whatever it is, however Samuel is doing it, not everybody seems to be affected. Chief Cavenaugh is about as far from incurious as you can get. And there are a few others I encountered during a stroll through the town. I haven't met Cavenaugh yet, but I can tell you that the others who seemed more...alert or anxious all had one thing in common."

"Which is?"

"Their own kind of energy. Not psychic, unless they're latents; I wouldn't necessarily pick up on that. But I could definitely sense shields of one kind or another."

Brooding, Bishop said, "Nonpsychics build shields all the time. To protect themselves. Mentally, emotionally, even physically. It's more common than not."

Bailey nodded. "Especially in small towns, where your business tends to be everybody else's."

"Were the shielded ones church members?"

She pursed her lips. "Don't think so, but I didn't exactly have a list to go by. Just from appearances...no. They didn't have that scrubbed and placid look about them."

"So the shielded ones tend to not be church members. And seemingly aren't affected, or aren't much affected, by whatever is affecting everybody else."

"That could be why," Bailey offered. "Samuel can't get to them, can't influence them, not by psychic means and not by more conventional . . . cultish means. But, if my casual walk through town is any indication, you're looking at only a small percentage of the town being . . . immune to Samuel."

"Which," Bishop said grimly, "argues an enormous amount of sheer energy expended. That has to be taking a toll."

"Worth the price, maybe, to him. It allows him to operate without worry. No stories in the newspaper or other media attention. Nobody questioning his people. Nobody bothering them." She paused, then added, "On the other hand, it might not be so deliberate. Those sensors we have in place now are showing an awful lot of random energy we can't really explain, and not just inside the Compound. If he's expending enough of it, leaving enough residue in the very air, it could be acting as a sort of dampening field over the whole area, including outside the Compound. Affecting anyone who's susceptible to electrical or magnetic energy."

"Affecting us," Bishop said. "In unpredictable ways."

She tilted her head slightly as she studied him. "Adding Tessa's experience to Sarah's, plus other reports, means this isn't exactly new information."

Answering the unspoken question, Bishop said slowly, "I've always believed an absolute psychic would be born. Eventually. Someday. A psychic born able to control his or her abilities completely."

"A good thing. Unless he or she is on the other team."

"That possibility dawned as we discovered, over time, more and more psychics *on* the other team," he admitted.

"Okay. Do you believe Samuel is an absolute psychic?"

"I'm afraid he might be."

Bailey waited a moment, then probed, "And?"

"And everything I know about profiling, all my experience, tells me that he might have been made, not born. Shaped by events in his life. Created."

"And?" Bailey repeated.

"We're born with limitations, Bailey. All of us. Our abilities evolve and change, but they have ultimate limits, even if it takes us years or a lifetime to find them. Something created, on the other hand, something... forged in the crucible of experiences may not have those kinds of limits. And the evolution of something like that could be consciously controlled, accelerated by will alone. Samuel could be growing stronger, literally, day by day."

"Which is why you said this couldn't go on for weeks or months."

He nodded. "Yes. We have to stop him."

"Even without evidence?"

"Even," Bishop said, "without evidence. And without evidence, we can't put him in a cage. We can't deal with him in a courtroom. Without evidence, we have to destroy him."

Tessa was frowning. "Sarah was a Haven operative, not a fed. And the FBI investigation into the church wasn't authorized?"

"Not by the Director. He's...not a big fan of the SCU. Or of Bishop. Things have been a little tense since his appointment."

"Why not a fan? From everything I've been told, the SCU has been incredibly successful in their investigations, especially in comparison to some other FBI cases."

"And it could be that. Bishop bends over backward to avoid publicizing our successes. And if we don't get credit—"

"—the FBI doesn't get credit. But does the Director really want to explain that the successes are due to a unit mostly made up of psychic agents?"

"I doubt it. Very much. So you could see how he'd have mixed emotions about us. Whatever other tensions are there, I don't know. But I know he's been watching the unit and Bishop very closely."

A bit dryly, Tessa said, "I doubt that going behind the Director's back to put agents inside a church would win any brownie points."

"I never said SCU agents were inside the church," Hollis said immediately. "Look, Tessa, any suspected cult leader is automatically on the FBI's watch list, *and* the

SCU's. Any suspected cult leader with even the possibility of psychic ability and we'd be nuts not to get eyes and ears on the inside, to gauge the danger, ASAP. A psychic cult leader suspected of murder calls for a full-scale investigation."

"But not an *official* investigation."

"If you're worried about the legalities, Haven is still officially working for Senator LeMott."

Tessa was shaking her head. "I'm not worried on that account. I know John and Maggie would never send one of us into any situation without legal cover."

"Then what are you worried about?"

A little laugh escaped Tessa.

Hollis grimaced. "Okay, dumb question. I mean, what's bugging you about the Haven/SCU connection in all this?"

"I'm just not sure of the boundaries. The limits."

"What do you mean?"

"We can watch. We can gather information. But we aren't—none of us is—authorized to actually arrest or even detain anyone."

"Well, that's debatable. But not the point. You want to take Chief Cavenaugh into our confidence, don't you?"

"Why not? He *does* have the authority, without question or debate, to openly investigate, to detain or arrest, even on suspicion. And he's certain Samuel and his church are involved in the murders."

"He's also about as subtle as neon in his suspicions, according to what you told me."

"Maybe that's not such a bad thing. Maybe Samuel and his church need to know someone's watching."

Hollis studied the other woman for a beat or two, then said quietly, "All that pain you felt. You believe we need to act quickly. To stop whatever is going on up there."

"Don't you?"

"Stop it, yes. As soon as possible, yes. But, Tessa, even with the chief on our side in this, the law isn't, and Cavenaugh has to follow the law. We have no hard evidence, remember? No proof that Samuel or anyone in his church had anything to do with Sarah's death, or Ellen Hodges's death. Or any of the others'."

"I know that. But at least the chief can ask his questions directly; we're . . . smiling and pretending."

"It's just another way to investigate, and you know it. You also know, I hope, that nobody would blame you if you decided it isn't a way you want to be involved in this."

Tessa shifted beneath the other woman's steady gaze. "I'm not going to bail. It's just—I guess that dream unsettled me even more than I thought."

"I'm not surprised. What Samuel is doing, if we're right about any of this, is about as unnatural as it comes. And whether his motivation is the usual—if more literal—power trip of a cult leader or something more, what we do know without question is that he's dangerous. And getting more so. Six of the eight known victims in this area died in the last two years—and that doesn't even begin to count the women killed last summer in

Boston, and last October in Venture, hideous murders we're convinced Samuel was ultimately responsible for."

"And all we have are questions."

"It's not all we have. We suspected he was a murderer. That he was killing with his mind, his abilities, if not with his own hands. This could be why he kills, this apparent need for energy. The hunger you sensed and saw in your dream. This could be one answer, or part of an answer. But it doesn't change anything. We have to find all the answers, like the critical one of how to stop him. Preferably before anyone else dies."

That final sentence served to focus Tessa and stiffen her resolve, to remind her of her part in all this. Her job.

"So he gets at least some of what he needs from them, from his followers. The women. He uses his abilities to stimulate them to orgasm and then draws the energy out of them. That's just . . . so hard to believe."

"It was your dream," Hollis noted.

"I don't have visions," Tessa said immediately.

"I don't think what you had was a vision."

"You don't believe what I saw was real?"

"Oh, I believe it was real. I believe it happened exactly as you saw it happen, probably when you saw it happen."

"How is that possible? I was here. I never pick up impressions at a distance, much less anything that detailed."

"Remember what I said about our abilities changing?"
Tessa nodded.

"Well, I believe yours have changed. Or are in the

process of changing. In this case, at least. You connected to something while you were in that compound. Maybe a person, maybe an energy source—I don't know. But you made a very real, tangible connection."

"What makes you believe that?"

Hollis studied the multicolored aura surrounding the other woman, fainter now than it had been when Tessa had awakened her but still glittering here and there, almost sparking, as if with electricity. Not an unusual aura for a psychic, in Hollis's rather limited and very recent experience. But one thing about it was unusual.

A tendril of energy, shifting, almost writhing, snaked out from the aura, through the kitchen doorway, and disappeared toward the front of the house. And out the front door.

"Call it a hunch," Hollis said.

"The problem," Special Agent Quentin Hayes said, "is that it takes so damn long to get anybody inside. And once they *are* inside, they're lucky if they can be alone in the john for five minutes. That doesn't really lend itself to any kind of a thorough recon."

"Tell me something I don't know," Bishop said.

Quentin looked up from the map spread out on the conference table and lifted an eyebrow. "Probably can't do that. But I can tell you one more thing you already know. You shouldn't be here."

"I'm covered. The Director's at a law-enforcement seminar in Paris."

"I wasn't talking about the Director." Quentin straightened, a rare frown crossing his face. "I'm a lot more worried about Senator LeMott."

Bishop leaned back in his chair at a workstation on the other side of the room and gazed steadily at one of his most trusted primary agents. "Whatever LeMott's doing, it's by remote control, through his own operatives. Me riding herd on him in D.C. won't change a thing."

"It might give us a shot at identifying his operatives, before they do something reckless and this whole situation goes to hell."

"We're a lot more likely to identify them on this end, with the people we have in place. I haven't been able to get a clear reading on LeMott in weeks, maybe longer."

Quentin's frown deepened. "That ever happen to you before? Not being able to read somebody all of a sudden when you started out being able to read them?"

"No."

"And that doesn't worry you?"

Bishop sighed. "Of course it worries me. But LeMott wouldn't be the first nonpsychic I've met who learned how to shield his thoughts from a telepath."

"If he learned to shield his thoughts from you, just over the space of a few weeks, that's not only rare but unnaturally fast."

"You think he's had help?"

"Isn't that more likely? I mean, mad makes a great shield, and mad and crazy with grief can make a stronger one—but he had that last summer, and you could read him then."

Bishop considered for a moment, then shook his head. "Whether he has help in blocking me isn't something I can do anything about right now. Things are moving too fast in Grace for any of us to shift our focus. At least two church members murdered in the last two weeks is either a deliberate escalation, a buildup of energy, or else a loss of control signaling something a lot worse."

"I really don't want to see this guy get worse," Quentin said dryly. "Either way."

"No. But unless we stop him soon, he undoubtedly will get worse. And these new energy readings are confirmation of what some of us have felt for months; now that we can actually measure what's happening, at least part of the increasing danger is clear."

"Well, it's obvious. But I don't know how clear it is. I've never seen anything like this before."

"Neither have I. But I don't need to be familiar with it to know that an electromagnetic field fluctuating like this one is as unnatural as it is potentially deadly."

"Yeah, I got that. It's one reason I didn't argue when you asked Diana to stay at Quantico."

"And I got that," Bishop murmured.

Quentin cleared his throat and bent once again over the map of the church's Compound, making rather a production of studying it. It was an unusual map only in that it was extremely detailed and had a clear film overlay on which were numerous cryptic symbols and mathematical formulas. "Okay, so I've been a little protective. Sue me."

"She'll be fine, Quentin. She's improving every day, more in command of her abilities, and healing in every way. You were right about how much strength she has."

"She's still got a long way to go."

"She's nearly completed her formal training."

"That's not what I meant and you know it."

"Fishing?"

"Well, I haven't seen anything about us. I was hoping you and Miranda might have."

"Sorry."

"Sorry you haven't seen anything? Or sorry you can't tell me what you've seen?"

"The former. We've been a bit preoccupied by this investigation, remember? And...the visions have been few and far between lately."

"Ah. I wondered why you wanted me along on this one. Not like you to bring in more than one primary, as a rule. Not from the early stages of the investigation, anyway."

"Precogs are in short supply, and if there's anything here to be seen ahead of time, I want that edge."

"If you and Miranda haven't seen anything, I'm not likely to."

"You might."

"I'm stronger with Diana around," Quentin pointed out.

"Yes. But she can't be here; she's a medium. A very powerful medium. Hollis wouldn't be here if it wasn't crystal clear she's meant to be. For whatever reason."

"I'm not arguing, not about Diana. But...no visions? At all?"

"Not in a while."

Pushing aside the personal ramifications of his unanswered question, Quentin said, "I really don't like the sound of that. It's one thing if some of the rest of us are affected psychically by Samuel or his people—or whoever the hell is generating some of these weird energy fields strong enough to scare away the wildlife—but you and Miranda have been solid and stable for a long time now, no matter what we've investigated. If this is affecting you guys..."

"We don't know that it is." Bishop hesitated, then added, "We don't know that it isn't. One reason why I have to be here—and Miranda stays away."

"And if it turns out part of Samuel's plan *is* to eliminate you? To try a little more divide-and-conquer where you and Miranda are concerned? You're not exactly making it harder for him."

"Miranda's shield is holding, and we've managed to amplify it recently. I shouldn't read as psychic; in the lab, our strongest team members couldn't pick up even my presence."

"In the lab."

"Yes."

"I guess it's useless to remind you that fieldwork

tends to explode a lot of the theories and beliefs we develop in the lab."

"It's all we have, Quentin. We have logic, and we have our theories, until experience proves us wrong."

"Yeah, that's what I'm afraid of. That experience will prove us wrong this time. Because it so often does. And if it does, it'll be a little late to adjust our theories."

"No choice. We have too many people at risk. Besides, if Samuel even knows I'm anywhere nearby... Well, let's just say if he's that powerful, it wouldn't make much difference where I was."

Half under his breath, Quentin muttered, "This just keeps getting better and better."

"We have good people on our side, Quentin."

"We have too many rookies. At best, they get distracted from the job, from the mission, the way Sarah did. At worst, they can be an active liability."

"Sarah did what she thought was right."

"I know. And I don't blame her for it. Hell, I might have done the same thing. But it cost her her life. And it cost us a valuable set of senses on the inside."

"I know."

Quentin shot his boss a sharp glance. Then he sighed. "I know you know. Look, I like Tessa, I really do, but she's under a hell of a lot of pressure, and I'm not at all sure she won't buckle."

"Tessa will do her best. Which is all any of us can do. And Hollis is with her."

Quentin finally stopped pretending to study the map. He straightened and cocked an eyebrow once again.

"Sort of had to reconfigure your plan when she showed up, didn't you?"

"It was . . . unexpected," Bishop allowed.

"A sign from the universe? A not-so-gentle nudge to remind you that whatever you know or think you know, none of us is really in control of our destiny?"

"Maybe. But after Venture I didn't need the reminder, believe me. I'm taking nothing for granted, not this time. We've already paid too high a price."

After a moment, Quentin looked down at the map again and said slowly, "Judging by all this . . . I'm thinking the cost so far may turn out to be only a down payment."

Nine

TESSA HADN'T PLANNED on returning to the Compound so soon, but when Ruth "just thought I'd stop by" on Thursday morning to check on her, Tessa allowed herself to be convinced to pay a second visit to the church later that day.

Hollis emerged as soon as the visitor had gone, saying, "I'm not sure going back so soon is a good idea, Tessa."

"Why not?"

"Because yesterday drained you, because you hardly got any rest last night, and because you've been up since before dawn," Hollis answered frankly.

"I look like hell?"

"You look...tired."

"Good. That's the way they're supposed to see me, remember? Tired. Unsure. Vulnerable."

"Yeah, but it's supposed to be a pretense. When you're tired, there's a danger your shields will weaken and leave you exposed to another psychic. In this case, a psychic we're reasonably sure can, at the very least, steal or siphon off abilities from someone else—and possibly kill with his own."

"Reasonably sure. But no evidence we're right."

"I wouldn't bet your life on the sliver of uncertainty, Tessa."

"No." Tessa drew a breath, trying to contain the impatience she felt even as she acknowledged the strangeness of it. "No, of course not."

"All I'm saying is that you have to be careful. Samuel has shown a lot of interest in bringing latents into his church, maybe because he's figured out their brains produce more electromagnetic energy than nonpsychics and sees them as another potential energy source. But we don't know how he deals with active psychics on the inside—unless we assume from what happened to Sarah."

"Can we assume from that? She reported her belief that at least one of Samuel's people is a powerful psychic, right?"

"Yes. But strongly shielded."

"Even so, if Sarah picked up on it, Samuel must have."

"My guess is, that person is a psychic Samuel controls. Someone he's able to dominate. But he couldn't dominate Sarah. She was on the inside, she was looking for information, and she was getting some of those kids out. And now she's dead. I say it's a safe assumption she posed a threat to Samuel, either because she was a psychic he couldn't control or because he figured out she was working against him."

"Hollis—"

"Either way, you're at risk. Especially when you're tired."

Tessa heard the concern in the other woman's voice and appreciated it. Nevertheless, she brushed it aside. She also pushed aside the guilty awareness that she probably should have told Hollis about the previous day's nosebleed. Or should now.

She didn't.

"That energy you saw a few hours ago, my aura with the connection to . . . something or someone else. Do you still see it?"

"Barely. It's just a thread now. Why?"

"Let me guess. It looks taut, not loose like before. As though something is pulling at it."

Hollis frowned. "That's what you're feeling?"

"So strongly I keep expecting to see a rope."

"Tessa, that isn't necessarily a good thing. In fact, it probably isn't a good thing. This could be Samuel pulling you back there. Or doing his damnedest to."

"I never even saw him yesterday."

"You dreamed about him last night, with all the vivid detail of a true vision. And, besides, trust me when I say you don't have to see him to be touched by him."

That reminder gave Tessa pause, but after only a moment she shook her head. "You said it yourself. Whatever is going on out there, it's getting worse. People are dying, Hollis. And all these extra senses of mine are telling me to get out there. Today. As soon as possible."

Hollis eyed her thoughtfully. "You're a lot more confident and certain than you were earlier this morning."

That was true enough, and Tessa knew it. However . . . "I can't explain it."

"I really wish you could," Hollis said.

"Look, one thing I've learned is to trust my instincts. Or intuition, or clairvoyance, or whatever it is that nudges me to do something when my rational mind tells me it's a bad idea. That's why I'm here, right? Because John and Bishop believe my abilities can help investigate this case?"

"Yeah. That's why you're here."

"Okay, then. I have to go out to the Compound. Now."

"You told Ruth it would be later today."

"I'll give her ten minutes' head start, and then I'm going."

Faced with that clear sense of urgency, Hollis stopped arguing, but she did offer a further word of warning.

"We know you'll be under observation most of the time you're there; if you do manage to do any exploring on your own, don't forget that. Someone will be watching. Count on it."

Ruby—

It was very early on Thursday morning, and Ruby

had found her attention wandering from her lessons. That clear voice in her mind brought her head up with a jerk and made her go suddenly cold.

She dared not answer; the four friends had decided weeks ago that it was dangerous, that Father could probably hear them if they practiced the abilities that had bloomed in them since October.

Ruby had cheated a bit on that agreement, though not with her friends. She had cheated because she needed to protect Lexie—but that was her cheat, her risk. If Father discovered what she had done, she'd be the only one in trouble.

In trouble. That was almost funny. Because if Father found out what she'd done, what she was still doing, the "trouble" she'd be in would be very, very bad.

And there was a good chance he *would* find out. He could do so much; surely, Ruby thought, he could mind-talk too. And if he knew she and her friends could do it . . .

People able to do things with their minds had a habit of disappearing from the Compound. Or else they became . . . different.

Ruby didn't want either of those things to happen to her or to any of her friends. And she knew they didn't either, knew that none of them would have even tried to reach out to her unless something was wrong. Very wrong.

She tried to be patient, and as soon as her mother became occupied—as usual—with her latest embroidery project, Ruby slipped from the house, driven by an overwhelming urge to go to whichever of her friends was in trouble.

But who was it? There had been no sense of identity, and the communication had ended so abruptly that she felt only the faintest idea even of the direction she should go.

She knew her friends were supposed to be at their lessons and were unlikely to be out openly roaming the Compound at this time of morning, and she knew her own roaming, if noticed by just about any of the adults, would likely end with her being escorted back home— which was one reason she dared not approach any of the houses in broad daylight.

She also knew better than to approach the church; she had watched and listened, and nobody had to explain to her that cameras just about everywhere made sure that Mr. DeMarco or one of the other men knew when anybody got close to the church.

Besides, that wasn't where she needed to be.

She followed whatever it was urging her on, and when she realized that she was nearing the barn in the west pasture, her heart sank. This was the side of the Compound nearest to the road to town, the shortest way out of the Compound.

Escape.

"Brooke, no," she whispered, her steps quickening. All she could think was that her friend had gotten this far in her escape plan and then panicked, maybe remembering that there was a fence and more cameras between here and freedom.

But something— instinct or her five senses or one of the extra ones—warned Ruby not to just go into the barn as she usually would. Instead, she worked her way around to the back, where a split plank provided a narrow, secret view into the barn.

At first, Ruby wasn't quite sure what was going on in there. She saw Brooke—just standing there, a few yards from Ruby's position, in the wide hall between rows of now-unoccupied stalls.

It took a moment for Ruby to make out that Brooke was shaking visibly.

It took another instant to see why.

Father.

Ruby caught her breath and instinctively put extra effort into making sure her shell was hard and thick, imagining herself encased in something unbreakable. So he wouldn't know she was there.

Then she realized there was an awful lot of *strange* in the barn. For one thing, she couldn't ever remember seeing Father alone, not outside the church. And for another thing...

He was shimmering oddly.

And his feet weren't touching the ground.

"Answer me, Brooke." His voice was quiet, even gentle, but something about it made the hair on the back of Ruby's neck stand straight out.

"Why would you want to leave us? Why would you want to leave me?"

"I...I wasn't." Her voice was small and broken.

He pointed silently to the ground beside her, where her bulging backpack lay.

"I . . . I . . . My aunt. I just wanted to go visit my aunt. That's all. That's all, Father."

"I don't believe you, child."

"I . . . I swear, Father. I swear I just wanted to see my aunt."

"I wish I could believe you."

His voice was sorrowful now, but there was something strange happening to his face. Something that made Ruby press her fists against her mouth to keep herself silent when everything inside her wanted to scream.

For the first time, she could see his true face.

The face his soul wore.

And it was something so black and hungry that Ruby had the terrifying notion it could swallow the whole world with room left over for even more.

"I would have much preferred to wait until God allowed your talents to fully blossom," Father was saying sadly. "Until you were ripe and ready for His holy work. But you've made that impossible now."

"Father, please—I'll be good. I promise I'll be good. I won't even try to leave, honest, and I won't say anything to anybody, I won't tell my parents or my friends, or anybody—"

Her words were tumbling over one another in her frightened haste to get them all out, and her legs were so wobbly it was a wonder she was still able to stand on them. She probably would have promised anything in that moment, anything at all.

But it was no use. Ruby could see that, and she bit down on her fist without even feeling it as the scream clawed its way up out of her soul and writhed around inside her, desperate to escape.

"I'm so sorry, child," Father said.

Brooke must have known what was going to happen, or perhaps she felt the first jolts of pain, because she opened her mouth to scream.

The sound was no more than a gurgle, a choked cry of terror and agony. As Father raised his hands, Brooke was lifted nearly a foot off the ground and hung there, her body jerking as though some invisible giant shook her angrily.

Father's head tipped back, his mouth opened slightly—

And Ruby could see the power leaving Brooke, being sucked out of her, coming out of her *eyes* and going into him in crackling white-hot threads, like lightning, sparking and sizzling.

But he wasn't burned.

He wasn't burned.

When Ruby saw Brooke begin to smolder, she turned away from the split plank and pressed her back against the other rough boards of the barn, too terrified to even try to run away. Her fist was still pressed to her mouth, and she could taste blood but still felt no pain.

All she felt was horror.

She listened to the awful crackling and sizzling sounds for what seemed like hours but was probably no more than a minute or two. Then, abruptly, there was silence.

Ruby counted to thirty, then forced herself to look into the barn again.

Father was gone.

Brooke was gone.

There was nothing to mark what had happened inside the barn except a scorched place where Brooke had stood.

Sawyer had no reason except obstinacy to return to the Compound late on Thursday morning, and when he called ahead he was more than a little surprised that DeMarco didn't offer an objection to the visit.

Maybe it amuses him to watch you fumble around and come up empty every time.

But when DeMarco met him at the Square as always, he was, if anything, more than usually stone-faced and seemed just the slightest bit distracted.

"What can I do for you today, Chief?"

"You can let me look around. Alone." Sawyer had made virtually the same request every time and fully expected the same polite refusal.

DeMarco looked at him for an unblinking moment. Then he said dryly, "It seems to be the day for it. Reverend Samuel is meditating, and most of the children are at their lessons. The residential floors of the church are, of course, private, as are the cottages; I would ask that you respect those limitations."

Too startled to hide it, Sawyer said, "No problem."

"Fine. Then look around to your heart's content, Chief." DeMarco half-turned away, then paused to add even more dryly, "Say hello to Mrs. Gray for me."

"She's here?" There were several cars parked around the Square; he hadn't noticed hers.

"Like you, she wanted to...wander around. Get a feeling for the place. Ruth didn't see the harm."

And you were too late to stop her without being obvious about it?

"I don't suppose you'd know where Mrs. Gray is now?" Sawyer fully supposed he did.

DeMarco almost smiled. "I actually don't, Chief. Though Ruth did say she believed Mrs. Gray wanted to see what we call the 'natural church,' where Reverend Samuel preaches when the weather is...just right. It's up on the hill behind the Compound. Follow the path through the old pasture. You'll have no trouble recognizing the place."

"Thank you," Sawyer said warily.

"You don't play poker, do you, Chief." It wasn't a question.

With deliberation, Sawyer replied, "No. Chess is my game."

"You'll have to give me a match sometime. Enjoy your wanderings. I'll be in my office."

Sawyer gazed after the other man until DeMarco disappeared into the church, then set off on a direct path past the church and toward the pasture that lay behind the cottages on the north side of the Compound.

He was under no illusions; escort or no escort, neither he nor Tessa Gray would be unobserved anywhere within the Compound.

He wondered if she knew that.

It took him no more than five minutes to reach the pasture gate, closed despite the lack of stock. Since he'd been raised in a rural area where livestock was plentiful, Sawyer passed through but left the gate as he'd found it, securely fastened.

The path up the hill was faint but visible, and he followed it, forcing himself to stroll rather than walk briskly, to pause and look around, not quite idly. At least twice he paused to look back down the hill, studying the layout of the Compound.

It would be expected.

Not that there was anything unusual to see, at least as far as he could tell. The Compound was quiet, peaceful. No kids in the playground, but it was not yet lunchtime and they would be, as DeMarco had said, inside their homes at their lessons.

He had wondered briefly why the church didn't just build its own school as part of the Compound but had decided it was a simple matter of wanting to avoid the red tape and regulations that even a private school had to contend with. Better to have the children of the church home-schooled by a parent; as long as the children passed the necessary state-mandated periodic tests, no one was going to interfere in the matter.

"Bad day?"

He hadn't realized he was scowling. Even more, he

hadn't realized until she spoke that he had reached the "natural church" just barely over the top of the hill.

It resembled a natural amphitheater, with a wide, solid granite ledge just to his right that would no doubt make an excellent stage—or pulpit. On the gentle downward slope below, curving terraces looked to Sawyer as though they'd been cut into the hillside, artificially set with scattered, mostly chair-sized boulders supplemented by numerous rustic benches.

Natural church my ass.

Unlike a true amphitheater, the shape was inverted, so that rather than gazing downward, all his followers would have to look up at Samuel while he preached.

Wonder if he does the loaves-and-fishes bit. And where the hell is the microphone?

"Chief?"

She was sitting on one of the larger boulders on the third terrace down. Casual in jeans and a sweater, her cheeks a bit rosy from the morning chill and big gray eyes solemn, she looked even more fragile than he remembered. The sight of her made something inside his chest tighten.

Don't be an idiot. She's your dead childhood friend's widow—and a recent widow at that.

"Bad week," Sawyer replied finally. He made his way down to her but hesitated rather than join her on the wide boulder. "I imagine services here would be impressive," he said.

"Probably. And I imagine it cost them a pretty

penny to make all this look so...natural. Rather than man-made." Her voice was quiet, thoughtful.

He was a little surprised, but pleasantly so.

So they haven't quite got their hooks into her yet. At least not completely.

Still, he kept his tone if not his words neutral when he said, "Keep the audience entertained and they'll be back."

Tessa smiled faintly. "I was just thinking something along those lines. Have a seat, Chief."

"Sawyer."

"Have a seat, Sawyer. Please."

He joined her on the cold and not-very-comfortable boulder, turning just a bit so he could look at her as they talked. The slight breeze brought him a very pleasant herbal scent that he realized must have been her. Her hair, he guessed. He wanted to lean toward her, and fought the urge. "I was surprised when DeMarco said you were up here."

"Did he tell you?" She frowned briefly. "I suppose Ruth had to report to him. They all seem to, don't they?"

"He does run things for Reverend Samuel," Sawyer replied, still cautiously feeling his way with her. "Security, at least."

Tessa nodded. "She didn't exactly say so, but I think Ruth was reluctant to let me explore on my own. Without his permission, I mean."

"Yeah, well. I got his permission. Which is unusual."

She turned her head and regarded him, those big

eyes still solemn. "Maybe he wants to put your suspicions to rest. Let you wander around on your own, and if—when—you don't find anything, you'd have no reason to come back here."

"Do you believe that would discourage me?" he asked, curious.

"No. I think you're convinced the church is connected to the deaths of those two poor women found in the river."

Sawyer wasn't surprised she had noted his suspicion; he had certainly not tried to hide it. Nevertheless, he heard the defensiveness in his tone when he said, "You think I'm wrong to keep pushing?"

"I think," Tessa Gray said, "you should push harder."

"They're just sitting there talking." Brian Seymour gestured toward the main monitor in the security room. "She said something, he said he was having a bad week—and then he moved away from the microphone, and that's all we got. They're just far enough away that we can't pick up their voices."

"Convenient," DeMarco said.

"Well, the microphone was placed just so we could record Father's sermons," Brian reminded him. "It wasn't intended as part of the security system."

"Yes. I know."

They were alone in the security room for the time being, so Brian didn't hesitate to be frank. "I know you want to keep a close eye on the chief, but Mrs. Gray as well? She walked through the scanner when she came into the church with Ruth, and nothing showed up. No weapon, no electronics. Not that I'd expect her to be carrying anything like that, anyway."

"No," DeMarco said. "Neither would I. But as long as she's with the chief and within range of any of the cameras, watch her."

"Copy that. I'll tell the guys as soon as they get back from their break. Should we record if any of the microphones pick them up again?"

DeMarco considered, then shook his head. "As amusing as it might be to listen to the chief try his hand at courting, I believe we'll leave them their privacy. That much of it, at least. As you say, audio isn't part of our security system out there, so we might as well save the tape. Turn the microphones off for the time being, Brian."

Brian grinned a little as he obeyed. "Courting? Way I hear it, Chief Cavenaugh's slippery as an eel; the matchmaking biddies in town have been trying to hook him up permanent for years without any luck."

"It remains to be seen whether he needs their help," DeMarco said dryly.

"Maybe his taste just runs to wealthy widows, and this is the first real shot he's had. They aren't all that common in Grace. Especially young and very good-looking ones."

"True."

Sobering, Brian said, "It could cause problems for us,

though, couldn't it? I mean, if Mrs. Gray decided to re-marry—and especially the chief?"

"You're jumping the gun just a bit, Brian, don't you think?"

"Well, yeah, sure. But—"

"I doubt the chief is ready to ask for a date, let alone propose." Without waiting for a response, DeMarco added, "I'll be in my office. Make sure I'm called if necessary, but otherwise I don't want to be disturbed."

"Yes, sir." Brian turned back to the monitor, not entirely relaxing until he heard the door close behind De-Marco. Then he leaned back in his chair and checked the other monitors before returning his idle gaze to the silent discussion going on just over the hill and supposedly out of sight of anyone in the Compound.

"Push harder?" Surprised yet again, Sawyer frowned at Tessa. "Why? Have you seen something?"

"I've seen what you've seen. Less, really, since this is only my second visit here."

"But you believe there's something here to see?"

It was her turn to frown, and she looked away to gaze up the hill toward the "natural" pulpit. Her eyes seemed unfocused for a moment, almost dreamy. "I'm not a cop," she said absently. "I'm not so sure I'd recognize anything unusual."

"Then why do you—"

"Except for the Stepford bit. They're all very . . . perfect, aren't they? Scrubbed and polite and smiling. Content." Her gaze returned to his face, the gray eyes sharp now. "I hear some people get that from their religion, but up here it seems a little excessive."

"Just a little?" he said almost involuntarily.

Tessa smiled. "Okay, more than a little. A nosy question, but are you religious, Sawyer?"

"Not really. Raised with it, of course. Hard not to be here in the South."

"But it didn't . . . speak to you?"

"The preachers yelled quite a bit, but, no, I didn't much care for the fire and brimstone."

"Me either. Do you think that's why what Samuel offers his flock is so seductive? Because he doesn't yell? Because he promises reward instead of punishment?"

Sawyer studied her for a moment, conscious of the very odd but strong impulse to tell her that they should both leave. Now. But he had no idea why, specifically, he felt a threat directed at them both.

"Sawyer?"

He actually turned his head and looked all around them, wary, realizing that the hairs on the back of his neck were stirring in warning, and not because of the damn camera.

"We should leave," he said.

"They turned the microphone off."

He looked quickly back at her. "Tessa, what are you talking about?"

"There's a microphone hidden up there just behind the pulpit. Didn't you feel it? Can't you feel it now?"

Carefully, he said, "How could I *feel* a microphone?"

She studied him, a tiny smile playing about her mouth. "That's your thing, isn't it? Electronics? So you always know when there's a camera around, when there's surveillance? I bet watches die on you within weeks or even days and cell phones lose their charge much faster than they're supposed to. And I'll bet you short out lamps and screw up computers from time to time. Unless you've learned more than basic control, at least."

Sawyer was rarely speechless, but at that moment he couldn't think of a damn thing to say. The sense of a threat was still there, hovering, but he honestly wasn't certain if it was the camera—or something else.

"Sorry. Under normal circumstances I wouldn't have said anything," Tessa continued. "It's your ability, after all, and your decision who to tell about it. I know from experience that keeping quiet is...usually the better way. People tend to fear what they don't understand, and—But we don't have a lot of time, so I have to be blunt."

"Blunt in saying what?" He wasn't giving in without a fight.

"That you're psychic. Probably since you were a kid, but you may not have been aware of it until you hit your teens."

"Tessa—"

"Most of us move from latent to active in our teens, unless there's some kind of traumatic event earlier than that. Or sometimes much later in life. We're the lucky ones. Our abilities aren't born in pain and suffering."

Again, Sawyer didn't know what to say.

Tessa smiled, this time a bit wry. "Technically, you have a heightened sensitivity to electrical and magnetic fields. We don't really have a name for that, other than a kind of clairvoyance. I don't know if you're able to manipulate the fields, but you do affect them, they affect you, and you could probably feel that microphone about the time you topped the hill." She nodded slightly to indicate something off to his right. "Just like you can feel the camera trained on us from that tree over there."

Sawyer didn't bother to turn his head to look at the camera thirty yards away from them but kept his gaze on her face. "And you know all this because . . . ?"

"Because I'm psychic too. And one of the things I'm really good at is sensing another psychic and knowing what abilities they have."

"*One* of the things?"

"I'm also clairvoyant, though not like you; I tend to pick up bits of information, emotions, snippets of thoughts. I have an unusual shield that hides my abilities from every other psychic I've ever encountered, and I'm mildly telepathic both ways."

"Both ways?"

Yes. Both ways.

"Shit. Was that—"

"Me, yeah. Sorry. It is, to say the least, intrusive to shove thoughts into other people's minds without so much as a by-your-leave, and I generally ask permission first." Her shoulders lifted and fell in a little shrug. "The ability only seems to work with other psychics. And even then I'm limited to very short phrases and sentences."

Sawyer thought about the sarcastic inner voice that had been nagging at him and had to ask. "You haven't been—you haven't done that before? Put thoughts in my head?"

Her eyebrows went up a bit. "No, that was the first time. Why? Has there been an alien voice in your head?"

"I assume you mean *alien* as in unfamiliar."

"Well, I'm not a big believer in visitations from little green men, so, yeah, that's what I mean."

"How could I have an unfamiliar voice in my head?"

Her mouth twisted slightly. "Around here? Pretty easily, I'd say. There's a weird sort of energy in this place, here in the Compound and even in Grace, and you can't tell me you don't feel it."

"Lots of places have weird energy. That doesn't translate to somebody else's thoughts in your head."

"It might here. I can't be absolutely sure of the number, but I can tell you there are quite a few psychics inside this Compound."

"I can't believe I'm having this conversation," he muttered.

"It gets worse," she told him.

Ten

JESUS. How does it get worse?"

"We believe Samuel is one of the strongest and most unusual psychics we've ever encountered. Extremely powerful and extremely dangerous. And probably at least one of the people closest to him is an unusually strong psychic as well. Maybe DeMarco." She shook her head. "I couldn't get a read on him, and that's rare for me."

Sawyer took a moment to sort through the questions rattling around in his mind and focused on one. "We believe. Who is *we*?"

Tessa answered readily, having clearly expected the question. "I work for a civilian investigative organization called Haven. We're called into cases that ... present difficulties for cops and federal agents, for whatever reason. Most of us are licensed P.I.s, but we obviously don't have quite as many rules and regulations to worry about during an investigation."

"You break the law?"

"Personally, no. Well, not so far, though I have to admit I've never been faced with that particular choice. And it isn't company policy, believe me; we also work with cops and federal agents, both of whom would be more than a little uncooperative if we didn't mostly play by the rules."

"Mostly."

She ignored the muttered word to add, "This time out, we're part of a federal investigation of the Church of the Everlasting Sin. And of Samuel."

"First I've heard of it." He tried to keep the suspicion out of his voice and undoubtedly failed, judging by her faint smile. *Or, hell, maybe she's just reading your mind.*

"You'll have to forgive us for that. We had reason to believe that Samuel could have people inside local law enforcement. Church members, perhaps. So we couldn't be sure who to trust. Until we had someone here who could..."

"Read me?"

Tessa nodded. "We had to be sure. We couldn't take the chance of confiding in the wrong person, not with so many lives potentially at stake. I'm sure you know enough about cults to know that if and when the cult leader is threatened, or even just feels threatened, the consequences can be devastating."

"Koresh," Sawyer said grimly. "Jim Jones."

She nodded again. "Probably something you've been worried about yourself, especially in recent weeks. You pulled those bodies out of the river. I'm betting you know there have been other victims as well. Victims someone else had to pull out of the river at some point downstream. Victims who died in . . . unnatural ways."

"Are you telling me that Samuel killed them? You know he killed them?"

"If we knew absolutely, if we could prove it, then you and I wouldn't be having this conversation. We're sure he's responsible. We just don't have courtroom proof. Yet."

"So . . . what? You're here to get that proof? By allowing them to recruit you, take you into the fold?" Before she could answer, he sat up straighter and said, "Wait a minute. If this is your job, then you aren't really Jared's widow. It's all a cover."

She cleared her throat and looked, for the first time, a bit uncomfortable. "Jared Gray is alive and well. Sailing somewhere off Bermuda, last I heard. I'm sorry, Sawyer, for the deception. That part of it, at least. He said—well, he didn't think there'd be anybody back here to grieve for him, especially since he left right after high school. He was in Florida trying to untangle his parents' estate months after they'd died in a car crash, hadn't even started thinking about what he'd do with the part of it here in Grace."

"You asked him to play dead."

"Not me personally. But, yes, that's what he was asked to do. And he was willing to disappear for a few months. More than willing; I think he was sick of dealing with legal matters and just wanted to get away. A sailing 'accident' was easy enough to arrange."

"And a wedding before that?"

"All the paperwork to indicate there had been a wedding, yes. An actual ceremony wasn't necessary."

"Just a lot of lying."

Grave now, she said, "I hate that part of the job. And if I didn't believe I was helping, doing something positive with my abilities, I couldn't pretend to be someone else."

Sawyer drew a breath and let it out slowly, honestly not sure if he was relieved or pissed. "So what's your real name?"

"Actually, my real name is Gray. Tessa Gray. One of the hardest things about going undercover is remembering a whole new name, so we try to avoid that as much as possible, keep at least our Christian names the same. This time it just happened to work out that I was able to keep both."

"Quite a coincidence."

"My boss says there are no coincidences. Just the universe arranging things."

Hollis Templeton would have been the first to admit that inactivity drove her nuts, so she considered it a cosmic joke that fate had placed her in the small town of Grace and in the Gray family home where she was virtually a prisoner.

She couldn't even go into town.

"You broadcast," Bishop told her frankly. "Especially since you began to see auras. We can't take the chance that Samuel or his people might see or sense you. It's enough of a risk just to have you in the house with Tessa when church members visit her."

"I know, I know. I wouldn't even be here if Ellen Hodges hadn't told me I needed to be. I just wish she'd told me *why* I needed to be here."

"You'll find out eventually. But until you have some sense of why, you have to keep a low profile."

"I don't have to like it."

"No, I wouldn't expect you to. But sit tight for the time being."

Hiding her abilities had never been an issue until recently, and since they were still evolving—seeing auras was a very new aspect—she had spent her time learning to cope with what was rather than worry about shielding it from other psychics.

She wished now that she had taken a few lessons in developing her personal shield and had in fact been practicing using the few basic instructions Bishop and others on the team had offered. But she was a long way yet from being able to hide her abilities.

In the meantime, since doing *something* was better than pacing the floor in worry about whatever Tessa might be doing inside the church Compound, Hollis had abandoned the smaller kitchen space to turn the big table in the formal dining room into her command center. Her laptop was set up there, and files, notepads, and maps vied for the remainder of the polished mahogany surface.

There was a very large, very grand book-lined study on the other side of the sprawling house, but Hollis, like

Tessa, was uncomfortably aware of being very much an outsider in someone else's home, and she preferred to work in the brighter and less personal dining room.

Not that there was a lot of work to do. She had gone over everything so many times that she felt like it was all branded in her mind, and staring at the bits and pieces of information was a bit like staring at blank jigsaw pieces: impossible to know how everything really fit together.

If it fit together.

Despite Bishop's certainty, Hollis was having a difficult time accepting that the Reverend Adam Deacon Samuel really had been the mastermind—literally—behind one of the most vicious, inhuman serial killers ever to rampage across American soil. It didn't seem possible, at least in a sane world, for an avowed man of God to deliberately unchain an evil, ravenous beast and set it loose to maim and kill innocents.

Even worse, to personally hunt for and virtually feed that monster its victims, one by one.

How could any man, after doing that, return to his church and preach to his congregation about God's love?

"It's a cult," she reminded herself aloud, needing more sound than that provided by the kitchen TV, on low and tuned to an MSNBC news show. "He's got himself a cult. Cults are all about power, not religion. All about control. Look at what he's doing now with the women of that church. Maybe he needs the energy, or maybe he just likes manipulating them. Controlling them. He gets the energy and the kicks—and the satisfaction of knowing he's the alpha among all the men of the congregation. That he can . . . pleasure the women in a way none of their men can. And . . . yuck," she added involuntarily.

Hollis had only recently begun her training in criminal profiling, but what she had learned so far told her to look for patterns, for a kind of logic in a personality so far outside accepted norms that trying to find something logical seemed irrational.

Seemed.

There was always logic, if only that of a twisted mind.

A twisted and impenetrable mind, at least to Hollis. She almost wished Dani were here; as far as Hollis knew, Dani Justice was the only person living who had first-hand experience with at least some of the thoughts in this twisted monster's mind. And was, moreover, possibly the only person who had ever hurt him in a psychic sense.

And therein lay the danger.

Dani was someone else too easily recognizable to Samuel, and she, unlike Hollis, posed a very real and deadly threat to him. Hollis he wouldn't be happy about; Dani might be able to destroy him, and that was a threat that could push him over the edge.

"Call me," Dani had said to Bishop. "If it comes to that. If you need me there. Call me. In the meantime, I'll keep practicing."

"What about Marc?" Bishop had asked, referring to the man with whom she was in the process of forming a unique partnership.

"Marc understands the stakes. And he knows how I

feel about finishing this, once and for all. Call me, Bishop. If you need me."

Hollis hoped they wouldn't need Dani. As remarkable as her ability was, Dani had not faced Samuel in a literal sense, had not pitted her strength against his directly. What she had done in Venture had been self-defense, not an offensive attack.

Facing him here would be...something very different.

Something deadly.

"He recharges," Hollis said aloud to herself as she stared down at a detailed drawing of the church Sarah had managed to get out to them weeks before. She fixed her gaze on the third-floor layout and Samuel's suite of rooms in the rear of the building. "He controls. He kills. Why does he kill? Because he can? Because he wants to? Because he has to? Why—"

The physical reaction was always the same. All the fine hairs on her body stood out as though electrical energy filled the room, and goose bumps rose on her flesh as if someone had suddenly opened a door into winter. And there was, still, a jolt of fear, a sense that some doors were really never intended to be opened by the living. Not, at least, without some dreadful cost.

Hollis looked up slowly.

The woman was young, pretty, with long fair hair, and her expression was unhappy.

Possibly because she was dead.

But she looked alive, looked flesh-and-blood real; Hollis had the uneasy suspicion that if she could reach across the table and touch this spirit, the woman would feel just as alive as she looked. Hollis always had that notion and probably would until—if—she put it to the test.

"I told you to look for her in the water. Why didn't you listen?" Her voice was low, anxious.

Hollis ignored the question to ask one of her own. "Who are you?"

"Andrea."

"Andrea who?"

"You have to look for her in the water."

"Look for who in the water?" Hollis countered, trying for once to get at least a few bits of useful information she could focus on.

"Ruby."

"Is Ruby in the water now?"

"I told you."

"You told me more than three months ago."

Andrea's expression turned uncertain. "Three months ago."

"Three months ago and in another town. Another state. I saw you in Venture, Georgia. At a murder scene. We're in North Carolina now. Don't you know when you are? Where you are?"

A breath of a laugh escaped Andrea. "I'm in hell, I think."

"Andrea, when did you die?"

"You don't know about me yet." She said it in an odd, automatic way, as if reciting something memorized.

"You said that before. In Venture."

"Did I?"

"Yes. When did you die?"

"Before."

"Andrea—"

"It's my fault. What he's doing. I should have made him understand. I should have ... He's made it so much worse, and it's all my fault."

"What's your fault?" Hollis's question was more insistent, because she could see that Andrea was fading, losing substance and energy, and knew the contact would last only seconds longer.

But Andrea was shaking her head. "Please, look for her in the water. Help Ruby."

Hollis drew a quick breath. "If she's already in the water, then I can't help her."

"You can. You have to. All of you have to." Even her voice was fading, the final words holding a curiously hollow sound. "You need her help to stop him."

Hollis stared at the empty space on the other side of the table, vaguely aware that the room was a normal temperature again and that the sensation of a live current in the air was gone. She pulled a legal pad from under one of the maps and made several quick notes, jotting down what had been said while it was still fresh in her mind.

Then, conscious of a nagging uneasiness, she searched among the folders for the right one and from it pulled a list of names Sarah had provided for them. Members of the Church of the Everlasting Sin.

One of Sarah's goals once inside the church had been to both compile this list and provide basic information about each person, trying to determine which of Samuel's followers might possibly be active or latent psychics. She had placed a check beside possible latent psychics and added a star if she had sensed a particular strength or awareness of their ability in the person.

There was a score of checks, which was an extraordinarily high percentage of potential psychic ability for such a small community. Several names boasted question marks. But there were no more than four names with stars beside them. Hollis ran her finger slowly down the list and was almost at the bottom when she found it.

Ruby Campbell had a check beside her name. And three stars.

She was twelve years old.

"I hesitate to interrupt the brooding," Tessa said, "but we really don't have time for it."

Sawyer felt his eyebrows climbing as he looked at her. "Well, forgive me for needing a minute or two to let it all soak in." She had spent the past ten minutes or so telling him about the Special Crimes Unit, the very concept of which he was having a hard time dealing with.

"I really am sorry. I know it's a lot—Haven, the SCU, what we believe about Samuel and his church. And you have every right to feel overwhelmed. You also have every right to mistrust me, and I wouldn't blame you if you did. But I'm afraid I need to know—now—whether I made a mistake in confiding in you."

"Wasn't sanctioned, huh?"

"It's not quite like that. Field operatives make judgment calls all the time, and one of those is often whether—and when—to take local law enforcement into our confidence. Nobody's going to second-guess me for making that decision. But I need to know if it was the right one."

After a moment, he said, "I honestly don't know how I feel about any of this, Tessa. But I'd be a liar if I said I wasn't happy to know that I'm not the only one suspicious of Samuel and his church."

"Good enough."

"Is it?" He didn't want to be accused again of brooding but couldn't do anything about the frown he knew he was wearing. "If Samuel is even half of what you say he is, then I'm a bit doubtful of my own control, my—what did you call it? shields?—my ability to keep him from sensing my thoughts. I don't know if I can keep your secrets."

"Just try to concentrate on your own suspicions of him whenever you're around him. That's no secret to him and could very well keep him from delving deeper."

"Delving? Into my mind? Jesus."

"Well, if it makes you feel any better, we aren't sure he can do that. Delve, I mean."

"It doesn't make me feel any better."

"Sorry. But, look, we're all in that boat, more or less. We don't know how powerful he is. Even worse, we don't know for certain what abilities he has. *Is* he telepathic? Is he precognitive? Empathic? What's his range? What are his limitations? He can...suck up energy from other sources to recharge his own, even from other people, but can he channel that energy? Literally? Make it a weapon? Or has he found some other way of killing with his mind?"

"Jesus," Sawyer repeated.

She nodded. "Scary, isn't it? The law doesn't cover what he is, what he can do. He doesn't use a knife or a gun or a garrote, or even a big stick. As far as we can tell, he doesn't have to be anywhere near his victims. He certainly doesn't have to touch them. And yet, somehow, he murders them. He steals their very life energy, and in a way that has to be unimaginably painful and terrifying."

"Why? Why is he killing?"

"I don't know. But I believe he won't stop. I believe every one of his followers is at risk."

"Nearly a hundred people live in this Compound."

"Yes."

"People who practically worship him."

"Don't kid yourself—they do worship him. He's spent a lot of time and expended a great deal of energy to make certain of it."

"Then why the hell isn't that enough for him? What more could he want than to be considered a god by his followers?"

"Maybe...to be considered a god by the world."

Sawyer drew a breath and let it out slowly. "I really, really hope you're wrong about that."

"So do I. But if you want to consider the textbook definition of a cult leader, he pretty much fits, and for a cult leader it's always, at the end of the day, about power. About controlling his followers. And about convincing them that only he can lead them to . . . peace, or heaven, or some version of utopia, of the promised land, whatever it is they want to believe in. I haven't heard his sermons yet, but I'm told they can turn on a dime from God Loves You to Those Who Don't Understand Will Try to Destroy Us."

"I've been told the same thing, though I've personally only heard the God Loves You version."

"And have you seen his effect on his female followers?"

"I've seen it. Creepy as hell. Whatever he's doing to them . . . if it isn't a crime, it's sure to God a sin."

"It's worse than a sin." She told him their theory.

Though it pretty much confirmed his own suspicions, Sawyer nevertheless felt queasy. "Christ. So he's killing some of them and regularly . . . feeding off others? Off the sexual pleasure of the women?"

"We think so."

"For energy? Literally?"

Tessa nodded.

"Why does he need so much energy?"

"We don't know. Maybe because he's using so much to control his followers. Maybe he's stockpiling for some . . . future need."

"What kind of need?"

"If he's paranoid, and cult leaders mostly are, he has to be afraid someone really will try to stop him. In his mind, that would be an ultimate battle. An apocalypse.

Armageddon. He may be trying to build up his power, strengthen his abilities, for that last stand against whoever is perceived to be attacking him. Most cults either explode or implode, sooner or later, and it's virtually always because the cult leader has lost it."

"If he's using so much energy, even if he's just storing it, won't that have an effect on his brain?"

"Probably. And we're pretty sure he was twisted to begin with. There's no telling what's happening inside his head, but I can pretty much guarantee you it isn't good."

"Maybe his own ambition will destroy him," Sawyer said. "I don't have to be a doctor to know that the human body was never intended to contain too much electrical energy. Whatever's building up inside him, sooner or later, it's gotta blow."

The morning meditations were always the most difficult for Samuel, at least these days. He thought it was because there was seldom an opportunity to recharge his energies so early in the day, but he also felt certain it was part of God's plan.

To keep him humble.

On this morning, however, he'd been forced to deal with the small problem of Brooke—poor child, to believe she could escape God's plans for her—and while he was saddened by her loss, her energy had certainly made his early meditations much easier on him than usual.

So it wasn't quite so difficult to work his way

through the memories one more time, to relive his child-hood. His slow, hesitant acceptance of God into his life. Until...

On a scorching hot July day when he was thirteen years old, God reached down and touched him.

It happened more or less in the middle of nowhere, in an area so rural the cows by far outnumbered the peo-ple. It happened at a summer tent revival being run by an older preacher, a thin, unshaven, intense-eyed man named Maddox who had long ago fallen out of the main-stream but felt compelled to preach his radical version of God's word to anyone who would listen.

Samuel had intended to pass through the tiny ex-cuse for a town the day before, but a flyer tacked to a power pole had drawn his attention, and he had decided rather idly to stay for the revival. In his experience, the ladies of the town often brought cakes or cookies along, and sometimes casseroles, turning the event into a sort of family picnic.

There wasn't much entertainment in such isolated areas, and a good preacher could brighten up an other-wise dull Saturday. And if he was really good, the crowd would return, possibly larger, on Sunday, choosing him as a onetime alternative to their more traditional churches.

So Samuel hung around the town, earning a few bucks sweeping out a couple of downtown stores forgot-ten by time and then hitching a ride out to the big pas-ture where a worn tent had been pitched, all the flaps pinned open because it was a sweltering day.

Inside were a few dozen folding chairs and benches, sitting unevenly on the harsh stubble of recently harvested hay. Someone had taken the trouble to rake up whatever manure had been on the ground beneath the tent, but there was nevertheless a pervasive odor of cow hanging heavily in the still, hot air.

Maddox passed out badly printed "programs" that consisted of a single sheet of cheap paper, folded once and filled with tiny, smudged type. His sermon, more or less. The highlights, at least. It was barely literate but filled with passionate belief.

Samuel settled onto a rickety chair at the back, happy that there had been a chicken and two beef casseroles but disgruntled because nobody had brought cookies. He listened to Maddox build slowly to a rant against government officials and established religions and anybody other than himself who believed they had the Answer.

Maddox alone had the Answer.

The Answer he cannily hinted at but never actually provided. Only the godly, he assured them, could hear the Answer.

He was good theater, Samuel thought. The couple dozen townsfolk who had come out to listen fanned themselves with his program and nodded and occasionally threw in an *amen* to keep the show going.

Thunder began to rumble distantly, then closer, and a hot breeze blew through the tent.

Samuel saw a few people consulting watches and beginning to grow restless, and he saw that Maddox had also noticed. The old man's words began to tumble and fall over one another as he rushed to get his sermon finished and reach the all-important ritual of passing the collection plates, which were, Samuel had noticed, old baskets.

But even with a storm approaching and his audience growing restive, Maddox took the time to ask if any wanted to come forward and offer their own testimony.

Samuel didn't have to look around to know that no one else in the audience was interested. It was too hot to bestir themselves. Besides, it was time to be leaving, what with a storm coming.

He realized afterward that it was God who made him get to his feet and move to the "front" of the tent, where Maddox had been pacing back and forth. God who made him face the audience filled with sweaty, distracted faces. And God's voice that thundered from his thirteen-year-old throat with all the passion Maddox possessed and all the power he lacked.

"God loves you!"

A few of the chairs lurched sideways as the people occupying them jumped in surprise.

"God loves you and wants you to be happy. God wants you to enjoy this life in all its abundance! God sent His son to *die* for you, for your sins, so that you need never fear punishment. God has *chosen* you, of all His children, to hear the Truth!"

From the corner of his eye, Samuel could see that Maddox was hardly pleased by having his spotlight stolen, but he didn't really care what the old man felt, because he was enjoying himself. Looking at the sweaty faces, intent now, some of them filled with a kind of wonder, he felt that sense of power that never failed to thrill him.

They listened to him. They believed what he told them. They believed he was special.

He lifted his arms, calling on God to verify the truth of his words and fill this congregation with that truth, and—

A freight train hit him.

Samuel opened his eyes to find himself on the ground, the hay stubble poking uncomfortably against his back. Above him was a ring of pale, sweating faces, most of them wearing anxious expressions that also, he realized in surprise, held more than a touch of awe.

"Son, are you all right?" It was Maddox, one of those worried faces. But his also held a curiously calculating expression.

Samuel struggled to his feet, aided by several hands, and instead of answering the question, he found himself staring at one of the men who had helped him up.

"You're going to lose your farm," he said.

The man started in suprise, his face going pale. "What?"

"Next year. Better get ready for it, if you don't want your family to starve."

"Son—" Maddox began.

But Samuel was looking at another face, this one younger and less careworn. "She did cheat on you, just like you thought. But she's not the real Judas. Talk to your best friend. It's his bed she's been in."

The man spun on his heel and walked away; he was nearly running by the time he left the tent.

Samuel turned his head and saw a woman's face and, again, without knowing where the knowledge came from, said, "Go see your doctor. There's something wrong with the child in your belly."

She gasped, her hands going first to her face, then to cup her only slightly rounded belly. And then she hurried away, nearly falling over one of the chairs in her haste to leave.

Maddox put his hand on Samuel's shoulder and gripped it for a moment. Hard. Addressing the murmuring crowd, he said, "Come back tomorrow, folks. Come tomorrow and listen to more of what this very special young man has to tell us. Come tomorrow, and bring your friends."

As the people began to back away and turn toward the exits, Maddox nodded to a thin dark girl who was perhaps a few years older than Samuel, a girl he hadn't even noticed until then. Silent, she picked up one of the offering baskets and moved among those leaving, collecting dollar bills and even a few tens and twenties.

"Son, you and me need to talk," Maddox said as soon as they were alone.

"What happened?" Samuel demanded.

Maddox pointed to the ground.

Samuel looked down, surprised to find a sort of

hourglass-shaped area of blackened earth and burned grass. Exactly where he had been standing. "I don't understand."

Maddox pointed up.

Above their heads and several feet from the center tent pole was a perfectly round hole in the canvas. It was, perhaps, six or eight inches across, and the edges were blackened.

"So hot it didn't even start a fire," Maddox told him. "Just punched right through the tent. Then through you and into the ground."

"What did?"

"A bolt of lightning, son." Maddox grinned, revealing large yellowed teeth. "You've been touched by God."

Samuel thought about that for a moment, absently watching as the dark girl returned with the basket of cash. He didn't feel different, really, except...stronger. And the air around him seemed clearer, not so heavy and oppressive.

"So what do I do now?" he asked, curious to hear the old man's answer.

Maddox grinned again "You're going to come with Ruth and me. This is Ruth—my daughter."

Samuel looked at her for a moment, nodded absently, then looked back at Maddox. "Why would I come with you?"

"Because we're going to start ourselves a real church, son. I've got the know-how, and you, well, you've been touched by God, haven't you? Touched—and given the gift of Sight." He reached out and again put his hand on Samuel's shoulder. "You know we're walking the path together now, don't you, son?"

Samuel studied that grinning face, the greedy gleam in those intense eyes, and wondered idly if Maddox had any idea at all that his path would end in blood and agony.

Not that it mattered.

That was at least a few years down the path.

"So when do we start?" he asked.

Samuel didn't come all the way out of his meditative trance as that particular memory faded from his mind. Other memories flashed by, like the pages of a book blown by a steady breeze, pages showing other tent revivals and small churches that were all but shacks slowly giving way to bigger, better churches. Until finally the church in Los Angeles, where everything had really begun coming together.

As his sermons had grown stronger, more powerful.

As he had grown stronger and more powerful.

As God had shown him the path he had to walk.

He meditated on that, going over it in his mind as he always did, until finally he was ready.

He was tired now, too tired, really, to do what he needed to do.

But he had no choice, because she was here. She was here, and he needed to reach out to her. Needed to touch her mind and find out if she was one of his Chosen few.

Or his enemy.

Eleven

TESSA LOOKED AT Sawyer steadily for a moment, then said, "We should probably move from here. Walk around. Take advantage of our . . . presumed solitude."

Sawyer got up from the boulder seat as she did, but said, "Avoiding an answer?"

"No, I think you're probably right. I also think Samuel can do a lot of damage before he finally destroys himself, even if that's the way this is going. I asked you once before, but can't you feel the energy of this place? How strange it is?"

They had turned with tacit agreement away from the natural church to continue down the slope, and Sawyer walked beside her for several steps in silence before answering. He still felt that wary sense of danger, but it was oddly unfocused.

It's not this place. It's more than that. Different. There's something else now.

It made him want to reach for his gun.

"I feel it," he answered finally. "Sets my teeth on edge. But it wasn't always like this. Years ago, I mean. It's only been in the last few months that I really noticed a difference up here in the way the air felt. The way I felt when I was here."

"Before then it was normal?"

"As far as that goes, yeah. What changed?"

"Him, probably."

"Do you know why?"

"Not really. Psychic abilities tend to evolve, or do when they're used. And they can be affected by everything from the person's mental and emotional state to a summer storm or other strong electromagnetic field."

"That's a wide range of possibilities."

"I don't have any easy answers, Sawyer." She sent him a look that was a little wry and more than a little reluctant. "Most of this is new to me too. Until about a year ago, all I knew about psychic abilities was what I was coping with myself."

"Alone?"

"Pretty much. No family to speak of, and I've been on my own since college." A frown flitted across her face and then vanished. "It wasn't until college that I really built my shields, and then it was from necessity. I kept picking up test answers, responses the professors wanted from us, stuff like that. It was cheating, and I didn't like it. So I learned to shut it out."

"What's wrong?" Sawyer asked.

"Well, cheating—"

"Not that. You winced. What is it?"

Tessa wasn't at all sure she was comfortable being observed so closely even though a part of her was keenly aware of *his* every move and expression , but heard herself replying, "A little headache, that's all."

"Starting when?"

"Just now. Probably this place."

With his own senses or instincts still nagging at him, Sawyer said, "Is the hair on the back of your neck standing up? Because mine is."

She looked at him, then looked around them. "The cameras. Probably. They're all over the place."

"And if it's not the cameras? Tessa, you told me Samuel can kill without touching someone. Without even being near them. So how would you know if you were a target? How would you know that sort of attack was coming?"

Tessa thought about the report of Sarah's death, of how quickly she had died, without warning, and drew a deep breath, aware now of building tension inside her. "I don't know," she replied.

"Could it start with a headache?"

"I don't know."

"Tessa—"

"He has no reason to consider me a threat. So why would he feel the need to kill me?"

"You don't know he doesn't consider you a threat," Sawyer countered. "He could have been...delving into your mind this whole time."

"He hasn't been. I'd know."

"Would you?"

"Yes." She thought so. She hoped so. But a chill stole over her, and it had nothing to do with the crisp winter day.

Sounding a little frustrated, Sawyer said, "So I guess that means I can't talk you into leaving right now?"

"I can't leave yet. Do you have any idea how difficult it's been to get someone inside the Compound, let alone the church?"

"Does it have to be you?"

"I'm here. The universe opens doors for a reason."

Sawyer quite abruptly took her hand, his fingers twining with hers.

Surprised, Tessa said, "Why did you—"

"You're not going through this door alone," he told her. "Whether you like it or not, I'm here too. That open door is as much mine as it is yours. And I'm a stubborn man."

She thought about protesting, but his hand was surprisingly warm, and surprisingly comforting. She liked it. She liked it too much. And all she could think of to say was "Better be careful. One thing I've learned is that when two psychics...make a connection, even a simple one...odd things can happen."

"Odd things are already happening," Sawyer said, sounding calmer now. "For instance, have you noticed there's no livestock here in the Compound? No pets visible?"

Tessa followed his lead obediently, even as she wondered if he meant this as a distraction—or if he was just able to keep his mind on business a lot easier than she could. "I noticed yesterday. Kept hoping today I'd see a few cows or horses, but no luck. There were once pets and livestock, I take it?"

"There were last fall."

"And they disappeared suddenly?"

"Well, sometime since late September. That was the last time I was up here until we pulled the first body from the river almost two weeks ago."

"What are you thinking?"

Sawyer didn't hesitate. "Sacrifice."

Tessa glanced at him, then allowed her gaze to roam around as they walked, for all the world as if she were mildly curious about her surroundings. Not that there was much to see except a large, unnervingly vacant pasture. She definitely had a sense of being watched but had to assume it was a camera somewhere nearby.

Needed to assume that.

Because the alternative was a lot more unnerving than the empty pasture. And, potentially, a lot more dangerous.

I see you.

Samuel reached out further, harder, irritated by his own weakness. He was tired, yes, but this should have been easy.

Relatively easy, at any rate. Because she was just a woman, and women were, after all, designed by nature to let men in.

This one was stubborn, though. Well guarded. He

could sense an open door there but couldn't seem to find it. He forced himself to draw back a bit, to probe more delicately, even though it meant fighting his own instincts.

He always wanted to break them. To reach inside and crush, rewarded by the incredible burst of energy they released when death took them.

But that was for his enemies and for those who wanted to leave him and leave God's grace, not his Chosen.

And he wasn't yet sure which this one was.

So he used up precious energy by testing her defenses with all the delicacy of years of practice, probing, searching for the door he could sense was already opening for him . . .

That simple statement again in her mind. Just that—and a sense of a presence that was incredibly strong but not threatening.

Still, Tessa felt a strong urge to shore up her shields, to protect herself. To close the door she had edged open in an effort to sense this place, to figure it out. Because she wasn't here to protect herself. She was here to gather information about the church and/or Samuel. And she was here to try to figure out who or what had made a connection with her yesterday.

I see you.

She looked down at their clasped hands and for just a moment wondered if Sawyer had made the connection.

But almost immediately she knew it wasn't him. Hadn't been him yesterday, at any rate; she wasn't at all sure a connection of some kind wasn't being made right this moment. Because his hand was warm and she liked it. Because he smelled of some spicy soap or aftershave, and she liked *that*.

Tessa pushed that away, not ready to deal with either her own feelings or some very basic emotions she could feel in Sawyer.

Man, he has a lousy sense of timing.

Or maybe it was her timing that was off. Way off. Or . . . was being affected?

Yesterday, and just now—who or what had connected with her? Was even now *there*, as though waiting for something. And even though she was conscious of no threat from it, why was she still unsure whether that connection was a good thing or a bad one?

It brought you back here. And maybe not for a good reason.

Probably not for a good reason.

"Tessa?"

"Are you thinking ritual sacrifice?" she asked, trying to focus thoughts that were becoming more scattered.

"No. I'm thinking that maybe it was an unexpected or at least unintended consequence of something else. Is that possible?"

"I suppose so."

She felt an odd tugging, an almost physical sensation, as real as Sawyer's hand holding hers. But it wasn't him. Something else tugged, pulled as though to get her attention. Tessa looked around, and immediately a flash, as though from sunlight off something metallic, caught her eye. It had originated, she thought, from just inside the woods that edged this pasture to the west.

"What is it?"

"Over there." She had turned in that direction without even thinking about it. "I saw something flash."

Since he hadn't released her hand, Sawyer also turned, remaining by her side as he lowered his voice to say, "It might be another damn camera."

"I don't think so." Tessa realized they were following a very faint path through the pasture and had a sudden almost overpowering sense of many feet walking it before them.

Small feet.

Be careful. He wants in. You mustn't let him.

"Tessa?"

She frowned but continued along the path. "This way."

"You're beginning to scare me," he said, following.

That was an odd thing to say. "I can't imagine why. I'm not very scary." She thought he swore beneath his breath, but her attention was fixed on the woods that lay just ahead.

Be careful, Tessa.

It was only a patch of sparse woods, maybe an acre in size, and in the center was a clearing that probably occupied half of that acre. Tessa stopped only a few feet inside the clearing, staring down at a cross that had been roughly fashioned from two sticks, a little crooked because of the weight on one arm of the cross.

She bent down and then straightened, holding a leather collar in her free hand. It had a rabies tag and a second, bone-shaped tag with the name *Buddy* engraved on it. As she moved the collar, the silvery tag caught a glint of sunlight and flashed, as it must have done to catch her attention in the field.

Vaguely aware of Sawyer standing just behind her, Tessa looked across the clearing at countless small mounds of dirt, most of them with a pile of stones or a rough stick-cross at one end, and almost all of them boasting a collar of some kind, either on the ground or draped over crosses and stones. There were bright plastic flowers here and there, stuck down into chipped, handleless coffee cups or in the ground, some of them faded by time but quite a lot of them not. There were even bedraggled toys and rawhide chews.

"It's a pet cemetery," Sawyer said. "But an awful lot of graves for a community that didn't exist barely a decade ago. And a lot of them look to be fairly recent."

Tessa hadn't intended to open the door in her mind wider, to open herself up. The opposite, if anything. But as she stood there holding the collar, she was abruptly conscious of sounds, of barks and meows and children laughing. The sounds grew louder and louder inside her head, and as they did, waves of pain and grief swept over her. And fear. Desperate fear.

"Tessa?"

"They thought it was an act of God," she whispered,

trying in vain to close down her senses, to protect herself from the assault. "An act of their God. He was...there was a storm, and...he was angry. They had sinned. And their God punished them."

He killed them. He killed them all.

Tessa felt the agony of that, the grief, and tried to cope, tried to ride out the ferocious emotions.

Stop it. He uses feelings to get in, don't you understand? He makes you feel things, and that opens the door for him. Don't feel, Tessa. Don't let him in—

She swayed on her feet, the collar dropping from suddenly nerveless fingers. As a wave of darkness swept abruptly over her, Tessa wasn't even aware of Sawyer catching her before she could fall and lifting her into his arms.

Reese DeMarco opened his eyes slowly and for a moment stared across his office at nothing. He finally pushed his chair back from the desk and rose, absently rubbing the nape of his neck as he crossed the spacious room to the door and unlocked it.

He made his way silently down the short, carpeted hallway that separated his office from the living quarters of Reverend Samuel, encountering no one else. It wasn't quite lunchtime, and everyone knew and respected Samuel's habit of meditating in mid-morning and mid-afternoon, so the upper floor of the church tended to be all but deserted at those times.

DeMarco reached a big, paneled wooden door and

opened it without knocking. He passed through the familiar foyer—spare and simple, as all these rooms were—and through the living room, notable only for the colorful light splashed all about from the stained-glass windows.

Off to the right, two more closed doors offered access to a study and a bedroom suite. DeMarco paused at the study door for a moment, then quietly opened it and stepped into the room.

This room, too, was alive with color from three large stained-glass windows, but the decor otherwise was very plain. Simple shelves held scores of books—not elegant leather-bound volumes but once brightly colored dust-jacketed books, obviously collected over time. A big desk sat with its back to the center window, and two low-backed visitor's chairs sat on the worn old rug before it. A leather sofa and matching chair and ottoman were positioned opposite the windows.

Samuel occupied the chair. He sat with his feet flat on the floor, hands relaxed in his lap, head slightly bowed. Eyes closed.

DeMarco waited silently.

It was at least a couple of minutes before Samuel finally opened his eyes and lifted his head. He didn't look like a man who had been meditating, resting; he looked like a man on the edge of exhaustion. His face was pale, haggard, and there were deep shadows beneath his dull eyes. When he drew a breath to speak, it appeared to require a tremendous effort.

"They're leaving," he said.

"Yes."

"Tell Carl to let them through the gate. No questions asked."

"I'll see to it."

Samuel drew another difficult breath. "The weather report?"

"Rain by the weekend. No mention of storms."

A ghost of a laugh escaped Samuel. "Murphy's Law."

In a measured tone, DeMarco said, "With all due respect, this is a waste of your energy."

"I have no choice."

"According to the Prophecy, we're safe for now. You said it was summer. You said she was older."

"I may have been wrong."

"Prophecies," DeMarco said, still in that deliberate voice, "are tricky beasts. By acting before it's time, you may bring about the very thing you hope to avoid."

"Perhaps I can't avoid it. Perhaps I never could." Samuel's lips twisted into something more grimace than smile. "They don't understand. They'll never understand. They want me dead, Reese. Worse than dead. Broken. Destroyed. Especially him."

"It doesn't have to end that way."

"It will—unless I destroy him before he can destroy me."

"They have no proof. No evidence. If they had, they would have come after you a long time ago. You're safe here."

"Among my people."

"Father—"

"They are my people, aren't they? Bound to me body and soul?"

"Of course, Father."

"Will they die for me, Reese? Will you?"

Steadily, without hesitation, DeMarco replied, "Of course, Father."

Samuel's mouth twisted into another of those not-quite-smiles. "Good. Now, let Carl know he's to allow the chief and Mrs. Gray to leave. And—send Ruth to me."

"Of course, Father." DeMarco withdrew from the study, closing the door quietly. He passed back through the apartment, and it wasn't until the main door was closed behind him that the tension in his shoulders eased.

Just a little.

He paused for an instant, almost leaning back against the door, then drew a deep breath, straightened, and went on to do Father's bidding.

"I would have put you in the backseat," Sawyer said, his voice more than a little grim. "But I thought there'd be fewer questions this way."

Tessa blinked at him, feeling a little dizzy and very confused. She looked down, realizing that she was buckled into the passenger side of his Jeep—tightly buckled. She eased the shoulder strap a little and tried to ask a baffled question. "Where ... ?"

"We just left the Compound. I'll send somebody to

get your car later. Nobody was around when I carried you to the Jeep, and for once Fisk just opened the gates without comment."

"Carried me?" *Well,* that's *disconcerting. And I missed it. Dammit.* She shoved the regret aside. *Not now. I can't think about this now.* "From where?"

"The pet cemetery. Don't you remember? What the hell happened to you back there? You were out. And I mean out. You didn't faint—you were almost comatose."

Tessa forced her sluggish mind off the subject of her apparently unconscious self being carried a goodly distance by a very attractive man she hardly knew, and tried to remember. It took a minute or two, but the fog in her brain seemed to be dissipating as they left the Compound behind. She felt bone-weary, but at least she could think again. And remember.

"The pet cemetery. Jesus. He killed them. All the pets, the livestock. It was . . . He was furious."

Sawyer let out a rough sigh, and his fingers tightened on the steering wheel. "That's what I thought you said. You had a vision?"

"Of sorts. I don't really have visions, usually, I just know things. And I know that. I felt it."

"Shit. He killed them? All at once?"

"I think so. Last October. He was away for a while, for weeks at least, and when he came back there was . . . some kind of power struggle going on inside the congregation. Somebody else wanted to run the church. Samuel was—"

"He was what?" Sawyer shot her a sharp glance but

then returned his attention to the road, intent on putting more distance between them and the church.

"Weakened." Tessa's voice was hardly more than a murmur, and she stared straight ahead, struggling to sort through the images and emotions she was remembering. "Hurt. He had tried to use his abilities in different ways, new ways, but there was somebody stronger fighting back. He lost that fight. Badly. And then came back home to . . . rebellion. It was more than he could stand. He called them all to that outside pulpit, even though there was a storm coming. Maybe because there was a storm coming. He didn't think he'd have the strength to tap in to it, but . . ."

"But?"

She shook her head. "Somehow he did. Somehow he drew energy from the storm. I'm not sure exactly what happened; it's all fuzzy and jumbled. All I know for sure is that the problem—the man who wanted to run the church his way—vanished. Samuel's congregation was convinced all over again that they should follow him. And all the animals died."

The words were barely out of her mouth when Tessa felt something move against her foot. Under normal circumstances, she probably would have jumped in alarm, but she was too tired to waste the energy. Instead, she merely leaned forward to see what it was.

A big shoulder bag, the type students sometimes carried their books or notebooks or laptops in. Heavy canvas, with a flap opening.

"Is this yours?" she asked, even though she knew as soon as she touched it that it didn't belong to him.

He looked over as she lifted the bag from the floorboard and held it in her lap. "No, I've never seen it before. Tessa, be careful."

"It's all right." She unfastened the big clasp and pushed the heavy flap back. Inside, shivering and staring up at her fearfully, was a tiny white poodle.

Sawyer frowned. "A dog? From inside the Compound?"

"Unless you brought her with you today." Tessa was cautious until the little dog licked her fingers. Then she lifted what was hardly more than a handful of curling fur out of the bag and held the delicate creature in the crook of her arm. Instantly, the dog snuggled against her and stopped shivering. "Which I gather you didn't."

"No, I didn't. And if all the animals were killed, how could that little thing survive?"

"I think she had help." Tessa had used her free hand to rummage in the side pockets of the bag and discovered a folded piece of paper. What gave her pause was the fact that her own name was block-printed on the outside.

"What?" Sawyer asked.

"Did you see anybody around the Jeep? Somebody who could have realized I wouldn't be going back to my own car?"

"No, I didn't see a soul. And I was watching all the way down the hill. I figured I'd have to explain myself, or at least answer a question or two, especially with that camera trained on the so-called natural church. Kept expecting DeMarco to show up."

"I wonder why he didn't," Tessa murmured as she opened the note. Then she read the brief message written in the same carefully printed handwriting that was on the outside of the note, and the question of why DeMarco had allowed them to leave without comment became the last thing on her mind.

> *Please, take care of Lexie.*
> *I can't protect her anymore.*
> *Father's started watching me.*

Twelve

FBI DIRECTOR MICAH HUGHES would never be accused of being an extrovert, so the fact that he was expected to socialize with other law-enforcement officials from all over the world was a trial, not a pleasure.

Even in Paris.

He would have preferred to attend the seminars during the day and then retreat to his hotel room, where he could review on his laptop the day's happenings back in D.C., but cocktail parties and dinners were an expected part of the trip, and he was nothing if not doggedly professional.

Still, he was more relieved than especially curious or anxious when the post-dinner small talk on this Thursday night was interrupted as one of the waiters slipped him a note that said he had a phone call. Another waiter directed him to the hotel's house phones, in an alcove outside the banquet room where this particular dinner was taking place.

It was blessedly quiet out in the hallway, and he took a moment to enjoy that before going in search of the house phones. The alcove was, as promised, nearby, but as soon as he turned into it, he stopped. Nobody was on one of the half dozen or so phones lining the desk-height counter that ran around all three walls, but the room had one occupant.

"What are you doing here?"

The man was tall, broad-shouldered, and athletic, and could have been any age between fifty and sixty-five. He had the sort of regular features and good bone structure that made for a handsome face, and striking green eyes made it even more memorable.

"You should know by now that I can turn up just about anywhere." He had a deep voice with a note in it that Hughes had heard many times in his life: the absolute assurance of a man who was very much accustomed to getting what he wanted.

"I just...thought you were back in the States." Hughes heard the slightly nervous note in his own voice and bitterly resented it.

"I was. Yesterday." He paused a moment, then went on calmly, "I take it you've made no progress?"

"Look, I warned you it would take time. Bishop may be ruthless, but he isn't reckless, at least not openly. He knows he's being watched, that his unit exists only as long as it's successful—and he keeps it out of the news. He's careful. Very careful. He knows just how far to bend the rules and the regs without breaking them. And until he does cross that line, I can't touch him. Not officially."

"I see. And were you aware that he's currently in North Carolina investigating a church?"

"What?"

"Ah. Not aware, I see. Clearly my spies are keeping a closer eye on Bishop than your own are."

Hughes did *not* like the idea of anyone outside the FBI employing spies within it, but he had spent enough time with this man over the last months to swallow any retort or objection he might have made. But that didn't stop an increasingly familiar jolt of profound uneasiness.

It had seemed so clear at first. But now he wasn't at all sure he was doing the right thing.

"You'll be receiving a packet via courier by morning. Background information on the church and its leader, details your own people could have easily discovered and, in fact, probably have filed away somewhere. Plus some additional information less easy to acquire concerning recent activities of the SCU. And Bishop."

Hughes was reasonably sure at least one of the "spies" this man had within the FBI was actually inside the SCU, but he had never asked and didn't now. He had no need to know that. "Is there anything in the information that's actionable?"

"Perhaps. It certainly does raise questions as to whether Bishop is working for the FBI—or is conducting a vendetta of his own."

"A vendetta?" *Like yours?* "You believe this church or its leader has done something to personally injure Bishop?"

"What I believe is that he's a dangerous man who's

pursuing an investigation based on absolutely no evidence whatsoever. And he's getting people killed."

"You know that for a fact?"

"I do. He hasn't reported the latest casualties, but I have good reason to believe that at least two have died within the last two weeks. One of his own agents, and an operative with that civilian organization he helped found."

"I've told you I can't do anything about Haven. Not as long as they keep their activities on the right side of legal. And so far, they have. John Garrett is also neither careless nor reckless."

"As far as you know, they've broken no laws."

Hughes nodded unwillingly. "As far as I know."

"I'll keep my people working on that. In the meantime, I would assume that the death of a federal agent, presumably in the line of duty, at the very least calls for an investigation."

"It's automatic."

"Then you might, when you return to the States, check into the whereabouts of Agent Galen."

"I'll do that." Hughes drew a breath. "The wild card in all this is still Senator LeMott. Bishop caught the murderer of the senator's daughter three months ago. Not just the SCU; Bishop himself was personally involved in the capture. LeMott is not going to forget that, and he's a powerful man."

"So am I."

"Yes. I know. But LeMott could cause me a lot of trouble. I have to be careful when and how I act."

"I doubt you'd have your present appointment had I not exerted considerable influence on your behalf."

"I know that too. Believe me, I'm...more than grateful."

"I didn't ask for much in return, did I, Micah? I didn't ask you to violate your oath, to break the law. I didn't ask you to betray your country or tarnish your office. All I asked was that you find a way to remove a dangerous man and his followers from an otherwise fine organization."

"Yes. And I have no problem with that request."

"Then we understand each other."

"We do."

"I'm glad to hear it. Enjoy the rest of your stay in Paris, Micah. It's a lovely city. Do yourself a favor and at least take the scenic route to the airport when you leave. Enjoy a few of the sights. Take your mind off business for a while."

"Thank you. I will." Hughes watched the other man stroll away, aware of his own tension only when he released a pent-up breath. He found himself actually looking around to make certain no one else had witnessed that telltale slump of relief.

And Micah Hughes resented that most of all.

Grace

"The only thing I can figure," Hollis said, "is that Lexie's owner has a pretty damn powerful personal shield—at the very least. That plus the obvious fact that this little dog has probably been carried around in that bag most if not all the time must have protected her from whatever killed the other pets."

Tessa glanced at the chair beside her own at the dining-room table, at the open bag in which the poodle was curled, sleeping. "I read somewhere that the tiny ones are bred to be companion animals, so that makes sense. I mean that she'd be carried around most of the time. And that bag seems to be her security blanket. The question is, who's her owner?"

"One of the questions," Sawyer corrected. He had been introduced to Hollis upon their arrival at the Gray home and was still trying to cope with the notion of an FBI agent who was also a professed medium. A professed medium who not only knew about his own secret but was utterly matter-of-fact about his abilities. "I have more than I can count."

"Join the club," Hollis advised, then said, "My money's on Ruby Campbell as being Lexie's person."

Tessa wondered if Ruby's had been the voice in her mind there at the pet cemetery, the presence that had warned her with such insistence to close her mind that Tessa was pretty sure she had knocked herself out—literally—to obey.

"Because?" Sawyer's tone was the very polite one of a man who had decided to be calm about things. No matter what.

"Because I don't believe in coincidence. Because just

about the time you guys were reading that note, I was being begged to help Ruby."

"Begged by a ghost," Sawyer said.

"You, of all people," Tessa told him, "should be able to accept the existence of spirits. You saw your grandmother when she died, didn't you?"

"Jesus, Tessa—"

Reaching up to rub her forehead fretfully, Tessa said, "Sorry. I wasn't looking for that, it just came to me."

Hollis looked at Sawyer. "She's right? You saw your grandmother's spirit?"

"Just that once," Sawyer replied, hoping it mattered.

"I told you that your abilities were evolving," Hollis reminded Tessa. "Your visits to the Compound must have...activated a new pathway in your brain. Or amped up the voltage somehow. Even with your shield in place, you're picking up stuff."

Sawyer muttered, "That weird energy up there. God only knows what effects it's having. On them and on us."

"I don't need any new pathways," Tessa announced. "I was just—barely—learning how to follow the ones I had."

"Doubt you've got a choice." Hollis shrugged.

"Great."

"It's another good reason for you to stay away from that place," Sawyer told her.

"No," Tessa said. "It isn't. We all take risks, Sawyer. You're in law enforcement—you *know* that."

"Not unnecessary risks."

"And how do you define unnecessary when a hundred men, women, and children are in danger?"

Sawyer didn't like the corner he'd been backed into. "Okay, then let's talk about effectiveness. There's no sense putting yourself at risk when you can't be effective in a dangerous situation. And from what I saw at the Compound, I'm thinking whatever is going on up there is not something you can handle without *unnecessary* risk. To you and possibly to everyone else."

"What's he talking about?" Hollis asked.

Sawyer continued to look steadily at Tessa. "What the hell happened to you at the Compound? There at the end, you were so distracted it was visible. As if you were . . . listening to somebody else."

"Maybe I was," Tessa said.

Hollis was looking at her with a frown. "I just assumed that when you opened yourself up at the pet cemetery, all the pain and grief there overwhelmed you."

"It started before we got to the cemetery," Sawyer told her. "She was a little . . . scatty."

"Scatty?"

"Distracted, like I said. I don't know what it was, but *something* affected her when we left that outdoor pulpit. Maybe sooner."

Tessa drew a breath and let it out. "Still here, guys."

Hollis's frown deepened. "Tessa, did you consciously drop your shields at that cemetery?"

She didn't want to answer, but Tessa knew she had to. "No. I opened a door, just a little bit. But I didn't drop my shields."

"Then something *was* affecting you? Something that got through your shields?"

"Maybe."

"Tessa."

"All right, yes. I heard . . . That same presence as before was in my mind. Not the dark one; the one who said, *I see you.* Only this time, it was warning me. To be careful. To not let my feelings overwhelm me, because *he*—Samuel, I assume—gets in that way. He makes people feel and gets in that way."

"How did you feel?"

It was Tessa's turn to frown as she tried to sort through the fragments of memory and emotion. "It's hard to separate things. At first I felt uneasy, as if someone was watching me. Sawyer felt the same thing."

He nodded when Hollis looked at him. "Tessa said maybe it was the cameras, but . . . it didn't feel like that." He hesitated, then added, "Cameras pointed at me feel a certain way. This was something else."

Tessa nodded. "I felt a tugging, a pull, and when I looked around, I saw something flash at the edge of the pet cemetery. Once we got there, the . . . pain and grief of the people, especially the children, started to overwhelm me. That's when that voice in my mind warned me to shut the door before he got in. So I shut it. Too hard, I guess."

Sawyer frowned at her. "That's why you went out? You did it to yourself?"

"Well, self-preservation. You asked me if I'd know if I was under the sort of attack Samuel is capable of; the insistence in that voice told me I had to protect myself, and fast. So I did."

"We're in trouble," Hollis said.

"Not necessarily."

"Tessa, you were chosen for this assignment partly for the strength of your shields and the fact that you don't read as psychic. No matter who that insistent voice belongs to, it shouldn't have been able to reach you so clearly, not through what was in effect only a chink in your shields. And you shouldn't have been overwhelmed by the emotions of those people, not with your shields up. *At all.* That's new, we both know that, and the new stuff is the hardest to handle. We are definitely in trouble."

"I was tired and distracted before I even went up there, Hollis, and you know it. I felt like I was being pulled long before I reached the Compound. You said I connected to someone or something up there yesterday, and I agree." She reached for the piece of paper lying on the table in front of her and looked at it again, read it again.

Please, take care of Lexie.
I can't protect her anymore.
Father's started watching me.

"This was addressed to me. Even more, it was placed in Sawyer's Jeep, not my car, when no one could have logically known I wouldn't be leaving the Compound the same way I came."

Hollis shook her head. "You didn't mention meeting any of the kids yesterday, not by name."

"I was introduced to a whole group of them pretty much at once. I barely spoke to them beyond saying hi. Until you told us about seeing Andrea's spirit and what she said about Ruby, I didn't remember picking up any names. But Ruby was there, a dark girl with really pale gray eyes. I think she's the one who touched me, physically touched me, and I'm almost positive she was carrying this bag."

"Almost?" Sawyer stared at her. "Wouldn't it have been obvious?"

Tessa thought about it and frowned again. "Now that you mention it, it should have, shouldn't it? A big bag for a little girl to be carrying, and unusual since they were all in that playground near the church. None of the other kids was carrying any sort of bag or backpack. But . . . Ruby was. I have to concentrate to remember actually seeing it, but when I concentrate, it's there, clear as day."

Softly, Hollis said, "You need her help to stop him."

"Excuse me?" Sawyer said.

"It's what Andrea said. 'You need her help to stop him.' And she was talking about Ruby."

"How could a twelve-year-old girl help stop someone like Samuel?"

Tessa looked at him for a moment, then returned her gaze to Hollis. "Maybe that's why Sarah was so convinced the children were important."

"Who's Sarah?" Sawyer asked.

Knowing that would be a long and probably difficult conversation, Tessa chose to postpone it. "I'll tell you about Sarah later. Right now I'm more worried about Ruby. Hollis, you said Sarah had managed to get three of the kids out, right?"

Hollis nodded.

"Latents. But what if she was picking up the strength of an active psychic and didn't know it, because Ruby has the ability to . . . obscure or disguise what's real?"

"That would be a hell of an ability," Hollis said slowly. "And one I've never heard of outside science fiction."

"But possible?"

"Sure, anything's possible. But how likely would it be that Samuel could miss something that unique?"

"Maybe because it's unique. Or maybe because he hadn't been paying attention. Until lately." Tessa looked down at the note and read the last chilling phrase out loud. *"Father's started watching me."*

"Christ," Sawyer said. "She's twelve—she's hitting puberty."

Hollis drew a deep breath and let it out slowly. *"Bastard.* If he's looking for another good source to tap, the chaos of adolescence also produces an enormous amount of energy. Sexually and otherwise. It's when a high percentage of latents become active for the first time— usually because of some kind of trauma. Just guessing, I'd say the simultaneous death of almost all the pets and livestock in the Compound would be very traumatic for a little girl. Especially one who loved her dog."

"She had to protect Lexie," Tessa told them. "So, instinctively, she did. Some kind of energy shield, for sure. But more than that, she must have tapped into her latent ability to hide or disguise an object. And she's been able to continue hiding Lexie all this time, hiding her in plain sight, from everyone in that Compound, including Samuel. She must have thought they were safe. Until she realized he was beginning to look at her the way he looked at the older women. Until she understood."

Quentin Hayes had been a seer most of his life but preferred the official SCU designation of *precog* or *precognitive* instead, since the ability to actually *see* the future was very new to him. Until he had crossed paths with an extremely powerful medium in an extremely dangerous situation not so long ago, all he had been able to claim was an occasional precognitive awareness that something was about to happen.

All that changed when he met Diana Brisco.

So it was less than a year since he'd begun actually seeing visions, and since they were still comparatively rare, he hadn't yet grown accustomed to the sheer power of them.

They still came out of nowhere with no warning, and they still brought him to his knees.

"*Christ.*"

"Quentin?"

He knew Bishop was there with him, in the same

room—but after the blinding burst of pain, the room shimmered and then faded, and in its place was . . . hell.

Dark clouds rolled and banked heavily above, so dark they shut out the sunlight, and thunder boomed and echoed. The air above his head crackled and sparked with pure energy; acrid smoke stung his nostrils with a smell that turned his stomach and caused his soul to flinch, because it was a smell he recognized.

Burnt flesh.

He didn't want to but forced himself to turn and look at what he only vaguely recognized as the outdoor amphitheater used by Samuel and his congregation. It was a charred and scorched place now, the large boulders intended to be seats blackened, still smoking. And among the rocks were other still-smoking shapes.

Human shapes.

They were twisted and contorted in mute agony, and it was obvious that many of the adults had tried in vain to protect children. But none of them had had a chance, Quentin realized sickly.

He heard a scream and pivoted sharply, finding himself looking up at the area of the granite "pulpit" where Samuel preached.

Samuel stood on the pulpit, staring down at his dead followers, his expression chillingly serene. His hands were smoking.

At his feet, staring up at him, sat a dark-haired little girl, her expression every bit as serene as his.

"Ruby!"

It was Tessa who had screamed, who cried out the

little girl's name. She was...she was bound to a cross, one of four placed on either side of the pulpit. Ropes at her wrists and ankles would have held her securely; the monstrous iron spikes driven through her hands and feet were clearly intended to maim and torture.

Two of the other three crosses held identically bound figures, but only Tessa was conscious; the others were unconscious—or dead. Hollis and Chief Cavenaugh hung motionless.

There was a lot of blood.

Samuel looked at the little girl, then smiled tenderly. He placed his left hand on the top of her head.

Before Quentin's horrified eyes, she began to smolder and, without a sound, she burst into flames.

Tessa screamed again. Samuel turned his head to look at her, his smile fading, replaced by a slight frown, just barely this side of indifference. He looked at her, Quentin thought, as one would look at a fly that annoyed with its buzzing. Then, with his left hand still on the head of the burning child, he extended his right hand, and a jagged bolt of pure energy shot from his fingers toward Tessa.

"Quentin."

Blinking, drawing in a gulp of blessedly normal air, Quentin looked down at the hand gripping his arm, then up to meet Bishop's concerned gaze. "Jesus. How do you and Miranda stand this?" The hoarse sound of his own voice startled him.

"Practice." Bishop helped him to his feet, and into a nearby chair. "What did you see?"

"I saw...hell. Listen, I need to get to the Gray house. Like ten minutes ago."

"Why?"

"Because they're about to make a very, very, *very* bad decision. Trust me on that. And I don't think anything short of an unexpected visit will dissuade them."

Bishop reached immediately for a phone. "The chopper can land in that clearing between the house and the road; that should get you close enough without alerting the farmhands."

"Can he get away this time of day?"

"He'll have to. I can't risk getting that close to the Compound, and we don't have another pilot available right now. Bring them back here."

"Sure?"

"Quentin, you're white as a sheet. I don't need it described to me to know you saw something we do *not* want to happen. So it's time we pool our resources. *All* of them."

Thirteen

SAMUEL WAS ALWAYS careful, when he used Ruth, not to drain her to the point of unconsciousness. Partly because he preferred to take the energy of younger women, and partly because Ruth's energy was...odd. He wasn't sure what was different about her, but over the years had come to understand that her role in his life and his ministry was different from the role other women played.

Perhaps it was because she had been with him longest and had known him through all the stages of his journey. Or perhaps it was simply that God had decreed she would stand with him in order to remind him, again and again, of the devil who had borne him.

Because he could never draw Ruth's energy without remembering—

He was nearly twenty before he truly began to master the gifts God had bestowed with that bolt of lightning years before. Until then, he was erratic, uncertain when he would be able to hold a congregation spellbound with his power and when he would be forced to rely on the knowledge and tricks he had gained when preaching had been merely a means to earn enough for a bed and a meal or two.

But that day, that particular day, had been one of the more frustrating he'd endured, with his gifts eluding his grasp, and in the dark night he had found himself walking the streets of a cold and dirty city a lot like the one in which he had last seen his mother alive.

Perhaps that was why.

The whores were easy to find, as they always were, and he chose one with little thought beyond the knowledge that she was cleaner than most and promised him a room.

The room turned out to be at a rundown motel that brought back too many ugly memories, and in a rage, in the middle of the furtive act for which he'd paid, Samuel put his hands on her throat and began to strangle her.

He probably wasn't the first john to like his sex rough, but she must have seen something on his face or in his eyes, because she choked out a quick protest before he could cut off her breath completely.

"Wait—don't! I can—do something for you. Something better—"

"You can die," he grunted, fingers tightening.

"No! I can—show you death."

That got his attention. And earned her a reprieve. But he finished with her first, his hands still at her throat, just tight enough so that the sight of her red, sweating face and panicked eyes brought him to orgasm.

He got off her once he was done, stripping the condom off and tossing it into a corner, then using his own handkerchief to clean himself. He straightened his clothing, then sat on the bed beside her and stared down at her. She was no longer gasping, but watched him warily, as if afraid to even move.

"What did you mean? That you could show me death?"

She licked her lips nervously. "It's just . . . my grandma could see spirits. So can I. Is there anybody you want to talk to, honey? Anybody from the other side? Because I can make it so's you can talk to them."

Disgusted, he said, "You really think I'm going to fall for that bullshit? Where do you keep your crystal ball?"

"It ain't like that, honey, I swear! I'm no phony. I think about it, about opening a door to the other side, and the spirits almost always come through. I can see them *and* hear them."

"Can you?" He laughed and, obeying an impulse, lunged to once again grip her throat. "I think I want to be able to do that, *honey*. I think you're going to give me that. Aren't you?"

This time, she couldn't answer, because he was strangling her in earnest. And as he choked the life out of her, he reached. Reached with his mind, thrusting into her as his body had thrust into her just minutes before. Thrust and thrust and thrust . . .

"*Sammy!* What're you up to now, you little bastard?"

He jerked his hands away from the whore, staring at her. But it wasn't she who had spoken. She was never going to speak again. Her face was so mottled it was almost blackened, her swollen tongue protruding between her lips, her eyes wide and so red they looked bloody.

Her body was stiff. Cold.

Time had passed. A lot of time.

Samuel pushed himself off the bed and scrambled to his feet. And it was only then that he saw her.

His mother.

She stood near the door, her smile the cruel one he remembered so well, looking every bit as real and alive as she had looked all those years before.

"You're still a bastard, Sammy," she said mockingly. "No matter how old you get, no matter how many people are stupid enough to believe you're God's little soldier, we both know the truth, don't we? We both know what you *really* are."

He stared at her, his head pounding, hands curling into fists at his sides. He wouldn't...*couldn't*...let her destroy what he was building. He couldn't.

"I'll tell you a little secret, Sammy." Her voice dropped to a whisper. "God knows too. And the devil's waiting, with a seat for you that's right in the fire—"

"No. *Noooo!*" Terror shot through him, and with all his will, with every last ounce of strength and determination he could muster, Samuel slammed the door he had opened.

The spirit of his mother vanished, popping like a soap bubble.

He stood there for an endless time, swaying, exhausted, mumbling over and over, "I can't see spirits. I can't see spirits. I can't see spirits."

Ruth came when he called. She never told a soul about the dead whore. And he refused to see spirits. Ever again.

"**H**ow do you propose we get her out of there?" Sawyer demanded. "I'm game to try something, but what? According to your list, Ruby Campbell has parents, both followers of Samuel, both living in the Compound. They're her legal guardians, and since we have squat in the way of evidence that she's at risk, no judge is going to issue an order allowing us to remove that child from her home and parents. I doubt very much the parents will consent. And taking her out of there any other way is kidnapping."

"I don't care," Tessa said. "That little girl reached out to me. I can't just stand by and do nothing."

"I know that. All I'm saying is that we need a plan. A reasonable plan with at least a reasonable chance of succeeding."

Hollis said, "I know someone who can get into the Compound at night, without being seen or detected by any of the monitors. And into any of the buildings, locked or not. But Sawyer has a good point, Tessa. We can't just go in there and snatch the girl."

"We can't wait until night."

"Tessa—"

Somebody banged on the front door, making them all jump.

Sawyer had his weapon in his hand and was at the dining-room window before either of the women could move. "No car. I can't see the porch from here, let alone the door."

Tessa frowned, closed her eyes for only a moment, then said, "Dammit," and headed for the foyer.

"Tessa—"

"It's okay. I know who's here." She pulled the front door open, aware as the others joined her that Sawyer still held his weapon and that Hollis had one hand behind her, undoubtedly holding her own gun.

"Quentin, what're you doing here?" Tessa demanded.

"Saving your ass," he responded politely. "*Believe* me. And not just yours."

Hollis said, "You do love to make an entrance, don't you?"

"Always. Chief Cavenaugh, I'm Special Agent Quentin Hayes. I know all this seems very abrupt, but if you wouldn't mind, my boss thinks it's time we all met up and talked about things."

"Quentin, there's a little girl—"

"Ruby. Yes, I know. You don't want to go charging up there right now to save her. You really, really don't."

"What did you see?" Hollis asked him.

"Something I don't want to see again. Ever. I'll explain, but right now we need to go. We don't have much time, because our pilot can't be AWOL more than an hour or so." He stepped back and gestured.

They exchanged glances, and Sawyer holstered his weapon, Tessa returned to the dining room long enough to pick up the bag that still held a sleepy poodle, and Hollis grabbed a jacket. Then they followed Quentin from the house.

After hearing that there would be a pilot, Sawyer wasn't all that surprised to find, awaiting them in a clearing no more than a couple hundred yards from the house, a sleek green and white helicopter. His first thought was that it was a M.A.M.A. chopper: one of the Mountain Area Medical Airlift choppers seen fairly often carrying patients from accidents and smaller hospitals to the major medical center that was in Asheville.

His second thought was the recognition that this was a much more powerful and unusual machine, and also that it was a hell of a nifty idea to make the aircraft look like one residents in the area wouldn't think twice about if they looked up and saw it. Most people would make an idle mental note to check the news and see if there'd been an accident but wouldn't be surprised if no later news report was forthcoming—patients were regularly ferried from one hospital to another, and that seldom made the news.

He was surprised at the almost eerie quiet of the machine, though it explained why they'd heard nothing. The rotors beat the air rhythmically, but that was virtually the only sound, and even that was oddly muted.

"Military?" he asked Quentin.

"They wish. Let's go."

Sawyer was the last to climb aboard, and it wasn't until he settled into his seat and accepted the headphones Quentin gave him that the pilot turned his head and offered a very faint smile.

It was Reese DeMarco.

Sawyer exchanged looks with Tessa, hoping that his eyes weren't as wide and baffled as he felt, and then hastily put on his headphones as the helicopter lifted into the air and headed north, so low it was practically skimming the treetops.

"What the hell?" Sawyer demanded. "He's on your team?"

"Afraid so." Quentin sounded amused. "I know he makes a rotten first impression, but given time you'll warm up to him."

"I doubt that," Sawyer snapped.

Tessa looked at Hollis, who merely shrugged.

"I've never met him," the agent told Tessa. "Knew we had somebody else on the inside, but that's as much as Bishop would tell me."

Through the headphones, Reese DeMarco's voice was cool. "And that was more than you needed to know."

Hollis shot him a none-too-friendly look, then shrugged again. "Looks like all the secrets are coming out today anyway."

After that, the passengers and pilot remained silent for what turned out to be about a ten-minute flight to a very large house perched high above Grace on the side of a mountain. What appeared to be a flat-roofed multicar garage sported a clear heliport, and DeMarco set the chopper down with a featherlight touch and switched off the engine.

Sawyer was in no mood to be impressed. He ignored their pilot as he helped Tessa out and then walked beside her across the landing pad, following Quentin, Hollis, and DeMarco into the building.

As soon as they stepped inside, Sawyer knew they were in someone's home rather than any sort of government or corporate structure. The rooms were open and expansive, towering windows provided spectacular views of the Blue Ridge Mountains, and the furnishings and artwork were, clearly, both expensive and tasteful.

They passed through a huge living area, seeing a gleaming state-of-the-art kitchen off to the left, and then into what was obviously an unusually large study. A massive conference table occupied the center of the space, while at least three discreet computer workstations were scattered around the outer areas of the room, each with a stunning mountain view.

Sawyer thought the room was deserted. For an instant.

He came out of nowhere, a big man whose powerful single punch knocked DeMarco to the floor without warning.

"You shot me," the big man bit out.

DeMarco didn't attempt to get up. Instead, he pushed himself onto an elbow and gingerly rubbed his jaw with one hand. He eyed the man standing above him with more than a hint of wariness. "Galen—"

"You fucking shot me. *Twice.*"

By the time Ruth left him, Samuel felt considerably better. Not fully energized, of course, but strong enough so that he could conduct the planned afternoon Ritual with a few of his Chosen.

After that, of course, he would be fine.

He needed the cleansing of the Ritual, especially after remembering . . . her. Not that she mattered, really. What mattered was that he had truly come of age that day, discovering that he could master his God-given abilities *and* acquire new ones.

It had required more long years of effort and practice, of course, before he learned to be confident. Years more before he began to cautiously explore his limits—only to discover that with enough time and power he could do almost anything.

Almost.

He didn't meditate again, because he wasn't strong enough to endure the trip back into his complete past, but he did remain in his quarters for a few more minutes before joining those in the church for lunch.

He thought about the Prophecy.

That had been given to him nearly two decades ago, long after Maddox had found his own bloody end on the path. Samuel had gone on, but not alone. Ruth had been his first disciple. Loyal through all the years since, it was

Maddox's daughter who quite often discovered and re-cruited the very best of Samuel's Chosen ones.

She had helped him through the test God had given him the previous summer, the test of his control over the Beast, though he thought she probably wouldn't have if she had not witnessed, all those years ago, God reaching down to touch him a second time, his gift the Prophecy.

After that, she had never doubted him.

And he had taken giant steps, this past year and more, toward becoming the perfect sword of God's wrath. He was almost there. Almost.

Only a bit more sharpening of his sword was needed, and then he would be ready.

Then the Prophecy would be fulfilled.

Then the world would be blasted clean by the pure white heat of God's chosen warrior. And the Chosen few would go on.

Soon.

"You should be glad I did," DeMarco retorted. "At least I knew where to put the bullets. Either of the guys with me would have gone for head shots, and not even *you* come back from that."

For several beats, it seemed as though Galen was in no mood to be reasoned with, but finally he swore under his breath and extended a hand to the man he had just decked.

"Well, it hurts, just in case you didn't know that. Getting shot. It hurts like hell."

DeMarco accepted the hand up, still visibly wary. "Sorry. And, actually, I do know it hurts. From experience. But what choice did I have? You were too damn close to miss, and there was no way you could make it to any kind of cover in time to avoid getting shot by one of us. I had about a second to act, and the best option for both of us seemed to be to put you down, fast and hard. Don't try to tell me you wouldn't have made exactly the same choice if the situation had been reversed."

"Yeah, yeah. Point taken. But it was—unpleasant. And that river was damn cold too." The grumble was obviously more automatic than anything else.

Sawyer looked at Tessa and asked, "Am I supposed to be following any of this?"

"I wouldn't expect so. I'm not."

Quentin grinned at both of them. "Agent Galen was inside the Compound a week or so ago in the predawn hours and ran afoul of DeMarco and two armed church members."

"Afoul?" DeMarco stared at him, brows rising. "Seriously?"

"You want to explain this?"

"Not really."

"Then don't criticize my choice of words."

"Armed?" Sawyer said.

"Just handguns," DeMarco told him. "Nothing heavy."

Galen said, "You mean aside from that silver cannon you carry?"

"It fits my hand."

"It's more firepower than any handgun needs. It's going to leave a mark—two marks, as a matter of fact—and not much does."

DeMarco rubbed his jaw again and dryly said, "Uh-huh."

"Oh, don't even compare bullets with a punch."

"I may not bruise easily, Galen, but I do bruise. How am I supposed to explain this?"

"Tell Samuel you ran into a door."

"Funny."

"Nobody up there is licensed," Sawyer said, his voice a bit louder than before.

To Tessa, Hollis said, "I feel like I'm at a tennis match. With a few extra players on the court."

"I know what you mean."

Another player came into the room just then, drawing Sawyer's still somewhat indignant attention. Yet another tall, wide-shouldered, and athletic man, this one moved with an easy, curiously feline grace, someone totally comfortable inside his own skin. He had jet-black hair with a rather dramatic widow's peak as well as a streak of pure white at the left temple, very pale and extremely sharp silvery-gray eyes, and a faint jagged scar down his left cheek that kept him from being quite as good-looking as DeMarco was but helped him look twice as dangerous.

Which was saying something, Sawyer thought, as those metallic eyes fixed immediately on him.

"Chief. I'm Special Agent Noah Bishop." The newcomer's voice was cool and calm.

"You're in charge?"

"Technically, you're in charge. Your jurisdiction."

Sawyer wondered how many times Bishop had made that little speech.

DeMarco said to Bishop, "You might have warned me Galen was on the warpath."

"I might have," Bishop agreed.

"Shit, Bishop."

"Hey, he was going to take his shot. I figured it'd be easier on you if you didn't know it was coming."

"Thanks a bunch."

"Anytime."

Galen said to DeMarco, "Want an ice bag for that jaw?"

"Don't gloat. It's unbecoming. Especially when you blindside a man." DeMarco gave his jaw a final rub, then squared his shoulders, clearly throwing off the subject. "Look, I'm on a tight timetable here, so unless everybody wants to find themselves some wheels or walk back down the mountain, I suggest we get to it."

Bishop said, "Samuel believes you're out alone, patrolling the perimeter of the Compound?"

"He calls it prowling. It is my long-standing habit to do so at irregular intervals, something he's accustomed to. I left word that's what I'd be doing for the next hour or so."

Clearly hearing or sensing something more, Bishop lifted a questioning brow.

"There are a couple of other people who've been paying unusually close attention to my movements recently, so I'm more than a little uneasy about being outside the Compound," DeMarco explained. "I'd really rather not give them any reason to be suspicious of me, not at this late stage."

"Sounds like they already are," Quentin pointed out.

"Maybe. Or maybe Samuel's growing paranoia is fueling it in others."

Bishop frowned, then gestured toward the oval conference table, and most everyone moved to take seats. Sawyer was interested to see that Bishop took the head of the table and DeMarco took the foot—both instinctive power positions—while Galen chose to lean a shoulder against the side of a bookcase, apart from the group, where he could watch everyone at the table as well as keep an eye on the doorway.

Someone on guard, Sawyer thought. Probably at all times.

"*Is* Samuel growing more paranoid?" Bishop asked DeMarco.

"I'm no profiler. But it doesn't take an expert to see that he's walking a very fine line right now."

"Between?" Sawyer asked.

"Between sanity and madness, Chief. The thing is, he's come down on the mad side too many times already. I don't even know how he can be sane at all, at any time, given the things he's done. Though I suppose monsters can always find justification."

"What's his?"

"That he's doing God's work, of course. The world is

overrun with sinners, and he's helped cull a few. That's how he looks at it. Just a warm-up for the big show."

"What show?" There were so many questions tumbling through Sawyer's brain that he had to start asking, and keep asking, even though he knew Tessa had only one concern right now and was impatient to steer the discussion to Ruby.

"Armageddon. An apocalypse. Whatever you want to call it. The End Times. The end of the world, Chief." The very lack of emotion in DeMarco's voice made his words all the more chilling. "Samuel believes he was given a Prophecy by God. And given the power, by God, to trigger the final destruction. To control it. And to survive it."

"He's also," Bishop said flatly, "a serial killer."

"Which you know," Sawyer reminded him, "but can't prove. Right?"

"Unfortunately."

DeMarco said, "There's been no confession. Not even something remotely resembling one. He might talk of culling sinners but not of killing them. What he did last summer in Boston—he did it partly just to see if he could, I think. If he could control the beast. If he could hunt and not get caught. But then the monster hunters got too close, and he set out to discover just how good they really were. He set out to explore and test the strengths and weaknesses of the only enemy he was truly afraid of." He nodded toward Bishop.

"You?" Sawyer asked Bishop. "He's afraid of you specifically?"

"The SCU. But, yes, me specifically. I was, thanks to the media, the public face of the task force and the SCU during the Boston investigation. So he saw me as a threat. Enough of a threat that it drove him to ground for a while. Until, as Reese said, he decided to test his limits and ours. In Venture, Georgia, this past October. And too many women died in both places before we managed to find and cage the monster."

"One of the monsters," DeMarco noted. "Unfortunately for everyone involved, when Samuel pushed himself—apparently in a series of attempts to steal from others psychic abilities he wanted to possess, needed to possess for this ultimate battle he believes is coming— the experiences changed him. And not for the better."

Bishop said to Sawyer, "It wasn't until near the end of the hunt that we realized what he might be capable of. And by then we could only react defensively, try to protect ourselves and our abilities. Dani Justice, a Haven operative, was the only one of us who possessed an ability that could be channeled and used as a weapon. She used it defensively."

"And it hurt Samuel," DeMarco said. "Badly. Shook his confidence *and* weakened him. And did something else to him. When he came back here...I didn't know what had happened, at first. I was so deep undercover that my check-ins were infrequent. All I knew was that he claimed to have had a transformative experience, that he'd walked through the wilderness, through the desert, like Moses."

"Seriously?" Sawyer asked.

"Oh, he was quite serious. And he had been changed. None of us knew how much until the rebellion that had been simmering in his flock while he was gone boiled over when he returned. One follower, a man named Frank Metcalf, had taken advantage of Samuel's absence over those many weeks to make his case as a better leader. More than a few were willing to follow him. Until Samuel came back. Changed. And literally put the fear of God into them."

"Is that when he killed all the animals?" Sawyer asked.

DeMarco looked at him, no expression at all on his face. "He killed more than the animals, Chief. He also killed Frank Metcalf. He killed him without so much as laying a finger on him."

"How?" Sawyer demanded.

"Lightning. He channeled lightning. I saw it with my own eyes."

Fourteen

RUBY CAMPBELL had lived with her secret for such a long time that it seemed to her there had never been anything else. That she had never just been a little girl who ran and played and complained about her lessons or her chores.

It hardly seemed possible to her now that such a simple life had once been hers.

Was it ever like that? Or do I just wish it had been?

Her head ached all the time now, because she had to concentrate so much, had to think so hard about the way she needed things to be. How she needed other people to see. What she needed them to see. Even after sending Lexie away to be safe with Tessa Gray, Ruby knew she couldn't let down her guard.

Father had noticed her. He was watching her.

And she knew now what he could do. What he had done.

Brooke . . .

There was a numb place where Brooke had been. A

dark spot in Ruby's memory of what had happened to her friend. She thought it was probably because she simply couldn't bear to remember it just yet.

Not all of it, at least.

But Brooke was gone. She was gone, and Ruby hadn't even been able to tell their friends about it yet.

And on top of suffering her own grief alone and in silence, Ruby was more terrified than she'd ever been in her life. Terrified that Father might know her secret. All her secrets.

He hadn't said anything about Lexie, hadn't appeared to notice, but that didn't reassure Ruby. Because the really, really scary part of her secret wasn't that she could make things look like other things or even seem to disappear. The really scary part was that *she saw* what was there. Even what was really underneath people's skin.

And now she had seen what was underneath Father's skin.

"Ruby?"

The little girl braced herself. She looked up from her afternoon lessons to see her mother standing in the doorway of the little den they'd turned into a schoolroom.

"Yes, Mama?" She tried hard to see her mama's face as it had been, once. Before the church. Before Father. Before last October.

"Father wants to have a Ritual before supper."

A chill crawled up and down Ruby's back, and she wondered if she'd ever feel warm again.

"So you'll need to finish your lessons and go take a

shower. I've laid out your robe for you, and I'll do your hair. Hurry up, now."

"Yes, Mama." She saw beneath the pleasant, pretty features to the cold, hard shell that lurked under the surface, the shell that was blackened, as though scorched, and contained only an emptiness so vast Ruby didn't have words for it. All she knew was that her mother no longer lived there.

Her mother, she knew now, had been gone for a long time.

"Hurry up," Emma Campbell repeated.

Ruby nodded but said, "Mama? Do I . . . do I have to be naked under the robe? Like last time?"

"Ruby, you know it's part of the Ritual." Emma Campbell smiled. "You're at the Youth Level. Even more, you're one of the Chosen. It's a great honor, and your father and I are so proud of you."

"Yes, Mama." Ruby didn't try to argue, didn't try to protest. It was useless. And it was dangerous.

"Use the special soap I bought for you when you shower. So you'll smell nice for the Ritual."

Ruby's stomach lurched, a reaction she tried to hide as she reached for normal, everyday things. Reassuring things. "I will. Is Daddy coming home in time for supper?"

"No, I'm afraid not. He called earlier to say the sales conference is going on longer than he expected, and he'll probably be gone a few more days. But he's signed up a dozen more accounts. I think they may make him Salesman of the Month after this trip."

Ruby looked down at her hand, watching the pencil she held wobble slightly before she regained her fierce control. Looking at the half-circle wound made by her own teeth hours before, a wound she was hiding from everyone. In a very soft voice, she said, "Mama? When did Daddy become a salesman?"

"Oh, Ruby, don't ask silly questions when you know the answers as well as I do. Your daddy's always been a salesman. Now, hurry up and finish your work."

"Yes, Mama." Ruby dared not look up until she was certain Emma Campbell had returned to the kitchen and her endless baking. And when she did look up, she didn't cry, even though her eyes stung and there was an aching lump in her throat.

Because her daddy had always been a mechanic.

And she was never going to see him again.

"That was when Reese called me," Bishop said. "That was when we started putting the pieces together."

"Lightning?" Sawyer cast about for something reasonable to say when presented with the fantastic. "That...doesn't sound like any kind of psychic ability I've ever heard of."

"It's about energy." Bishop's tone was remote, the scar standing out whitely against the tanned skin of his cheek. "From what little we've been able to find out, Samuel was struck by lightning when he was a teenager. Not only did he survive, but he came out of the experience profoundly changed."

DeMarco said, "He was already preaching his version of the Bible, not because he'd found God but because he'd found a way to make money. And a way to make people listen to him and respect him. After the lightning he was, as Bishop says, changed. He must have been a latent or even active psychic before then; we have no way to be sure. After that experience, he was very obviously psychic, clairvoyant, and precognitive."

"Miracles," Hollis murmured. "There will always be followers of people who claim to know the secrets of the universe."

"And people who claim to be touched by God," De-Marco said. "I don't know if he believed that when the lightning struck, but eventually, over time, he certainly came to believe it. After that, the only laws he obeyed were the ones God supposedly gave him, and those were remarkably flexible. I don't know much about his journey before he settled here, but I think it's safe to say he discovered a long time ago how easy it was to kill."

The sick feeling in Sawyer's stomach intensified. "Those bodies in the river. Others that washed farther downstream. How long has he been killing here?"

"It was happening when I got inside, so I can't tell you when it started, not for certain. My guess would be that it's been going on for at least five or six years, maybe longer. But I was witness to none of it, he has never confessed any of it to me, and I have no proof whatsoever that would justify even a search warrant or an arrest, let alone a trial and conviction. Not for any of the murders he's committed. Which is why I haven't been able to take any action despite what I know absolutely."

"You said you witnessed a murder last October," Sawyer objected.

"I witnessed a man being struck by lightning," DeMarco said flatly. "Samuel was yards away when it happened. Do I believe he killed that man? Yes. Do I believe I could convince a court of law that Samuel, for want of a better word, summoned a lightning bolt to do it? I don't think so. Any more than I can prove that the enormous energies he released that day also destroyed virtually all the pets and livestock within the Compound. In an instant."

"Which is our theory," Bishop said. "It's also our theory that his use of electromagnetic energy has so affected the very atmosphere above the Compound that even the birds stay away."

Sawyer struggled to let all that sink in. Finally he asked DeMarco, "How long have you been inside the church?"

"You should know. We met shortly after you took office, two years ago."

"Wait," Hollis said. "You've been under that long?"

"Twenty-six months," he said.

Frowning, Hollis turned her gaze to Bishop. "You knew about Samuel that long ago?"

Bishop shook his head. "You heard Reese. It wasn't until last October that I began to suspect Samuel."

"Then why was he sent in?"

"There are presently more than a dozen suspected

cults on the FBI watch list because they're believed to be dangerous or potentially dangerous. The FBI, ATF, or Homeland Security has undercover agents in six of them. The SCU has agents inside two of those—plus Reese here. We knew Samuel posed a danger almost from the moment Reese was inside and able to report. We suspected Samuel was psychic, but since he doesn't read as psychic and has never openly displayed abilities we can define, we were never sure of his capabilities. I had no idea he had any connection to the murders in Boston last summer, or the murders in Georgia a few months later. Not then."

"And now? Are you absolutely sure?" Hollis asked him.

"Ask Reese."

Without waiting to be asked, DeMarco said, "Until about ten years ago, Samuel was fairly harmless, as cult leaders go. Like many of them, as I said, he started preaching young. Then lightning struck, literally. And suddenly he had a mission. To save his followers. He saw himself as their healer, their savior. Over time, he became convinced that he was God's instrument on earth, chosen and set on a path that would lead his people through the dangerous days ahead."

Sawyer grunted and said, "Sounds like most of the preachers I've heard in my life."

DeMarco nodded. "Yeah, not much difference in the early days. But then, gradually, his sermons began to be less about God and more about the role of his flock in the coming End Days. They were, he taught them, persecuted or, worse, ignored by blind and faithless outsiders. The world was a perilous place and would become even more perilous. Only he could protect them; only he could lead them to salvation. They had to trust him, had to believe in him. Utterly."

"And that," Quentin said, "crosses over the line. From legitimate spiritual leader to the first dangerous stages of a cult."

Again, DeMarco nodded. "Still, he wasn't preaching violence as far as any outsider could tell—and by then some watch groups were paying attention. He preached the usual dire warnings of the approaching End Times, of how the ungodly would be punished, but he wasn't encouraging anyone to do anything about it, other than pray. No abuse reported, no stories from former church members that indicated any openly dangerous tendencies. They didn't even isolate themselves particularly from the communities around them. Only thing that really stood out that long ago was the fact that he left his first small, fairly remote church outside L.A. in the hands of one of his trusted followers and took his act on the road.

"He didn't seem to want to settle anywhere over the next eight or ten years. He traveled around the country. He'd spend maybe a year in a likely spot, usually a small town or other remote area, gathering a few converts and then choosing one of them to run that branch of his church. Then he'd move on to the next likely spot."

"Why?" Sawyer asked. "That doesn't make sense."

"It does seem weirdly random," Hollis agreed. "I've

always thought so. If the branches he founded end up anything like the one we found in Venture, it was hardly more than a shack with a handful of loyal members."

"A shack—plus a lot of property," Bishop pointed out.

"Well, yeah, but mostly worthless property. Abandoned buildings, defunct businesses, and not a lot of land. What's the good of owning stuff like that? Especially when you don't even bother taking steps to improve the property?"

"I wish I knew."

Hollis frowned again at Bishop, then turned her gaze to DeMarco. "You don't know why he wants the land?"

"No."

"His right-hand man doesn't know?" Sarcasm tinted her tone.

DeMarco appeared to ignore the dig. "No, his right-hand man doesn't have a clue. Samuel plays his cards close to the chest. Very close. He doesn't confide his thoughts to anyone, far as I know—with the possible exception of Ruth Hardin, who's been with him longer than anyone else. As Bishop said, he doesn't read as psychic, and so far we haven't found a psychic who's able to read him. At all."

"Including you?"

"Including me."

Ruby lingered in the shower as long as she dared, using the special soap her mama had bought. It smelled like roses, so sickly sweet that her already queasy stomach churned even more as she soaped herself from head to toe and then just stood underneath the steaming hot water.

The Ritual.

She hated the Ritual.

Two of the other girls loved it, she knew that. Amy and Theresa. She saw it in their wide, dazed eyes and flushed cheeks. She heard it in their nervous, excited giggles.

They were Becoming, and it thrilled them.

Father thrilled them.

But Ruby and Brooke knew the truth, and what they knew had made their skin crawl.

Ruby's skin was crawling even in the shower, a cold pit of dread lay heavy in her stomach, and she wasn't certain how much longer she would be able to pretend otherwise. She wasn't even *absolutely* sure Father believed her pretense, except . . .

He seemed to get what he wanted from her. What he needed. He seemed pleased. So maybe she could make Father see what wasn't there as well. She allowed herself to hope that was true. That she could make even him see what she wanted him to see, believe what she wished him to believe . . .

Maybe.

And if she could do that—

"Ruby, hurry up! You'll be late."

She reluctantly turned the water off, then stepped out of the shower and began to towel herself dry. And it wasn't until that moment, dripping on the mat with her wet hair in her eyes, that it occurred to her what she had done.

She had sent Lexie away.

She had sent Lexie to an outsider.

What if Father sees that? What if he knows?

What have I done?

"Ruby?"

All she could do was concentrate harder, to try her best to make the protective shell she had fashioned for herself even stronger. Stronger than it had ever needed to be before, even when she watched Brooke die. Her head began to pound, to throb, and she could feel her own heartbeat, first racing and then gradually slowing, growing more steady as she regained control over herself.

He can't know where I've sent Lexie. He can't.

"Ruby!"

Her fingers felt a little numb as she hurriedly finished drying herself and wrapped the damp towel around her. She went out into the bedroom, her parents' bedroom, where Emma Campbell waited.

"Here, sweetie, come sit down at my dressing table while I do your hair."

Ruby obeyed, keeping her gaze fixed on her own reflection in the oval mirror. Still her face, thank goodness, with nothing dark and empty underneath. She checked every day, always worried that it could happen at night, when she slept. When she couldn't concentrate to keep her shell around her for protection. She dreaded looking into the mirror every single morning.

She didn't know what she would do if she saw beneath her own skin what she saw beneath the skin of so many of those around her.

Except that I wouldn't be here to see that. I'd be gone. Only my empty shell would be left.

She glanced up at Emma Campbell's reflection, then just as swiftly returned her gaze to the reflection of her own face. She didn't know where they went, the people who'd once lived inside their skins. She wished she could believe they'd gone to heaven but knew that wasn't the case. People went to heaven when their bodies died naturally; their souls went to heaven. That was what Ruby believed.

But what Father did—what Father took—that was something else.

Something horribly *un*natural.

He took it, Ruby was sure, from the people who no longer believed, the people who just . . . went away.

And he took it from his Chosen ones.

Emma Campbell had been a Chosen one.

And now Ruby was Becoming. Almost ready. Almost old enough to endure the True Ritual. That was when she would lose herself. Give herself, Father said, to God.

That was when she would stop being Ruby Campbell and become just an empty shell with a pretend person inside.

"I believe I'll put your hair up this time, Ruby. You look so pretty when your hair is up."

She braced herself and looked steadily at the reflection of Emma Campbell's face. The face that her mother had worn and that the pretend person wore now. The face that was so familiar, and yet so alien.

This isn't my mother. Not anymore.

"You can't read him because he has a shield?" Sawyer asked.

DeMarco shrugged. "Maybe. Though I've come to think of it more like a black hole. He draws energy in, constantly. It seemed a fairly minor characteristic at first, possibly an interesting variation on a shield, negative energy, but over time it's grown stronger, to the point that if you're within ten or twelve feet of him it's an actual physical sensation of being pulled toward him."

Hollis muttered, "Bet his congregation calls that charisma."

"They call it part of his divine gift," DeMarco said calmly. "And either he's hardwired for it or else he has amazing concentration and focus, because while he's pulling energy in, nothing of himself escapes. Nothing of his personality. None of his thoughts or emotions. Even when he's . . . stimulating female members of his flock in order to feed off their energy, he still reads as a null field. As if there's no person, no mind, no soul there."

"How is that even possible?"

"I don't know."

Sawyer said, "But you do know that's one thing Samuel is doing? Feeding off those women?"

"I believe he's been doing that for a long time. But it wasn't so obvious at first, and I doubt he was pulling much of their energy then. I think he was doing more giving than taking, at least in the beginning, with the members of his congregation, whether that was building their trust or somehow making them ... dependent on him. Maybe even addicted to him.

"I spent a lot of time trying to understand how he was able to control them so thoroughly. There were none of the typical signs or methods of a cult leader brainwashing his followers. And yet those followers were devoted to him, and way beyond any normal sort of devotion. That was obvious. That was why I was sent in twenty-six months ago."

Bishop said, "As a group, they had become even more isolated, more reclusive. We try to learn from history, Chief, and from our mistakes. We needed to know what was going on inside the church."

"To avoid another Waco. Another Jonestown."

"Exactly. But since cults *are*, by nature, isolationist and highly suspicious of outsiders, the only way to really know what goes on inside is to get someone inside. Not an easy thing to do, especially with a paranoid leader already warning his congregation about enemies everywhere and a looming apocalypse."

Sawyer looked back at DeMarco. "So how did you get in?"

"The same way most of his followers did. I hung

around church shelters and halfway houses in Asheville for weeks, obviously one of the castoffs of society, homeless and unemployed. I was a loner, bitter, openly . . . disenchanted with our government, and though I didn't have property to tempt the church, I made sure what I had to offer Samuel was visible to all."

"Which was?"

"My army jacket, bearing the kind of service patches and insignia you don't find in pawnshops. I'm ex-military. We had a hunch Samuel might be interested in building himself an army."

"And?"

"And he was."

Sawyer said, "An army? He's building an army up there?"

DeMarco shook his head. "Not the way you think. Not the way we expected. There are a few handguns in the Compound, a few shotguns. Nothing more than that. He's convinced his followers—most of them—that they won't need weapons to defeat their enemies. Not manmade weapons, at any rate. His followers are his army, and he's been building that army carefully for at least the last few years."

Sawyer thought about that and decided it needed to sink in a bit more before he tried to do something with that particular puzzle piece. "But you were still valuable to him. Your nonpsychic skills were valuable." He realized suddenly that he had no idea what psychic skills DeMarco could boast, and the realization made him acutely uncomfortable.

"He had no one with any experience to run his security. Until recently, it hadn't been a concern, but by the time I was recruited, he was growing more and more security-conscious."

"Paranoid."

DeMarco nodded. "I gather he felt he'd been making enemies, but whether he had already focused on the SCU then, I have no way of knowing."

Hollis glanced at Bishop, then said, "We're pretty sure he was focused on at least one of us as long as eighteen months ago."

"He let us find those photographs with his pet monster," Bishop said. "In fact, I believe he made sure we'd find them. He wanted us to know he'd been watching. Following. My bet is that the reason there were only pictures of you was because he wanted us to wonder just exactly what we *are* wondering. Was he tracking you as a potential victim or because you're SCU?"

"And it could be either," she agreed. "Considering where I wound up."

"Which is?" Sawyer asked.

"Let's just say that I got to meet the pet monster up close and personal." Before anyone could comment, she frowned at DeMarco. "Does Samuel leave the Compound often? Because I had the sense he was pretty reclusive up there."

"He is now. Has been since last fall. Before then he'd go off for a few days or a week now and then, with an especially long trip occasionally. Last summer he was gone the better part of six weeks, even though he came back here several times over that stretch. It was usual for him to come back with a new recruit or two and say he'd been a guest preacher at this church or that revival. We'd no reason to suspect he was doing anything else."

"He wasn't followed when he left here?"

"No. My instructions were to infiltrate the cult and do as much as I could to make myself indispensable to Samuel and his operations. That meant staying here and keeping things running whenever he left."

"And fomenting a little rebellion?" Hollis suggested.

"I didn't discourage it. In hindsight, I should have." He wasn't apologetic or regretful, merely matter-of-fact.

She nodded.

Sawyer said to DeMarco, "I gather you're responsible for the electronic security up at the Compound?"

"Samuel wanted some state-of-the-art gadgets installed, and I know a bit about that sort of thing. I also have contacts. Military contacts. He liked that."

Hollis said, "Which is all well and good, but how did you manage to convince him you're a believer? Unless you are?" She was looking steadily at him, clearly bothered by that point.

"You won't see it," DeMarco told her.

"See what?"

"My aura."

When her blue eyes narrowed, sharpened, it was Quentin who said, "Give it up, Hollis, before you get a headache. Or have a stroke. Reese has a double shield."

"I've never heard of anything like that before," Hollis said, clearly dubious.

"I'm unique," DeMarco drawled.

Half under his breath, Sawyer said, "Jesus, I'm the one getting the headache."

Quentin offered him a faint smile. "Information overload? Well, the main thing you need to understand is that Reese, like Tessa, doesn't read as psychic, but he has an uncanny ability to create a . . . persona that *is* readable when he allows it to be."

"Convenient," Hollis remarked.

"Useful," Quentin corrected. "Any psychic who manages to get through his primary shield isn't likely to look for a secondary one, especially when they discover that manufactured persona—in this case, the bitter ex-military guy entirely willing to kill for, or possibly die for, a charismatic pseudoreligious leader."

Fifteen

THE "ROBE" WAS actually more like a dress—or a nightgown. It was long, so thin it was nearly transparent, and sleeveless. It was white.

"The color of purity," Emma Campbell said softly as she stood back and smiled at Ruby.

Ruby shivered, wondering again if she would ever feel warm. "I can wear your cloak to the church, can't I, Mama? It's getting colder outside."

"I suppose so. But you be sure to take it off once you're inside."

"Yes, Mama." Ruby was grateful for the warmth of the ankle-length stark black cloak and even more grateful that it covered the thin robe, but despite that she always felt uneasy wearing it. She didn't know for sure, but something told her that her mama had been wearing the cloak when she finally just . . . went away.

Smiling, Emma Campbell said, "You do as Ruth tells you, just like before. And do as Father tells you, of course. I'm so proud of you. Your daddy and I are both so proud of you."

The painful lump rose in Ruby's throat again, so she merely nodded and tried not to think about her daddy. Or about her mama. Instead, she walked through the house and to the front door beside the shell named Emma Campbell.

"Be good. Remember."

"Yes, Mama." She went out into the chilly afternoon, walking steadily toward the church, concentrating hard on making her protective shell so strong even Father wouldn't be able to touch her through it.

Not the real her, at least.

And she didn't look back because she knew Emma Campbell had already returned to her sewing room.

It's needlework for her. And sewing for Amy's mom. Theresa's mom does quilts. Brooke's mom has all those jigsaw puzzles . . . I know it all means something. Maybe he gives them things to do. So they don't have time to think.

So they don't want to think.

Maybe he found out what they like to do best and let them keep that.

Only that.

Ruby walked steadily to the church, seeing the other girls waiting on the steps for her. Seeing, with a catch inside, that Father had already replaced Brooke, as easily as though she had never existed.

Mara. Little Mara, only eleven, and visibly nervous

at this, her first Ritual. And unlike the other two, she was wearing a long sweater over her robe.

Amy and Theresa, both thirteen, wore only the thin robes despite the cold.

They felt grown up in the robes, Ruby knew. They felt grown up, and special, and important to Father.

They felt Chosen.

"Hurry up, Ruby," Amy called out to her impatiently.

"I'm coming," Ruby responded, hearing the bright sparkle in her own voice, the sound of eagerness that was every bit as fake as the smile that curved her lips. She began to climb the steps to join her friends.

But she didn't hurry.

"Sure that's just a persona?" Hollis muttered. "Because the way I hear it, people who stay undercover for too long can get really . . . lost in their role-playing."

DeMarco glanced at her, then looked at Sawyer. "That ability plus a few other characteristics make me an ideal candidate for undercover work. As Bishop discovered a few years ago."

"So you're SCU?"

It was Bishop who replied. "He's not FBI. But we realized early on that having operatives . . . off the books would be helpful if not necessary in some situations."

"I thought that's why you helped found Haven," Tessa said, speaking up finally. She looked at Bishop. "As a civilian offshoot of the SCU," she added.

"A sister organization," Bishop said. "But Haven was set up primarily to provide short-term support, with operatives called in for specific, usually brief periods of time, to assist in criminal investigations. Most lead perfectly ordinary, normal lives the majority of the time, with their Haven work more like a series of temp jobs than anything else."

"True enough," Tessa agreed. "On my last assignment, I didn't even have to unpack. And in my normal life, I design Web sites. Easy to set my own hours, work from home or on the road with a laptop, and take time 'off' whenever I need to. Tailor-made for someone with a whole other life."

Bishop nodded. "It's different for those of us inside the FBI, and not just because it's a full-time job. Being an SCU agent means we're employees of the federal government all the time, with laws, rules, and regulations we're duty-bound to uphold."

"Which can sometimes present problems," Quentin murmured. "For some of us."

Sawyer wondered if he was talking about himself but didn't ask. On his long list of questions, that one seemed relatively unimportant.

Bishop didn't comment on Quentin's aside but continued, "It became obvious that we needed operatives able to bridge the gap between cop and civilian. Operatives trained in both law enforcement and military tactics, with strong investigative instincts and abilities—and with some kind of psychic edge. People capable of going undercover, possibly long term, with little or no backup, and not necessarily with government sanction."

Hollis let out an odd little sound and said, "You do like to walk the edge, don't you?"

"I have to sometimes. Whether I like it or not." Bishop shrugged. "Reese, like a number of our civilian operatives, is a licensed private investigator—and his military background is legit."

"And I like working alone," DeMarco said.

"What about your normal life?" Hollis asked.

"Don't really have one."

Hollis looked curious, but before she could ask the obvious question, Tessa lost patience with the lot of them.

"Ruby," she said in the tone of one who was not going to be ignored. "That little girl is in trouble."

"Ruby isn't in immediate danger," DeMarco told her.

"But you know she *is* in danger?"

He looked at her, those pale blue eyes not warming at all. "They're all in danger. Samuel's Prophecy, remember?"

"Armageddon." Quentin's voice was wry. "All the best prophecies seem to predict Armageddon."

"Yes," DeMarco said. "But the difference is that Samuel, unlike all the prophets of the past, might actually have a shot at seeing his vision, his Prophecy, come true. Even if he has to light the conflagration with his own hands. Or his own mind."

"You don't mean literally?" Sawyer said. "That he

could create—with his mind—destruction on a scale that could be even loosely termed apocalyptic?"

"Afraid so."

"But you said—Wait. The lightning?"

"Why not? He's used it to kill on a small scale. Who's to say he can't eventually gain or channel enough energy to be able to destroy on a truly massive scale?"

Quentin murmured, "Welcome to our world."

"Shit," Sawyer said. "No offense, but I'm finding it very difficult to think in apocalyptic terms. That was never a brand of religion I bought into."

"Perfectly understandable," Quentin told him. "I've been having trouble with it myself. And I saw it. I think."

"That was your vision?" Tessa stared at him. "That Samuel destroyed the world?"

"Well, a goodly piece of this part of the world. All his followers. And Ruby. You, the chief, Hollis. Maybe only the beginning of his apocalypse, because my sense was that he was just getting started. There was sure as hell nobody stopping him."

Bishop spoke suddenly. "And Ruby."

Quentin lifted a brow at his boss. "Yeah. So?"

"You aren't including Ruby as one of his followers. Why not?"

Considering the question, Quentin said, "I have no idea. From all appearances, she *was* one of his followers. At least...she was sitting at his feet, almost like an acolyte. But he killed her too."

Bishop was frowning. "Are you sure that's what you saw?"

"No. I mean, the visions are new to me, we both know that. They only last a few seconds, and I'm trying to see as much as I can, remember what I see, because so far everything's been literal rather than symbolic."

"So what did you see?" Hollis asked.

Since Quentin hadn't yet given Bishop the actual details of his vision, he tried to remember and relate every one; if he'd learned anything in his years with the SCU, it was that details could be and often were very important in their understanding of abilities and events.

"It was that outside pulpit of his, energy crackling in the air, hellish storm clouds overhead—and smoldering bodies everywhere. Samuel standing on that ledge of granite, his hands smoking, Ruby kneeling at his feet. And behind him . . ."

"Behind him?"

Quentin looked at Hollis, Tessa, and Sawyer in turn and grimaced. "You three, crucified."

"Literally?" Sawyer wondered how many times he had asked that incredulous question.

"Yeah. Crosses, ropes, iron spikes. The works. Everything but Roman centurions. Four crosses, three occupied. You and Hollis weren't conscious. Tessa was. Tessa cried out Ruby's name. Samuel looked down at Ruby, smiled, put his hand on her head—and she burst into flames. Tessa screamed. Samuel turned his head and looked at her, then stretched out his free hand toward her, and what looked like a blast of pure energy shot out of his fingers. That was it. All I saw."

Ruth took Mara's sweater and Ruby's cloak as soon as the girls entered the church. She hung both garments in the cloakroom, then rejoined the girls in the vestibule. "Your shoes, girls."

Obediently, they removed their shoes, lining them up just outside the cloakroom. Mara had to remove socks as well.

The giggling had quieted by now. All the girls were solemn as Ruth made sure everything was as it should be. That robes were clean and pressed, hair tidy, nails trimmed and neat.

Then Ruth led the way from the vestibule and down into one of the side hallways that ran the length of the church, just below ground level. The hallway was rather institutional, with plain walls, plain carpet, and rather ugly wall sconces. At the end of the hallway was a locked door. Ruth produced a ring of keys and unlocked the door, revealing another set of stairs that led down to yet another level.

The girls went ahead of Ruth down the stairs, all of them hearing the sounds of the door being closed and once again locked behind them. She joined them at the foot of the stairs, and the girls stood silently as the older woman, with the deliberation of ceremony, unlocked a small room just past the stairs. The interior of the room was lined with cabinetry, everything metal and frosted glass so that only vague shapes could be seen inside.

Why? Because it has to seem mysterious to us? Or is there something here in the Ceremony Room that's really important?

Ruby didn't know. But she hated this level of the church, where there were only hushed rituals and secrecy. Where she had to fight so hard to protect herself.

Using another key, Ruth unlocked a big stainless-steel cooler. Inside, on a glass shelf, they could all see four white roses in individual crystal vases. One at a time, Ruth brought out a rose and fastened it into a girl's hair, just above the left ear. Each girl bowed her head as the rose was affixed.

Ruby was last and bowed her head obediently while the rose was placed in her hair. *Perfect roses. Except that they have no scent.* Not that it mattered today, since Ruby could still smell the sickly-sweet fake rose perfume from the soap she had used.

Ruth didn't appear to notice. She went back into the Ceremony Room, opened another cabinet, and emerged with four white candles, which she gave to them. Each girl held a candle in both hands while Ruth ceremoniously lit them—with a plastic disposable lighter.

Ruby almost giggled. *Ridiculous. It's all so ridiculous.*

And yet she was so afraid. Her hands were cold, her bare feet were cold, and her head was pounding because she was trying so hard to keep her protective shell in place. She was afraid she'd made a mistake in sending Lexie away to be safe, afraid Father would know about that, that he'd know she'd been hiding Lexie.

Afraid that he would know all the secrets she had done her best to keep from him.

There was nothing at all funny about that.

"Ready, girls?"

Ruby looked up fleetingly, and for an instant she saw the empty shell behind Ruth Hardin's solemn, serene face. That hard, ugly, scorched shell holding so much emptiness there couldn't have been much of Ruth left in there.

If any of her was left.

Ruby fixed her gaze on the flame of her candle and, along with the other girls, murmured, "Yes, Ruth."

Ruth led them single file down the hallway. Unlike the level above, this one was thickly carpeted, the plush wool soft against their bare feet. The walls were covered with fabric rather than paint or wallpaper, and the wall sconces were alight with dripping beads of crystal.

For the first time, it occurred to Ruby that the room they were nearing, the Ritual Room, was directly beneath the pulpit area of the church. She wondered why she had never realized that before, and even as she did, she understood.

Because her shell was stronger. She'd been making it stronger, concentrating harder—and without Lexie to protect, without Lexie needing to be unseen, all Ruby's energy had been able to focus on protecting herself.

And inside her shell, she was able to think clearly now, more clearly than she had ever been able to before. To wonder about things. She didn't have to see the faces of the girls ahead of her to know that they were becoming slack and expressionless, that their eyes were going dark and dazed.

Because it was always like that.

They didn't have shells. They couldn't protect themselves.

She felt a jab of guilt that she could protect herself and they couldn't, but she pushed that aside because she had to. She could only do so much; even protecting just Lexie had taken nearly everything she had, so she couldn't help her friends.

At least, she couldn't help them right now. She couldn't fold them inside her shell with her. But maybe she could do something else. Maybe she could bring help *to* them.

Maybe.

She wasn't sure how she could do that, not exactly. She wasn't even sure *if* she could. But she knew she was still connected to Tessa Gray. Not as strongly as she had been before she drew Tessa back here to the Compound so she could rescue Lexie, not as strong as she had been when she had warned Tessa not to feel so much out at the pet cemetery, but the tie was still there.

She could feel it.

And maybe . . . maybe she could use it.

Ruth paused outside the door of the Ritual Room and looked at the four girls in turn, making sure each still held their candle correctly, that each was still properly solemn.

Ruby wondered if she even noticed that Amy swayed slightly, her eyes wide and almost unseeing.

No. Because Ruth nodded in satisfaction, then used

yet another key to unlock the door and lead the way inside.

Ruby drew a deep breath and followed the others.

"**A**ll," Sawyer muttered. "That's *all* he saw."

Tessa said to Quentin, "What in that vision told you that you were seeing what would happen if we tried to help Ruby?"

"It wasn't anything I saw. But it was a certainty. I *knew* you guys would try to get Ruby out of the Compound today. And I knew that if you tried, what I saw would happen."

"No question? No doubt?"

Quentin shook his head. "Not a single one. I knew. And I've learned that I can trust that kind of certainty, because it's as rare as hen's teeth."

Hollis looked at Bishop. "You've dealt with visions longer, you and Miranda. Did Quentin see a possible future we've avoided because you guys chose to act? Or was it a prophecy we've only temporarily averted?"

Sawyer all but groaned. "A prophecy like Samuel's Prophecy? End-of-the-world stuff?"

Bishop said, "Only in the sense of being . . . ultimate. Unchangeable in its inevitability. We've come to realize over the years that some things we see, some visions of the future, can be changed—if we act at the right time and in the right way. But sometimes our . . . interference is exactly the catalyst necessary to bring about the very events we try to stop. Some things have to happen just the way they happen. And they will happen. No matter what we do or try to do. So we tend to be very, very cautious in acting on a vision."

"And as far as we've been able to tell," Quentin added, "there's no good, consistently reliable way to determine whether one of us is looking at a *possible* future—or an *inevitable* one. There's always a choice of whether we try to change what we see or just work to try and minimize the train wreck heading our way. Quite often, the precog who has the vision isn't certain whether to act. Sometimes, on the other hand, we feel quite strongly about it. Though I've never been sure whether it's gut instinct or, hell, just a guess."

"Cosmic Russian roulette?" Sawyer looked around the table, hoping somebody would offer a less deadly analogy.

Nobody did.

Tessa said to Quentin, "But you're sure this time that by stopping us, you prevented the events in your vision?"

Quentin frowned slightly and his eyes went a bit distant, as though he was listening to some sound only he could hear. Then he blinked, shook his head, and replied, "I'm sure what I saw won't happen. Not the way I saw it happen, at least. But every instinct I can claim is telling me that Reese is right. Samuel intends to bring about whatever prophecy he saw, his version of an apocalypse. I don't know when it will happen, and I don't know why he needs it to happen, but I know that's his plan. And I know it's going to be soon. Very soon."

"How?" Sawyer asked finally. "How could he hope to have enough power to do anything on a scale like that? And don't anybody say lightning. I mean besides lightning."

"His army," DeMarco said. "Somehow, he means to use his followers to bring about his vision."

"In what way?" Sawyer demanded. "I mean, how could those ordinary people become a . . . a power source for a megalomaniac?"

It was Bishop who replied. "Psychics. We're virtually certain that in recent years Samuel's focused his recruitment efforts on active and latent psychics. Even aside from the abilities themselves, we always have a higher-than-normal amount of electrical energy in our brains."

"Maybe a fun bonus for Samuel," Quentin suggested. "Abilities he wants to steal and more energy to help fuel his efforts."

DeMarco said, "He's already stolen abilities from some of the latents, I think. People who likely never had a clue that a vital part of themselves was taken away. But the fact that he hasn't gone after the abilities of a few psychics in the church I *know* are active tells me that he has something else in mind for them. Maybe it has to do with his growing need for energy, or maybe he does intend to use them to bring about his Prophecy. I don't know."

"What about the people whose abilities he went after?" Sawyer was bewildered. "Were they destroyed in the process?"

"Some simply disappear. One of the reasons law enforcement—including you, Chief—hasn't had to deal with missing persons is because those who disappear tend to be new recruits, from outside this area. When they vanish, nobody outside the Compound knows or cares. And those inside are told and believe that whoever it was just didn't fit in and chose to leave. There's never any proof otherwise."

"But some are known," Sawyer insisted. "Some who go missing are either from this area or else have family and friends who notice they're missing. Like Ellen Hodges."

"Yes."

"If he's killed so many, why have we found so few bodies?"

"I don't know. The bodies you have found, most of them, were people that appeared to me to be killed in haste, without much if any forethought. They posed some kind of threat to Samuel, and so he acted. Each murder was less about stealing abilities than it was about protecting himself. Unfortunately, I was never able to see just *how* he acted, how he was able to do what he did; I only saw the results, and only on some occasions, not all of them. A body, virtually always with no visible wound. Each time, I was merely informed that there was a 'problem' I needed to deal with. Samuel suggested the river rather than burial. I don't know why."

Galen spoke up for the first time to say, "You showed up within minutes of Sarah being killed." It wasn't an accusation, merely a comment.

"Sarah?" Sawyer looked around the table. "Are you talking about the most recent Jane Doe in my morgue?"

Hollis drew a breath. "Sarah Warren. A Haven operative." Her voice was toneless. "Until today, nobody could really come forward and I.D. her for you. The fact that she was undercover there can't come out until this is over. Sorry."

Sawyer decided not to get angry about that. Yet. "Okay. I trust this woman's family has been notified?"

"Yes," Bishop said. "And they understand why they can't claim her body yet or even publicly mourn her."

"Do they?"

Bishop looked at him steadily. "They understand, Chief."

Sawyer nodded. "Okay," he repeated, then said to DeMarco, "So how come you were able to show up within minutes of her death, as Agent Galen says?"

"Because Sarah made a mistake," DeMarco replied, something bleak in his tone. "She was spotted on one of the security cameras at the outer perimeter of the Compound, carrying one of the children. It was the middle of the night, and she was obviously leaving with the child. A child who didn't belong to her. Security alerted me. I had no intention of alerting Samuel, but a guard had already done so. He didn't come out but called me into his private quarters. And he was angry. He rarely shows anger, but that night it was clear he was furious."

"Why?" Sawyer asked.

"Because Sarah was taking Wendy Hodges."

Sixteen

HODGES? ELLEN'S DAUGHTER? You told me her father had taken her from the Compound."

Rather dryly, DeMarco said, "You might want to take anything I told you inside the Compound with a grain of skepticism, Chief."

"You're a great liar," Sawyer said finally.

"One of the best attributes of a deep-cover operative. Although I do think it was unfair of you to call me a ghoul."

"I never called you that."

"Not out loud."

Sawyer scowled at him. "That *really* doesn't help your case, you know. Just tell me I haven't had your voice in my head during the last few days."

"Excuse me?"

Either he's really a hell of a liar or he doesn't have a clue what I'm talking about.

It was Tessa who said, "He's asking if you're telepathic both ways."

DeMarco shook his head. "I just read. Can't send."

"Technically," Bishop said, "Tessa is the only one here who can send as well as read."

"Technically?" Sawyer asked.

"My wife and I are telepathic both ways, but only with each other. Sending is generally much more difficult even for powerful telepaths, though sometimes we can manage it in extreme situations."

"Like death," Hollis murmured. She looked up to find Bishop staring at her and added hastily, "Sorry. Just . . . thinking out loud. I mean, with so many telepaths around most of the time, what's the use of keeping things to myself?"

Sawyer didn't want to add another question to those still rattling around in his mind, so he decided to ignore the byplay. "Getting back to Ellen Hodges's daughter," he prompted DeMarco.

"Sorry. As I was saying, the little girl Sarah took that night—Wendy—was a very special child, highly valued by Samuel. A born, active psychic. Telekinetic. Far as I know, the only telekinetic he's ever found."

"They're rare," Bishop said. "Extremely rare."

DeMarco nodded. "And he was losing the only one he'd found, before she was old enough to come fully into her abilities. Before she could play whatever part Samuel intended her to play in his . . . end game."

"So he—what? Sent you after the child?"

"He told me to take a security detail and cut through

the woods, try to get to Sarah before she could take Wendy out of the Compound. I honestly believed he meant that we were to bring them both back to the church. But I think he knew she already had Wendy safe. That's why he was so enraged. I think he knew even as he was issuing those orders to me that he was going to kill Sarah. But I still don't know how he was able to do it. He never left the church. Never left his quarters. Sarah was two miles from the church when she died. We heard her scream."

"Yes," Galen said. "So did I. Her body was still warm when I got to her. And all I can tell you about how she died is that she died terrified and in agony."

Sawyer remembered the body he had found in the river, remembered the M.E.'s report that the dead woman's bones had been virtually crushed, and he couldn't even begin to imagine how painful and terrifying that must have been. And he couldn't begin to imagine how Samuel had done that to her.

"You're sure Samuel killed her?"

"I'm sure," DeMarco said bluntly. "Nobody else up there has anything like enough power to kill, let alone do it at such a distance. But I believe Samuel can. And he's getting better at it. Faster. More brutal. I believe he kills them and then draws every bit of energy from them."

DeMarco paused, then said deliberately, "Hell, for all I know, he takes their souls." His gaze was on Hollis. "We haven't had a medium close enough to tell us that for sure."

"He didn't take Ellen Hodges's soul."

"You saw her?"

"Yes. And a long way from here. That took amazing determination and made what she had to tell me more than usually worth paying attention to."

"What did she tell you?"

"That I needed to be here in order to help stop Samuel."

With a glance at Bishop, DeMarco said, "I wondered. Having a medium even this close is dicey. It's the one ability he does *not* want."

"Yeah," Hollis said. "I know. It's why he tried to feed me to his pet monster. He really, really doesn't want to be able to tap into the spirit world. Which means he knows he doesn't get their souls—or he believes there's something else on the other side that could destroy him."

"Something else he's afraid of," Tessa said. "Bishop, the SCU, and, specifically, mediums. Weaknesses we can exploit?"

"Let's hope so," Bishop said.

Sawyer looked around the table. "You got a plan?"

Quentin said, "We're working on one."

Sawyer wanted to say that it was a little late in the day to only be "working" on a plan but instead directed his attention back to DeMarco. "You said *some* of the psychics whose abilities he steals turn up dead or go missing. But not all of them?"

"No. Some are still there, part of his congregation."

Tessa said, "But changed. Right? Different from the way they used to be."

DeMarco looked at her. "Yeah."

"Changed how?" Sawyer wanted to know.

"Hard to say precisely. They no longer read as psychic, but . . . It's more than that. If I had to guess, I'd say that they lost more than their psychic abilities to Samuel. Maybe a lot more. Maybe as much as a person could lose and still be able to walk and talk and be almost human."

"Stepford people," Tessa murmured. "Going through the motions, all scrubbed and nice. But empty inside."

She was wearing a slight frown, and Sawyer could still feel her impatience; in fact, he could feel it growing. She had Ruby's bag on her lap, open wide enough so that the tiny white poodle's head was visible as Tessa petted her gently.

Odd, Sawyer thought for the first time. *Nobody's said a word about the dog. Or even seemed to notice her.*

"Pretty much," DeMarco said, agreeing with Tessa. "They smile and talk to you, and they're *almost* the people they used to be. Only not quite."

"All of them?" Sawyer asked, distracted by this new horror.

"No. But a majority of them now. Including the non-psychics." He shook his head. "The women can maybe be explained by the way Samuel sucks energy from them. Maybe there's a point of no return. Maybe they can only lose so much energy, so much of the essence of what makes them unique, before the person they were just . . . dissolves."

Maybe the creepiest thing yet, Sawyer thought. "And the men?"

"It's the same result; I'm just not sure how he does it. If he's drawing energy from the men, it isn't such an open, visible thing and not part of any kind of formal ceremony or pseudoreligious ritual. Not like the Testimony ritual, where one or more women are obviously stimulated to the brink of orgasm." His voice was matter-of-fact.

Tessa told them then about the "dream" she had had the night before. She kept her eyes on DeMarco the whole time, and when she finished he was nodding his head.

"Yeah, that happened last night. Exactly as you described it—my part of it, at least. I'm never present when he has one of the women in his office, but it always ends the same way. I'm called in, and I carry an unconscious woman back to her bed."

The Ritual Room was about twenty feet by twenty feet, Ruby guessed, though the size was deceptive because of the dark, floor-to-ceiling velvet draperies that hid the walls and the thick, dark carpet that cushioned underfoot. Though the ceiling of the room was far higher than was normal for a belowground level, the five pendant lights that were the room's only illumination hung low, no more than six feet or so above the floor, and each cast below it a perfect circle of light: one in the center and four encircling it.

About three feet out beyond the outer four circles stood a copper candle holder taller than Ruby, fashioned to hold a single candle. The copper gleamed even though it lay outside the light.

Ruby knew, because it had been explained to them, that each of the four outer lights and the tall candle holders were placed precisely to represent the four directions—north, south, east, and west—while the light in the center represented just that.

The *center*. The *center* of *everything*.

That was where Father stood waiting for them.

Ruby had wondered more than once if there was another door hidden somewhere behind the draperies, because Ruth always unlocked the door to usher the girls in, and it didn't seem likely that Father would be waiting inside a locked room for his Chosen ones. But Ruby had never gotten the chance to look around; Ceremonies and Rituals were always carefully controlled, usually by Ruth, this one especially.

The four girls silently took their assigned places. Ruby was north; Mara was south; Theresa was east; and Amy was west. Each went to the circle of light and knelt on a little velvet pillow facing the center, heads bowed, flickering candles held steadily before them.

With hardly a sound, Ruth left the room, drawing the long draperies across to hide the door and then disappearing behind them.

Ruby didn't have to look up to know that Father was smiling, that his face wore the serene expression it always wore.

His outer face, at least.

She didn't want to think about his other face, and she most certainly didn't want to see it again.

It terrified her.

"You are the Chosen," Father said, his voice unutterably loving as he spoke steadily while he turned in a slow circle.

"We are the Chosen," Ruby heard herself repeat, as the other three girls did. Ruby fought the strange, wordless urge to give in to him, no matter what he asked of her, no matter what he did to her.

It was always so hard to fight him.

"Loved by God."

The girls repeated the words.

"Given by Him to bless this world."

Again, they repeated the words after him.

"Given by Him to serve this world."

Ruby was trying not to think about anything except making her shell harder, repeating the familiar words and phrases without even listening to them.

"Given by Him to save this world."

The last sentence was repeated, over and over, a mantra or a prayer or an offering, spoken in low voices but faster and faster until the words seemed to blur together, until the sound was almost...a moan.

And as she repeated it, Ruby kept her eyes half closed. She refused to watch what she knew was happening.

He always began with Amy, in the west, though Ruby had no idea why. Perhaps it had nothing to do with the direction and was only because Amy was oldest.

But I can't look. It makes me weak when I look. It scares me so much that I forget to keep my shell wrapped around me.

Above the steady chanting came a sudden loud moan, and the sound made her look despite herself.

He was standing behind Amy, both hands folded on top of her head. His eyes were closed, and he continued to chant, his face lifted toward the ceiling—or toward heaven.

No, not toward heaven. God didn't choose him. God wouldn't want this, I'm sure of it.

Amy knelt, her head bowed. Eyes closed. She had stopped chanting; her mouth was open, slack, wet. She moaned again, her body visibly shivering, jerking.

Ruby knew what was happening to her friend. Ruth and Father and her mother might call it something holy, but she knew better. It wasn't holy at all. It was obscene. And the fact that Amy remained a virgin and that she felt nothing but pleasure during the act didn't change the fact that it was rape.

Nobody needed to explain that to Ruby.

And nobody needed to explain to her the terrifying fact that Father stole more than just his Chosen ones' innocence. Every time she looked at her mother's face, or Ruth's face, or the faces of so many of the women of the church, the women who had once been Chosen themselves, Ruby was offered a stark reminder.

Father stole *life*.

Father stole *self*.

A little bit at a time. A Ceremony. A *Youth* Ritual. A

Testimony. Whatever he chose to call it, the end result was the same.

He destroyed.

"So Bambi is okay?" Tessa asked.

"She was at breakfast this morning and seemed the same as always."

"So he hasn't drained away her personality yet."

"No. That process seems to take at least a dozen private visits with Samuel, over a span of months. Or, at least, it did. Things do seem to be moving faster now, happening quicker or more often. Like that black hole I compared him to, he's sucking in energy at an ever-increasing rate."

Hollis muttered, "A psychic vampire. Tessa and I talked about that after she told me about the dream, but in the sane light of day it sounds a lot worse."

"It is worse," Sawyer said. "Dracula seems sweet and cuddly by comparison."

Nobody laughed.

DeMarco checked his watch and swore softly. "I need to get back. If everybody's reasonably up to speed, I suggest we start talking about what we're going to do next."

"We have to help Ruby," Tessa said.

"She does seem to be one of the keys," Hollis said. "The other spirit that visited me—this Andrea I haven't been able to identify—told me back in Venture that we had to help Ruby. Wasn't by name then, but this morning she was a lot clearer about it being Ruby. Though I don't have a clue what 'Look for her in the water' means, Andrea definitely said Ruby could help us stop Samuel."

"Ruby's only twelve," DeMarco said. "How can she help?"

"I don't know." Hollis frowned at him. "Can't you read her?"

"No. Until I caught Samuel watching her a couple of times in the last few weeks, I wasn't even sure she was a latent."

"She's not a latent, she's active. And we think she may have a really nifty ability or two—"

Tessa interrupted to say, "My car's still up there; that's my excuse for going back. Not to try to get her out today," she added quickly. "But maybe if I can talk to her—"

"You need to be very careful anywhere near the Compound," DeMarco warned, and all of them heard the faint emphasis on the first word.

"Why? The vulnerability is just pretend, you know. It—"

"No," DeMarco said. "It isn't. You are vulnerable, Tessa. What happened to you in the Compound today, that uneasy sense of being watched, of being threatened? That was Samuel."

"How do you know that?"

"Because while he was trying to push his way into your mind, trying to affect and influence you, I was trying to hold him off."

"You weren't in my mind. Either of you. I would have known."

DeMarco shook his head. "That's not what I was doing. Like I said, I can't send, which means I don't have the ability to reach into someone else's mind, not like that. But my shielding ability has been . . . evolving."

"Fancy that," Quentin murmured.

DeMarco ignored him. "Several times in recent weeks, I've been able to project a kind of shield, a barrier, between Samuel and his target. It's not much more than a dampening field, but I believe it has had some protective effect. I have to know who his target is, and I have to have some time to prepare. And to even attempt it, I always make sure I'm alone and likely to be undisturbed, because every time I try, I take the chance of being discovered."

Tessa was pale. "How did you know I was his target this morning?"

"Because he knew you were coming."

"What?"

"Before Ruth got back to the Compound, he knew you were coming. He told me you'd ask to look around by yourself and that it was to be allowed." DeMarco's smile was hardly worthy of the name. "He does that sort of thing sometimes, casually with one or another of us, as though reminding us of his . . . divine powers."

"Well," Quentin said in a practical tone, "if he really has had some kind of vision of his apocalypse, an actual prophecy, then it's a given he's a functional precog. And, I'm guessing, an exceptionally powerful one. Which means it could very well be all but impossible to catch him by surprise."

Galen said matter-of-factly, "We may not be able to sneak up on him, but we can surprise him. I can shut down his entire security net with the push of one button."

DeMarco looked over at him. "I saw you, by the way. Last night. You're slipping."

"Bullshit. You just sensed me because you can do that—and because my shield happens to be tuned to your frequency."

"That sounds vaguely—" Sawyer decided not to finish that sentence. Even in his mind.

"Maybe it's an odd frequency," Hollis said almost absently, "because you have one of the strangest auras I've ever seen. It's almost pure white."

Polite, DeMarco said, "And why are you wasting energy trying to see auras right now?"

"I wasn't trying to—until Tessa's got my attention. Tessa, what're you doing? Because your aura's gone all strange."

"Strange how?" Sawyer asked, wondering what it would be like to see people bathed in various colors of light.

"Sparkly. Like she's expending an unusual amount of energy. Tessa?"

"Just a little experiment," Tessa said. She drew a breath and let it out slowly, as though relieving some strain, then looked at the serious faces around the table. "Aside from Sawyer and Hollis, do any of the rest of you see anything unusual about me?"

DeMarco said, "Only if you mean the dog. And I didn't see that until the chief thought about it."

"Still creepy," Sawyer told him.

"Sorry. You were thinking loudly."

Sawyer wasn't quite sure how to deny that, so he didn't try.

Bishop frowned at Sawyer for a moment, then looked at Tessa. He went utterly still, his eyes narrowing. Then, softly, he said, "I'll be damned."

"Huh," Quentin said. "Maybe we do have a plan. Or at least a better start to one."

Seventeen

AMY LET OUT a long, guttural moan and began to sway. Before she could topple over, Father smoothly took her candle and Ruth appeared out of nowhere to catch her. Held in the older woman's arms, Amy continued to jerk and moan for seconds longer. Her face was flushed, her slack mouth wore a blissful smile, and she ran her shaking hands down over her body from breasts to thighs in a gesture so sensual it made Ruby's stomach lurch sickly.

Still chanting, Father placed Amy's candle in the tall copper holder closest to her circle. And while he did that, Ruth was silently arranging Amy's limp body on the floor—faceup, her head on the little velvet pillow and her arms spread wide, feet together and just touching the base of the copper stand holding her candle.

Amy's lips began to move as she resumed chanting.

Theresa was next, and though Ruby tried not to watch it all happen again, she was unable to look away. Her heart was thudding as if she'd been running and running, and her mouth was so dry it was difficult to keep chanting, and she was desperately afraid that her shell was not going to be enough to protect her this time.

When Father was done with Theresa, Ruth laid her out on the floor in the same way, arms wide, toes touching the candle holder, and Theresa also resumed the chant, her voice languid.

Always before, Father had come to Ruby next, but this time he went to Mara instead. And her experience was visibly different from that of the other girls. Father took more time with her, and it seemed to Ruby that Mara was slower to respond to...whatever it was he was doing to her. Maybe because she was only eleven and this was her first time.

Ruby and Brooke had talked about their first times, and both agreed that it was weird and scary—and not at all pleasant. Their skin tingled, their scalps crawled, and it was difficult to breathe. But both of them had shells, and they hadn't been at all sure what a first time was supposed to feel like.

They had simply copied what the other girls did, how they behaved, and they pretended to enjoy their Becoming. Father had seemed satisfied by that.

But Ruby was alone now, the only one of the girls with a protective shell, and she wasn't at all sure it was going to protect her this time.

All she did know was that she was next.

She was last.

And when Father turned toward her finally, there

was something in his face she had never seen before, an odd smile, a curious light in his eyes.

Then she saw something in his true face, in that mask over the dark and hungry thing she had seen earlier, that thing she felt sure could swallow the world.

It was knowledge, awareness.

He knows.

"Ruby," he said softly. "You've been naughty, my child. I'm afraid you must be punished." And he stepped around behind her.

"I think the so-called plan stinks," Sawyer said.

Hollis looked at him with slightly lifted brows, then glanced at Tessa. "You know, I think I'll take my laptop up to my room. Check in at the office. Do a few other things to kill a little time. Or maybe I'll take a nap, because it's been a really long and eventful day."

"Don't go on my account," Sawyer called after her.

Tessa leaned back against the kitchen counter, waiting for the coffeemaker to finish its work, and said mildly, "We really don't have a lot of options, you know. When it comes to a plan."

Despite her seeming calm, he knew she was tense and on edge. He could feel it. Almost as if he had a hand on her. Which he very badly wanted. Even though he knew that, once again, his timing was, to say the least, off.

"We're assuming too much," Sawyer said, doing his best to keep his mind on business. And even as he forced himself to remember that, all the risks of what they were going to attempt flooded in and nearly stole his breath. *Christ, we're all out of our minds.* "For starters, we're assuming that the weird energy inside the Compound is going to affect *every* psychic's abilities."

"Because energy fields do affect us. And that one certainly affected me. It's affected DeMarco. And it affected you."

"I'm still not so sure about that."

"I'm sure. And so is Bishop."

"Yeah? And what makes you both so sure I can control it?"

"You're—what? Thirty-eight?"

"Thirty-six."

Tessa nodded. "And became an active psychic in your teens."

"I started shorting out electronics, is what I did."

"It's all about energy, Sawyer. You've spent about twenty years learning how to dampen down your own energy field. That can be a very valuable ability, especially when it's enhanced by what's going on in the Compound."

"Yeah, right. Assuming it works like that. Assuming I can do what I need to do at will. And there's no guarantee of either."

"No guarantee anywhere." Tessa shook her head. "But the one thing we're all agreed on is that we can't just wait around for Samuel to make his next move. Because someone is likely to die and because he's *not* likely to suddenly begin leaving evidence lying around for one of us to find.

"Besides, like Bishop said, the law can't touch him. The courts wouldn't know what to do with him. But we know how dangerous he is. We know he's either going to continue to get more powerful until he reaches some kind of critical mass—or he's going to explode trying to get there and kill an awful lot of people."

"So we have to destroy him. Yeah, I got that. Fairly ruthless, your Bishop."

"He isn't mine. And the thought of doing something like that...isn't an easy one for me. But in this case, I happen to agree with him. We have to make absolutely certain that Samuel can't hurt anybody ever again. With his mind, at least."

"Because he's dangerous. And because you're worried about Ruby."

"I'm worried about all of them. But, yes, Ruby especially." Tessa rummaged in the cabinets for coffee cups. "I hope she doesn't mind that I left Lexie up at the mountain house."

"Bishop was right; the farther she is from the Compound, the safer she's likely to be. Plus she's not being a drain on your shiny new ability to hide things." Sawyer paused, then added, "Interesting that she took right to Bishop."

"Yeah, Hollis says he has that effect on animals and kids. They trust him instantly. Says something good about his character."

"Or about his abilities." Sawyer shrugged when she

looked at him. "Well, it could be that, you know. Bishop's a telepath, so he could be . . . using a shortcut to win their trust."

"Cynic."

"Realist." He watched her pour coffee, then added wryly, "Though how I can call myself that after a day of talking about psychic abilities and—what's the plural of apocalypse?"

"I don't know. Apocalypses?"

Sawyer repeated the word aloud, trying it on for size, and accepted the cup she handed him. "Thanks. Apocalypses. Spending the day talking about psychic abilities and apocalypses, and I call myself a realist."

"That's the real situation. No sense in pretending otherwise."

"I guess. But it's still just so damn hard to believe. That Samuel could have killed so many over *years* without anyone noticing. And that he could kill them without even laying a finger on them. That's not supposed to be humanly possible."

"Maybe he's not human."

Sawyer eyed her. "Serious?"

Tessa sipped her coffee, then sighed. "No, not really. Whatever he is now, he's the human variety of monster. We do seem to turn them out from time to time."

"Yeah, but not many of them decide to be God Almighty. Literally."

"Well, not only am I *not* a profiler, I also have no intuitive feel for the minds of cult leaders or other monsters, so I really don't get the whole messiah complex.

First, why would anybody *want* to rule over the world? And, second, if that's what someone wanted, then why want to destroy the world over which one rules? I mean, what's the point of that?"

"Absolute power."

"I still don't get it."

Sawyer smiled at her faintly. "Probably just as well. That Nietzsche quote about hunting monsters and looking into the abyss is all too true. There are some dark places in the human mind, Tessa. Don't go there if you don't have to."

"Spoken from experience." It wasn't a question.

"An experience most every cop has." He shrugged. "The things people do to each other, often for the stupidest reasons, is more than enough to keep us up nights. Even in a small town like Grace, we get our fair share of lunatics and losers."

"So all this is . . . the extreme end of nightmare for you."

"Well, not all of it is."

The comment seemed to hang in the air between them, possibly flashing in neon. Sawyer could see that he had surprised Tessa, taken her off guard, and he swore at himself mentally.

Oh, yeah, idiot, a day spent talking about monsters and apocalypses is just a perfect day to cap off things with a totally awkward and uncalled-for hint that you're glad you spent the day with her.

The only positive aspect of his seemingly chronic foot-in-mouth disease where this woman was concerned was that he was now reasonably sure that the sarcastic voice in his head was entirely his own.

He finished his coffee so quickly that he burned his tongue, then set the cup on the kitchen counter, saying, "Hollis was right—it's been a long day. And no matter how tomorrow goes, I think we should all rest while we can get it."

"Yes. You're probably right."

She set her own cup aside and walked him to the front door, her slight frown worrying him until she said, "On second thought, maybe we should spend some of our time tonight practicing. Whose idea was it to do this tomorrow, instead of waiting a few days? Oh, right— mine."

Sawyer wanted to put his arms around her but fought off the impulse, determined not to make a second mistake on the heels of the first one. Instead, he said, "Well, you and the weather forecasters seem to be in agreement on this one. Get some rest, Tessa. I have to go see a friendly judge about some paperwork."

"See you tomorrow."

"Yeah."

Tessa closed the door behind him and leaned back against it.

"That," Hollis said from the stairs, "was mean."

"I thought you were going to take a nap."

"I changed my mind. Besides, it's so late now I might as well just wait for bedtime. And don't change the subject. Why didn't you throw the poor chief a crumb or two? In my book, he gets points for *not* being a practiced smooth talker."

"In my book too. But...wrong time and place. Maybe when all this is over and the dust settles..."

"Seize the day," Hollis advised. "When all this is over and the dust settles, there may be only a few of us left standing."

"Yeah," Tessa said. "That's what I'm afraid of."

"**S**ure you want to do this?" Galen asked.

Bishop looked up from the map he'd been studying to find both Galen and Quentin watching him. "I'm sure."

"We're banking on an awfully big maybe," Quentin pointed out. "A whole series of them, in fact. Maybe the weather will cooperate. Maybe our abilities will be affected in ways we can use—hell, just *control*—inside the Compound. Maybe Samuel won't figure out what we're up to until too late."

"My favorite maybe," Galen offered.

"It's a doozy," Quentin agreed.

Dryly, Bishop said, "If either of you has a better idea, now's the time."

The other two exchanged looks, then Galen shrugged. "I've got nothing."

"No," Quentin said. "Me either. Sadly."

"Then we go with what we've got."

Quentin sighed. "Reese hasn't been able to find evidence in that place in more than two years of trying, and he's good."

Galen muttered something under his breath.

Quentin ignored him, keeping his attention fixed on his boss. "If there was anything there to hang a warrant on, he would have found it. So even if your friendly federal judge agrees we have cause and signs a warrant, all that does is get us inside legally. And since we're trying to avoid Samuel's apocalyptic version of Waco, we go in low-key and casual."

"Wouldn't do any good to go in heavily armed anyway," Galen pointed out. "Not against Samuel."

"Which will probably reassure the judge, since he has no idea we're dealing with something a lot more dangerous than guns."

"Actually," Bishop said, "Judge Ryan knows all about psychics and how dangerous psychic abilities can be."

"Judge Ryan." Quentin stared at him. "Ben Ryan?"

"Ben Ryan. He was appointed a federal judge a year or so ago, and we're in his district."

"So how's Cassie?"

"Cassie's flourishing. And so are the girls."

"Ah," Galen said, making the connection. "Your cousin Cassie. Did she ever get her abilities back?"

"She's telepathic with Ben, but with no one else. Which suits both of them completely."

Quentin was thinking along different lines. "So Ben's out on this limb with you. I mean, if we leave that Compound without Samuel in custody and/or without enough evidence or enough willing witnesses to make a case against him, there's going to be egg on a lot of faces."

"Worth the risk," Bishop said briefly. "And Ben agreed with me."

"The Director could use any failure against you, Bishop. Especially something as potentially explosive as going after a religious leader, cult or no cult. It's exactly the kind of thing he's been waiting for."

"I know."

Looking at Galen, Quentin said, "But no pressure."

"We should be used to it by now. How many times have we gone into a high-stakes situation functionally blind?"

"A few. And yet we prevail. So far, at least." Quentin frowned. "But I sort of wish Hollis wasn't here. She's got more lives than a cat, granted, but she's used up most of them by now. And with Samuel's fear of mediums—"

"It's a weakness," Bishop said. "We use it against him if we have to."

"And how do we do that?" Quentin inquired politely.

"Hollis knows what to do."

"Yeah, and knowing that is fine and dandy *if* the energy in the Compound affects us the way we hope it will. But if it doesn't—if things go horribly wrong, as things so often do in the kind of confrontation we're setting up—then what? Hollis is standing in the open doorway between this world and the next—and one good shove the wrong way means we lose her."

"I know," Bishop said.

"My guess is that Samuel won't hesitate to shove. In fact, I'm guessing that'll be his knee-jerk response."

"I know," Bishop repeated.

"And then there's Tessa. Not only will she be going into that place alone, but the chances are damn good Samuel will know she's coming and have the time to conjure a nice little welcome for her."

Bishop didn't repeat his words, but merely waited.

Galen murmured, "Making your point the hard way."

"I don't know any other way to make it," Quentin told him.

Galen opened his mouth to comment, but the summons of his cell phone distracted him.

"That's another thing," Quentin said in a lowered tone as Galen took the call. "Cell reception down in the valley seriously sucks, and Sawyer said the police radios weren't much better. Especially now, with all the fluctuating energies trapped in that valley. The very energies we're hoping will enhance our abilities are going to make it tricky as hell for us to time this thing, especially when we aren't sure how much time Tessa will need to do her part."

"I have an idea about that," Bishop said.

Galen snapped his cell phone closed and said, "Huh."

The other two looked at him.

"Reports of my death," he said, "have apparently reached the Director."

"He's still in Paris," Bishop said slowly.

"Yeah. But my question is, how would that information have gotten to Washington, let alone Paris? Nobody here reported it. Aside from Reese, only two people witnessed me being shot and killed. Neither of them could have known I was FBI. And both are supposedly loyal members of Reverend Samuel's church."

Washington

It was nearly midnight when the phone rang, but Senator LeMott was still awake, propped up in bed, not reading.

He tossed the unread newspaper aside, pulled off his reading glasses, and answered the phone. "LeMott."

"I have a message for you, Senator. From down South." The voice was muffled, not even clearly identifiable as male or female.

"What's the message?"

"He found himself a friendly judge. A federal judge. The warrant was signed about an hour ago. They're going into the Compound late tomorrow morning."

"In force?"

"Not exactly."

LeMott listened to the muffled voice for another minute or two, then merely said, "Thank you." And hung up.

He sat there in bed for several more minutes, staring at the wood fire crackling in his bedroom's fireplace without seeing it. Then he reached into the drawer of his nightstand and pulled out a cell phone. He pressed one number and waited while the call went through. When it was answered on the other end, he spoke a single word, very clearly.

"Viper."

Then he closed the phone. Without hesitation, and with unerring aim, he threw it across the room and into the fire.

He wasted no time in pushing newspapers and covers aside so he could sit on the edge of the bed and use the phone on his nightstand for the second time that night. Again, his call was answered promptly.

"Yes, Senator?"

"Get the jet ready. I'm on my way."

"Yes, sir."

Senator Abe LeMott hung up the phone, then went into his dressing room, turning on lights as he went. He drew an already-packed bag from a shelf in one of his closets and set it near to hand.

It had been packed for quite a while.

He drew a deep breath and let it out slowly, flexing his shoulders as though shifting a burden.

Then he began getting dressed.

Eighteen

AT FIRST, Ruby wasn't even sure she was awake. It was pitch black, for one thing, the sort of darkness that was only possible in sleep. And the silence was curiously muffled, the way it was when thick snow lay on the ground and covered the trees.

And then there was the fact that she couldn't seem to move a muscle other than her eyelids.

"You've been naughty, my child. I'm afraid you must be punished."

With that memory came the pain that had followed his words, and Ruby felt hot tears leaking from the corners of her eyes. Pain, not pleasure, not any kind of pleasure, not even the pretend kind. It had felt as though a white-hot knife had jabbed at her head, again and again.

She had tried to keep her shell as hard as she could, had fought with everything inside her, and something told her now that it was only because of that struggle that she was still *her*.

But as hard as she'd fought, Father had managed to steal something from her, she understood that dimly. He had managed to steal some of her strength. Maybe most of her strength.

She thought that was why she couldn't move. Because it didn't feel like she was tied up or anything like that. It was just that her arms and legs felt incredibly heavy and a bit numb, as though they'd been asleep.

Ruby tried to call out for help, but only a bare whisper of air escaped her lips, and she had the sudden terrified notion that he had stolen her voice when he took her strength. He had stolen her voice and left her here—

Where?

Was she still in the Ritual Room?

She had no sense of space above her or around her. In fact, she could have been in a coffin for all she knew.

Another terrifying possibility.

She squeezed her eyes shut, hoping it would be better that way, but the blackness and the panic and terror were the same. She had no idea how much time had passed, how much time was passing. She had no idea whether this—surely part of Father's punishment—was temporary or whether she would just disappear, as so many others had disappeared.

Her mother was gone. Her father. Brooke. She had even sent Lexie away.

Ruby had never felt so alone in her life.

The only taxi Grace could boast pulled up to the gates of the Compound, and Tessa rolled down her window to speak to Carl Fisk.

"Good morning, Mrs. Gray." He was, as always, polite.

"Mr. Fisk. I called ahead and talked to Mr. DeMarco; I came to get my car. And to see Ruth, if possible."

"He said you were expected, Mrs. Gray. Joe, you might want to check with DeMarco after you let Mrs. Gray out; he said something about a couple of the women wanting to go into town this morning."

"Okay, I'll check with him. See you, Carl." The middle-aged driver was also polite, but disinterested enough that Tessa had concluded he probably wasn't a church member. Probably.

As the taxi passed through the gates, Tessa concentrated on shoring up her shields. Even just barely into the Compound, she could feel the skin-tingling effects of the odd energy fields. She thought it was stronger than it had been the day before and wondered if it was caused by the approaching storm system that had surprised the local weather people—or by something else.

DeMarco met the taxi at his accustomed spot in the Square; beside him, two of the young wives of the church waited, scrubbed and smiling and curiously indistinguishable from each other.

Tessa paid her driver and got out of the taxi, and the two young women got in. She stood beside DeMarco and watched the car pull away.

"Friday shopping?" she asked him quietly.

"They were discussing whether to go tomorrow. Since the taxi was bringing you, I suggested they go today." His voice was just as quiet as hers.

"So there's two away safe."

"I hope so."

"What about the others?"

"Usual routine. Most of the children will be at their lessons, in their homes. Well out of the way, at least initially. There are probably less than a dozen people inside the church, most of them in the recreation area or upstairs in the office space."

"Where's Samuel?"

"Meditating, as he does every day at this time. Tessa, you need to be very careful. There was something different about him this morning."

"Does he know I'm here?"

"I don't know. What I do know is that he held a Youth Ritual yesterday while I was gone."

"Is that—"

"Call it an initiation, in stages. As the girls reach puberty, he begins to lead them through a series of Ceremonies supposedly intended to purify their path to womanhood."

Tessa felt queasy. "He begins stimulating them?"

"So I gather. The Ceremonies for his Chosen ones are attended only by Samuel, Ruth, and the girls—four each time. But I've seen the afterglow."

"Christ."

Calmly, DeMarco said, "For that alone he deserves to

burn in hell. But something unusual happened yesterday, or at least I think it did. This group is the one including Ruby."

"You never said she—"

DeMarco cut her off. "I wasn't about to tell you something that would only make you more determined to rescue her as soon as possible. And I had no reason to suppose this Ceremony would be any different from the two or three Ruby has already endured."

Not nearly as calm, Tessa said, "So something was different this time?"

"I haven't seen Ruby this morning. Or one of the other girls who was in her group. Brooke."

"Would you, normally?"

"A communal breakfast, with prayers, in the church's dining hall. Not everyone attends, but many do. Ruby's mother was there, smiling. But no Ruby. And no Brooke. I gather the group has a new girl, Mara, but no explanation was offered as to why she apparently replaced Brooke or what happened to Brooke or to Ruby."

Tessa had a horrible feeling in the pit of her stomach. "You think he hurt them this time?"

"Brooke's gone," he said simply.

"What?"

"I knew it as soon as I saw Samuel this morning. I could feel it in him, that particular energy. He destroyed Brooke."

Tessa swallowed hard. "And Ruby?"

"I don't think so. You still feel the connection, don't you?"

She didn't have to think about that. "Yes."

"Then she's still alive. But I have no idea where she is."

"I have to find her."

"I know. And I can't help you, except by making sure the chief's distraction is felt all through the Compound." DeMarco checked his watch. "We have about half an hour. The cameras are already cutting in and out, but they always do when a storm's on the way, so no alarm."

"And no watching eyes?"

"Give me five minutes to get to the control room and take care of that."

"What about Ruth?"

"She was busy. I didn't want to disturb her. Be careful, Tessa." DeMarco turned and went into the church.

Tessa glanced up at the clouds thickening in the sky, drew a shaky breath of the cold morning air, and slid her hands in the pockets of her lightweight jacket. She tried to open herself just enough to get a sense of the place but not enough to be vulnerable—and immediately felt once again the skin-tingling sensation of energy.

It was almost automatic to instantly retreat, to shore up her shields. To protect herself.

But her determination to do her part today, coupled with her growing worry for Ruby, overrode that impulse for self-preservation. Or just made Tessa more stubborn; she wasn't sure which.

She kept that door in her mind open just a little bit. And listened with every sense she had.

Tessa began to wander around the church grounds,

taking the long way to her car as she kept that narrow opening in her shields and tried to probe through it.

"Come on, Ruby," she murmured, "where are you? You've reached me before. Reach me now...."

She walked slowly and probed as cautiously as she could, sensing people inside the church, inside the neat little houses, all of them with the eerie sameness that had struck her from her first visit.

All the scrubbed and nice people—

Help me! Please help me...

Ruby.

"I just think you could have mentioned it, Chief, that's all," Robin Keever said somewhat stiffly.

Sawyer closed the Jeep's hatch and faced her, sighing. "Robin, I've already explained that I didn't *know* feds were in the area until yesterday. Literally, yesterday. And I told you about it last night when I got back to the station and found you still hanging around."

"I was off the clock," she muttered.

"That's not the point. The point is that I told you about the feds as soon as I could."

Her gaze slid past him to the Jeep and, still obviously disgruntled, she began, "Well, I just—"

"So," he cut her off, "do you want to play or take your marbles and go home?"

She blinked at him, and a small smile worked at the corners of her mouth. "You mean be in on the operation?"

"Yeah. Such as it is." Before she could leap on the offer, he added sternly, "Listen to me. We don't want anybody up there in the Compound getting spooked. That means you keep your hand *away* from your weapon, you keep things casual, and you do exactly what I tell you to do. No more, no less. Got it?"

"Yes, Chief."

"The feds just want to have a quiet look around without making a big fuss about it." He hoped to hell he was as good a liar as DeMarco was. "So they go in as locals. I drive this Jeep, you drive yours, and we each have a couple of uniformed officers with us as we serve the warrant." He glanced up at the grayish sky as a rumble of thunder sounded in the distance. "Damn, the weather's moving in earlier than we expected."

"Do feds melt?"

He stared at her.

"Sorry. Sorry, Chief. Is the weather important?"

"You'd be surprised." He paused. "Really surprised. Robin, I need a familiar officer driving the other vehicle, somebody Fisk—or whoever's manning the gate—will recognize. But you are not to interfere in any way with the agents, understand?"

"Yeah, I get it." She was frowning now. "I'm not a rookie, and I won't do something stupid."

"I'm not worried about you doing something stupid," he said patiently. "I'm worried about you getting hurt. So stick close to the Jeep, and if anything...weird happens, you hit the deck and keep your head down until it's all over."

"Until what's all over? Chief, if you don't believe they have weapons stockpiled up there—"

"They don't."

"Then what am I hitting the deck to avoid?" Her voice was getting stiff again.

Sawyer didn't have a clue how to warn her, at least in part because he didn't know what to expect himself. Not that he could confess that, of course. "Just stick close to the Jeep," he repeated finally. "Let's go. We have to meet up with our temporary officers."

By the time Tessa circled the church, she was convinced that the faint whisper she'd heard twice more was coming from somewhere inside. She had met no one on her stroll, which didn't strike her as particularly odd— here—but she was wary of going inside.

Help me . . .

Not wary enough to ignore the plea, however.

Crossing her fingers that, between them, DeMarco and Galen had muddled up the security system enough so that she didn't have to worry about being watched, Tessa simply walked up the steps to the open front doors of the church and went inside.

She passed through the vestibule, stepping with more caution into the church proper. As far as she could tell, it was deserted. She walked slowly down the center aisle, looking around, trying to both reach out with her senses and keep herself protected.

Because, at the extreme edge of her awareness, she

could feel something...probing. Seeking a way in. And the sensation was the creepiest thing she had ever felt in her life.

It was Samuel, she was certain of it. It was him because that probing touch was cold and dark and lifeless. Soulless.

But hungry.

She drew a deep breath and closed her eyes briefly, fighting not to slam that door shut and curl up in a ball deep inside her own mind so he would never be able to find her—

Reese, interrupt his meditation now.

Tessa nearly jumped, that inner voice was so clear and strong. But it wasn't Ruby's voice; it was Bishop's. And it was virtual proof that the energy field here in the Compound *was* affecting all their abilities.

But it also left wide open the question of just how— and how much—they would be affected.

And how well they would be able to control those changes. Bishop, at least, appeared to be handling the change well, but as for the rest of them...

Tessa stood where she was, near the altar, and waited several moments until that probing touch at the edge of her awareness abruptly vanished.

Okay, Ruby—where are you, sweetie?

She heard no inner voice in response and felt a chill of anxiety. Had she waited too long?

Look for her in the water, Tessa.

Bishop again, reminding her of the instruction that had come from a spirit.

Tessa realized she was staring at the baptistery behind the pulpit. Like many she had seen, the room had a clear glass window overlooking the church so that baptisms could be witnessed by the congregation.

It struck her even before she reached the glass that the tank should have been drained, and yet it was filled. She dreaded looking inside—and was immeasurably relieved to find it filled only with water.

She slumped a little, but anxiety swiftly replaced relief. *Look for her in the water? If not here, then where?*

Tessa ...

Faint—but close. Very, very close.

Tessa stared at the baptistery for an instant and then began looking for the way back there.

Hurry, Tessa.

Not daring to think it, Tessa whispered, "I'm hurrying."

You don't understand. None of you really understands what he can do.

"Ruby—"

Hurry. We need Cody. Cody can help us.

Tessa didn't have a clue who Cody was, but she hurried—and found, at last, the door she'd been seeking.

"**I**t's a legal warrant," Sawyer told Fisk at the gate. "Signed by a judge last night. After we obtained positive identification that the woman's body found in the river Wednesday morning is that of Sarah Warren. One of your members, and last seen here at the Compound."

Fisk grimaced slightly as he returned the document

to Sawyer, but the only thing he said was "Mr. DeMarco will be waiting for you at the Square, Chief."

Sawyer drove through the open gates, keeping an eye to the rearview mirror until the Jeep driven by Robin had also cleared the gates. Good; Fisk hadn't recognized Galen. They'd been fairly sure he wouldn't—but only fairly sure. Sawyer didn't relax even then and heard the tension in his own voice when he said, "The gates aren't closing. I take that to mean the security system is down?"

"Should be, by now. Knowing Galen."

"Admittedly I don't know much about this stuff— but aren't you taking a hell of a risk?"

From her position in the backseat on the passenger side, Hollis said, "Yes. He is."

"So are you," Bishop pointed out, beside her.

"He doesn't want *my* ability," she retorted.

"No. He just wants to kill you."

"Then let's hope Quentin is right and I still have a life or two left to risk."

Sawyer muttered, "You two are really boosting my confidence here."

"Sorry," Bishop said, not sounding it.

Hollis said, "Don't worry, our makeshift shield is holding. More or less."

"It's the less that's making me nervous," Sawyer told her.

"We'll hope we can shore it up a bit as time passes."

"There isn't all that much time left."

Bishop said, "We're working on it, Chief. It's . . . a bit

difficult for us." There was a rare strain in his voice. "We've never before been able to build on or share one another's abilities."

"*Now* you're telling me this?"

"It was a chance we had to take."

"That we could share," Hollis explained. "And damn if it isn't working. So far, anyway. The communication thing is amazingly clear; even I can hear it. Faintly. But I've gotta tell you—everybody's aura is beginning to look a bit metallic. There's a hell of a lot of energy here."

Sawyer checked the clock on the dash and said, "And more coming. I just want to make damn sure we get to the Square before Samuel decides to have one of his outdoor sermons as the storm approaches. I don't want him anywhere near that so-called natural church, not considering Quentin's vision." Even at second hand, "remembering" that vision was enough to make Sawyer's entire being flinch. Smoldering bodies, Tessa and Hollis crucified and worse. Himself crucified. No. No, they were not going to allow that to happen.

He was sure they weren't.

They made it, the Jeeps pulling into the Square just as Samuel came out of the church, with DeMarco at his side.

"Hang back," Sawyer advised Bishop quickly. "I don't think either one of us wants to put your makeshift shield to the test until we absolutely have to."

"Amen," Hollis murmured.

Sawyer got out of the Jeep and walked quickly to meet Samuel and DeMarco, reminding himself over and over again as he looked at the *reverend* that he couldn't even begin thinking about the things this benign-looking man had done. He had to stick to the plan, no matter how much he wanted to pull out his gun and—

"Reverend Samuel. DeMarco."

Pleasantly, Samuel replied, "I understand you have a federal warrant, Chief. Needless to say, we'll cooperate fully. I was most saddened and deeply disturbed to hear of Sarah's death. She was a wonderful young woman."

Sawyer had to get a grip on himself before he could respond as calmly as he needed to. "I appreciate your co-operation, Reverend." He handed over the warrant, which Samuel no more than glanced at before passing it on to DeMarco.

DeMarco, Sawyer saw, was more stony-faced than usual but otherwise seemed the same, the habitual faint smile meaningless.

"Just tell us what you need," Samuel said smoothly.

Sawyer looked back over his shoulder, relieved to see that Robin was standing by the driver's door of her Jeep, as instructed, the bulk of the vehicle between her and . . . whatever might happen here near the steps of the church. Her face was, finally, inscrutable.

And about damn time too.

Quentin was leaning negligently against the passenger door, looking quite unlike himself in the uniform, hat—and mirrored sunglasses that Sawyer had always disliked seeing on his officers. And, beyond him, Galen had taken a couple of steps away from the Jeep and was looking around with apparent idleness.

Bishop had his back to the group near the church steps; he and Hollis, both hatless and without sunglasses but otherwise dressed as Grace police officers, appeared to be talking casually, with Hollis turned just enough so that no one on the steps could see her face.

It was a very relaxed scene, as intended. And the few church members who had noticed something going on and come to see what it was appeared merely curious and rather wary but not upset.

Good. Good. Everything low-key and casual. And leisurely. Because they had to have time for everyone to get in position. That was the tricky part. The timing.

Almost ready.

Thunder rumbled.

Stall. Tessa's voice, faint but clear. *I need just a few more minutes.*

Sawyer felt a jab of cold panic.

"We'd like to take a look around," he said to Reverend Samuel, hoping to hell he sounded calmer than he felt. "Talk to your people. We need to know who last saw Sarah. We need to find out if anyone has any information they may not realize is important." Deliberately, he added, "You know the drill. We've been through this before, Reverend."

"We have nothing to hide, Chief, I do assure you." Samuel glanced up at the lowering sky, adding mildly, "Though we might, perhaps, be well advised to take this discussion indoors."

Either he was another superb liar or else he really didn't sense a threat. Which meant that DeMarco's dampening field—and possibly Sawyer's—was having the desired effect. But Sawyer's feeling of triumph was cut short when they all heard another vehicle coming up the neat graveled drive. He turned without even thinking about it, staring at the gleaming black sedan as it pulled up near the police Jeeps.

Jesus, not now. Who the hell...?

A chauffeur who looked like a cross between a navy SEAL and a retired heavyweight boxer slid from the driver's seat and, expressionless, opened the car's back door.

Senator Abe LeMott stepped out.

Nineteen

*O*H, SHIT. *Definitely not part of the plan.*

Sawyer had certainly never met the senator, but he recognized him instantly; LeMott's face had been all over the news the previous summer. His face, and his wife's—until she had committed suicide not long after the savage murder of their daughter, Annie.

A murder investigated by a task force led by Bishop. A murder that had been, tragically, only one of many during that hot Boston summer. Her murderer had escaped the city but had not, in the end, escaped the determined efforts of Bishop, the SCU, and Haven operatives.

Not that all that had made it into media reports, but certainly the capture of a vicious serial killer had been reported. And there was plenty of evidence that he was, indeed, the Boston serial. Some of that evidence had been leaked to the media, and few had any doubt at all of his guilt.

So what was Senator Abe LeMott doing here—now?

Before Sawyer could ask that baffling question, Galen said roughly, "LeMott, you should not be here."

The senator looked at him with mild curiosity, glanced at a silent Bishop, then fixed his gaze on Samuel.

"I wanted to meet you," he said, his voice both courteous and cold. "To look into your eyes. Before you're destroyed, I want to know what kind of man could so easily kill."

Samuel smiled. "I don't know what you're talking about, Senator. I'm a man of God."

"You're a monster. Worse than that creature you kept on a leash while he killed for you. Man of God?" LeMott drew a breath and released it in a sound of unutterable disgust. "God won't have you, Samuel. Hell won't have you."

"Senator, you have my deepest sympathy. The loss of your daughter and your wife must be almost beyond bearing."

LeMott's face hardened.

Oh, Christ. He's going to do something. Sawyer didn't know what, but he was very much afraid that what was left of their careful plan was about to be scattered to hell and gone.

"Samuel, I don't believe you have an ounce of sympathy in what passes for your soul. In fact, I don't believe you have a soul. I'd feel more reluctance to put a mad dog out of its misery than I feel in ridding the world of you."

"Senator." His smile widened as Samuel shook his head. "Did you really believe it would be so easy?"

He lifted one hand in a quick, practiced gesture.

With shocking suddenness, the chauffeur who had stood so still and silent near LeMott was lifted off his feet as though an invisible rope were attached to his body. He literally flew backward for yards, until he slammed into a parked car with so much force the hood of the vehicle was nearly bisected. The chauffeur stiffened for only an instant and then slumped, his hand slipping out of the lapel of his jacket, the gun he held falling to the ground.

Beneath the crumpled hood of the car, blood trickled onto pristine gravel.

"God's punishment for the wicked," Samuel said.

Of all the people in the Square, LeMott appeared least surprised. The senator turned his head to look toward the dead man, then his gaze returned to Samuel's face.

"Freeze!"

Sawyer nearly jumped out of his skin, and even as he absorbed the ridiculous command, he knew he had made a horrible mistake in bringing Robin along on this "operation."

"Robin," he said, "don't—"

She didn't fly backward as the chauffeur did. But her weapon clattered against the hood of the Jeep, she let out a strangled cry that chilled Sawyer to the bone, and then she went down.

By the time he got to her, she was already gone, her face contorted in agony and wide eyes going white.

He rose slowly to his feet, numbly aware of the frozen tableau around him. So fast. It had all happened so damn fast.

Sawyer. It isn't over. And he'll go on killing unless we stop him now. Here.

"Poor thing," Samuel said, his voice as smooth and pleasant as always. "Poor little thing. I wonder what she did to earn God's wrath. Can you tell me, Chief?"

His eyes were beginning to glow.

"No." Sawyer took a step toward the church. Then another. Thunder rumbled, louder now. The storm was closer. He stared at Samuel. "I can't tell you that. She was a good officer. She was a good person." The choked sound of his own voice was hardly professional, and he didn't give a shit.

"Such a shame. You have my sympathy."

Sawyer glanced at LeMott, understanding in that moment the other man's icy rage. The senator was motionless, expressionless.

Thunder rumbled again, and a chilly breeze sprang up. A flash of lightning crackled across the dark, heavy clouds.

Almost time, Sawyer. We're almost ready.

Samuel tilted his head to one side suddenly, an alertness stealing over his benign features. "Someone's talking," he remarked softly.

It wasn't time for Samuel to become aware of what was happening. Sawyer knew it, knew they weren't yet ready, knew Tessa wasn't ready.

Their plan was in tatters, and all he could think to do was draw his weapon and—

Sawyer began to feel a prickling sensation crawling over him, from his scalp down his neck, spreading outward from his spine. And to his shock he realized that he couldn't move. It was as if his body no longer recognized the direction of his brain.

"I don't think so, Sawyer." Samuel was smiling at him, a little sadly. "I really did hope you'd know who your friends were when the time came. I told you so, remember? I'm sorry you made a different choice, truly I am."

His hand began to lift, and Sawyer watched it with the cold realization that he was going to die. The tingling sensation disappeared, replaced by a slow constriction that sent fiery pain all along his nerve endings.

"Don't," a woman's voice said.

Samuel paused, his expression at first a sort of amused indifference. But then he turned his head and saw Hollis.

"I really wouldn't," she said.

Sawyer realized he could breathe again, that the pain had diminished—though not disappeared—as Samuel's attention shifted to the woman who had taken a couple of steps away from the Jeep to face him.

Samuel's hand began to swing toward her, something flickering in his glowing eyes.

"I've opened a door," Hollis said.

Samuel froze, his eyes still flickering.

Not part of the plan, this isn't part of the plan.... Sawyer realized he could turn his head just far enough to see Hollis, and even with everything that had happened, he was astonished to see an odd sort of radiance around her.

Her aura. Somehow, she had made it visible.

"A door," she said to Samuel, her expression intent, eyes narrowed. "Between our world—and the next."

Thunder rumbled and lightning laced the darkening sky.

"Hollis," Galen breathed, "be careful."

She never took her eyes off Samuel. "I'm in the doorway," she told him. "Holding them back. Holding back the one thing you know damn well won't be denied to you in that world. Punishment."

Samuel studied her for a moment, his expression first wary and then certain. "I don't believe you," he said, and moved his hand.

Hollis jerked as though from a powerful blow, her aura beginning to shift from a metallic blue to a darker blue shot through with red threads. A thin line of blood trickled from her nose. "I'll let them through," she warned him, the words emerging almost in a cough. It was obvious she was in pain. A lot of pain.

"No." Samuel shook his head. "You won't."

His hand lifted, clenching into a fist.

She didn't fly backward as the chauffeur had done, but Hollis jerked again. Her aura vanished with a loud crackle that rivaled the lightning, and she was slammed backward to the ground.

And lay motionless.

Oh, Christ . . . this wasn't supposed to happen . . .

"Someone's talking," Samuel repeated, turning his attention from the fallen medium as though he had brushed away a bothersome insect. "Bishop, is that you? Have I finally lured you to me?"

Bishop faced him, wearing a tight, grim smile—and on his very dangerous face it wasn't a pleasant expression. "I thought it was time we finally met. We came so close last time, but you didn't stick around for the grand finale."

Move.

Sawyer realized suddenly that he could move, that he could take a step away. He wasn't sure in that moment whether Samuel had released him or someone stronger had pulled him loose, but either way he was able to move to the side and allow the two combatants room.

Doing the only thing he could do for Robin now, for Hollis, for all those Samuel had murdered, he focused his cold rage on his part of what was left of their plan, concentrating on directing all the energy he could muster to help contain Samuel's building energies.

It was like trying to catch lightning in a box.

The real thing crackled across the sky again, and the prickling, uncomfortable sensation of electricity filled the chilly, heavy air.

"I had to be somewhere else," Samuel said to Bishop, apparently unaffected and unworried. "I knew you'd understand."

"What I understood is that we managed to hurt you. Dani managed to hurt you."

"Yes, well. Dani isn't here."

Again, Bishop smiled. "Wrong. She is here."

Samuel's smile faltered for the first time, and his eyes began to dart around as he searched the faces of the dozens of people who had gathered nearby in the Square. Puzzled, curious faces, the only oddity about them the fact that they seemed unaffected by the brutal murders committed before their very eyes.

And all familiar faces. Faces Samuel knew well.

"You're lying, Bishop. Not that I give a damn." His hand raised abruptly, palm out, and Bishop was lifted off his feet and slammed back against the Jeep with an incredible force that shattered glass and crunched metal. He hung there, suspended, the vehicle almost wrapped around him as if it had run full speed into an immovable object.

Just like the chauffeur.

For a moment, Bishop's body seemed stiff, but then, abruptly, it went limp. Blood trickled down to stain the gravel.

"I'm almost disappointed," Samuel said, sounding it. "I expected more of a fight."

"Then you'll get one," Tessa said.

Samuel's head turned quickly, and he frowned as he saw her standing only a few feet away to his right. Standing in front of her, pressing against her, was Ruby.

His hand lifted again, but this time a literal shower of sparks cascaded out from Tessa and Ruby, the residue of the deflected energy.

"Try again," she invited.

He did, his frown deepening, his face twisting with

effort as this time he lifted a hand straight up—and caught the lightning.

He became a living conduit. A crackling bolt speared his upraised hand and shot out from the hand extended toward Tessa and Ruby. It lasted only seconds.

And again, astonishingly, the force he directed at them was deflected, sparks and threads of energy hissing off in all directions.

"It's amazing what you can hide, especially in a place like this," Tessa said conversationally. No strain at all showed in her face or in her voice. "Like Ruby, under the baptistery. Left there to die, slowly, among the trophies you kept. I guess at the end of the day, a serial killer is just . . . a serial killer. For all your fine talk of doing God's work, in the end you're no more than a butcher."

He let out a sound so primitive it could only have come from an animal and, with both hands, sent a white-hot stream of pure energy to strike them.

This time, it was deflected—and returned to the source, slamming him back against the stone column at the foot of the steps. He hung on, panting a little, his face pale, furious eyes narrowed.

"It's amazing what you can hide," Tessa said again.

Samuel's head snapped around, because her voice came from his left now. And there she was, with Ruby as before. With Ruby and a dark, solemn-eyed boy. Cody.

"If you only know how," Ruby said gravely. "We know how, Tessa and me. And Cody knows how to help us. Cody has a lot of power, but he hid it from you. Until now."

Samuel, for the first time genuinely baffled and shaken, looked to his right again. Where Tessa and Ruby had stood seconds before, Dani Justice stood now.

"Hi," she said. "Remember me? You took away somebody I loved a lot. And you can't get away with that. You don't get to hole up here, growing stronger and stronger by feeding off people. By killing people. You don't get to be God. Not today."

Her hands were at her sides, and as they slowly lifted she appeared to be inside a bubble of shifting, sparking energies. Her energies. Sawyer's. DeMarco's. Tessa's. Ruby's. Cody's. And more.

Much, much more.

Lightning crackled in the sky above her. Then bolts of it struck her aura of energy, intensifying it in a wild explosion of sheer, raw power.

"Not today," she repeated, and thrust her hands forward.

The sound was like an explosion. Was an explosion. A literal wave of incandescent energy surged forward from Dani and struck Samuel with the same kind of force he had used against Bishop—times ten.

The stone column crumbled to shards and dust, and he lay among the shattered remnants. He wasn't dead, but his face was twisted with agony, blood trickled from his nose and mouth, and when he tried to lift his hands in another attack, it was clear he had nothing left. Not even sparks.

His hands trembled, then fell.

"Father!" Bambi stumbled from the small group of church members standing nearest the steps and knelt among the broken remnants of the stone column, cradling his head. "Father..."

Looking down at Samuel, DeMarco said calmly, "I can read him now. It. There won't be another attack. Not today, at least. Maybe not ever." He shifted his gaze to Dani. "Nice shot."

"Thank you." She sagged, a little pale but composed. "I'd been saving that up for a while. And I had a lot of help."

A tall, whipcord-lean man emerged from another small knot of people and folded her in his arms. "Jesus, I wish you'd stop doing this to me," Marc Purcell told her.

"Hey, you hitched your wagon. Your choice. Don't blame me for the consequences."

"Yeah, yeah." He kissed her.

Even though all three were smiling at him, Sawyer made sure Tessa and Ruby and the boy were okay before turning quickly to start toward the ruined Jeep.

"Bishop..."

To his astonishment, Bishop, unhurt, was hurrying toward the crumpled vehicle that still held a man in its deadly grip.

"Galen, are you all right?" he asked, reaching his team member.

"Of course I'm not all right. I don't know why you all think this dying shit is painless. Just because I can heal myself does *not* mean it's a day at the park. Goddammit, somebody get a crowbar or something and get me out of here."

"It's amazing what you can hide," Tessa said. "What you can change. If you only know how."

Indignant, Sawyer said, "But why'd you hide that from me?"

"The same reason...they hid it from me. I broadcast...and Samuel was...reading you. Either one...of us...would have...given away...the plan." The thin voice caused all of them to jerk around, but Bishop was the first one to reach Hollis's side.

"Hey, boss," she said, her voice still weak. She was lying as she'd gone down, motionless. But her eyes were open—and were their normal blue color, if a bit darker than usual.

"Christ, Hollis," Bishop muttered.

"Another...fun new toy...for me." She winced and closed her eyes. "Sorry...busy now..."

All Sawyer could think to say was "What the hell?"

Resting on one knee beside his team member, Bishop explained, "Some mediums are healers." The relief in his voice was obvious. "The energies here must have triggered it in Hollis."

"Good thing...too," she murmured.

"Will she be okay?" Sawyer asked.

"I think so." Bishop put a hand on her shoulder for a moment and then rose to his feet. Leaving Quentin to work on extricating Galen from the Jeep's unloving embrace, he turned to face LeMott. Both men were expressionless, but the whitened scar on Bishop's cheek was as good as a neon sign.

"Senator, two people died today, and neither one of them had to. What the *hell* did you think you were doing?"

"I'm sorry for them," LeMott said, his tone flat. "Especially Officer Keever. She was only supposed to relay information, you know."

Sawyer took a step toward him, conscious once again of rage. "Information? You were paying Robin to spy for you?"

"She had dreams of leaving this small-town life." LeMott shrugged. "Dreams cost money. And I convinced her it was her chance to help you, Chief. To put Samuel away, once and for all. So she called me last night. To tell me what would happen here today."

"You son of a bitch," Sawyer snarled.

Bishop said, "I'm sorry, Sawyer. We were all but certain that he had eyes inside your department. We just didn't know who it was."

Sawyer turned his head to look toward Robin's lifeless body, then felt a hand slip into his. Tessa.

"I'm sorry," she said quietly, her other hand still holding Ruby close to her side. "We knew he'd go after Bishop and after me once he saw me with Ruby, but we didn't think he'd see anybody else as a threat. So we weren't protecting her. I'm so sorry."

"Yeah." His fingers tightened on hers. "So am I. You . . . said something about trophies?"

"He kept them in a space underneath the baptistery," she said. "Where he left Ruby."

"Awful things," the little girl with eyes that were old now said gravely. "Locks of hair, bits of clothes and stuff."

"DNA," Bishop said. "With that, we can nail him."

Senator Abe LeMott laughed. "You mean put him in prison? Allow him to live?"

"Justice," Bishop said.

"You were willing to destroy him."

"Yes," Bishop admitted evenly. "I was. And if in destroying his abilities we had killed him, I wouldn't have lost a night's sleep. But this way is the right way. His abilities are gone and he'll live the rest of his life in a cage. That's good enough for me."

"But not for me." LeMott turned his head to look at the broken remnants of the man who had been Adam Deacon Samuel and said simply, "Viper."

Still cradling Samuel's head against her, Bambi used her free hand and drew from underneath her long, prim skirt a gleaming knife. Without a moment's hesitation, she plunged it to the hilt in his chest.

Gazing steadily into his infinitely surprised eyes, her own icy, she said, "Say hello to Lucifer for me. And tell him a whore never forgets how to fake it. You should know that. Right, Sammy?"

Samuel died without making a sound, his life taken by a woman very much like the one who had given it.

Bambi pushed herself away from his body. She left him lying there in the rubble as she got to her feet, saying calmly to Sawyer, "It was self-defense, you know. Any jury will believe that."

"I'll make sure they do," LeMott said. He looked at Bishop. "I was afraid that, in the end, you wouldn't be quite as ruthless as you're often painted, Bishop. So I had a backup plan."

Epilogue

TESSA EASED Sawyer's office door closed and joined the others in the conference room of the police station. "Ruby's asleep. Worn out."

Hollis shifted in her chair to look at a clock high on the wall, murmuring, "God, it's only a little after five. This day's gone on for a lifetime." She was pale and obviously still in pain, but just as obviously well on her way to completely healing the damage Samuel had inflicted.

"On the plus side," Quentin pointed out, "you emerged with a fun new ability. Thank God. Be honest— did you know about it when you decided to face off with Samuel?"

"Wish I could say yes. It would have saved me a lot of being, you know, scared half out of my mind. But, no. When I hit the ground, I thought I was dead. I didn't even know what I was doing, until I actually started to feel bones knit." She paused and frowned. "Which is a very creepy sort of feeling, I have to say."

"Creepy, maybe. But useful in our line of work." It was Quentin's turn to frown. "And maybe that explains all your near-death experiences so far."

"Probably," Bishop said. "Medium–healers tend to have an incredibly strong will to survive."

Quentin said, "I think it was the medium part that tipped the balance. It shook Samuel just enough to give Tessa and Dani the time they needed to get into position. Nice going," he added to Hollis.

With a grimace, she said, "Yeah, well, he called my bluff."

"You were bluffing?"

A soft laugh escaped her. "Had to. Either all the energies out there weren't enhancing my abilities for once, or the spirits decided to stay out of it. Either way, I was sooo bluffing. Hard as I tried, I could *not* open a door."

"Damn," Quentin said blankly. "I mean . . . *damn*, Hollis. Thank the universe for that new ability and the will to survive."

"Yeah. I really did."

Tessa shook her head wonderingly, then looked at Sawyer. "Speaking of the will to survive, what's going to happen to Ruby?"

"I don't know. Her mother and so many of the others seem . . . almost catatonic now. I wonder if, in the end, Samuel will have as many living victims as dead ones."

"Bailey will do what she can up there," Bishop said. "The guardians in the SCU are, among other things, psychologists or counselors. And we have others on the team who can help."

"Can they?" Tessa asked steadily.

"Some. I don't know how much, to be honest. Samuel was . . . a wholly destructive force."

"Will he destroy Bambi?"

It was Sawyer who answered, with a faint grimace. "If Senator LeMott buys her the best defense money *can* buy, I doubt she'll spend a day in prison. The bastard was abusive, and most of his followers look and sound dazed at best and brainwashed at worst. Hell, I didn't want to have to put her in my jail. Even if I did see her kill him with my own eyes, I'd defend her in court."

"I think we all would," Bishop said. "Even Reese."

"How long will he stay at the Compound?" Hollis asked.

"Probably not long, if I know him. He'll make sure there's someone to run things up there, assuming the congregation wants to continue. He and Galen will make certain all the evidence Tessa found is collected. Not that we need it for a prosecution, but perhaps for Bambi's defense. And to tie up a few loose ends for us."

"You know," Quentin said, "we still have a few unanswered questions." He realized he was being stared at, and qualified, "Even more than usual, I mean. Like, who was Andrea, our spirit who told Hollis where Ruby could be found?"

"Why did Samuel have an obsession about buying up mostly worthless property?" Hollis added. "And did he *really* intend to destroy the world?"

Tessa joined in. "How was Bambi able to hide her

true intentions from Samuel? She didn't read as psychic, and her mind seemed to be an open book."

Bishop had an answer for that one. "It was because she wasn't psychic, ironically. He'll never admit it on the record, but Senator LeMott had her hypnotized, and planted very deeply and very carefully some post-hypnotic suggestions. That word he used out there today, 'viper'? That was the trigger, what activated the order to kill. Until that moment, even Bambi wasn't conscious of what she was going to do. Because she wasn't conscious of it, Samuel didn't read it."

Quentin said, "I thought a person couldn't be hyp-notized to do something as drastic as killing against their will."

"They can't, according to all the research." Bishop shrugged. "LeMott found himself someone entirely willing to kill. For a price."

"The female of the species," Quentin said, adding a hasty "Present company excepted, obviously."

Sawyer said, "Do my questions count? Because I've got a lot of 'em, beginning with why all my officers act like they're finally awake and ending with the signifi-cance of that medallion DeMarco said Sarah Warren had on her when she was killed."

"I can only answer the ones about Haven," Tessa told him. "And probably not all of those. But the medal-lion is something we all carry when we're on assign-ment."

"It's a start," the chief said with a sigh.

Slowly, Bishop said, "What I really want to know is, who told the Director that Galen was shot and killed?"

Abruptly serious, Quentin said, "Only three witnesses were there that night. We both know it wasn't Reese."

Bishop nodded. "Which leaves the two church members he was with—Carl Fisk and Brian Seymour."

"Funny thing," Quentin said. "Brian Seymour hasn't been seen since his last shift in the security control room late last night."

"So...was he working for the Director?" Sawyer wondered out loud. "Or for somebody else who wanted to keep an eye on the SCU? Just how many enemies do you have, Bishop?"

"At least one more than I need," Bishop answered. "And that's the one I'm going to have to find."

Read on for
a special preview of the
third thrilling novel in
Kay Hooper's Blood trilogy. . . .

BLOOD TIES

*Coming from Bantam
in Spring 2010*

NEW YORK TIMES BESTSELLING AUTHOR OF *BLOOD SINS*

KAY HOOPER

BLOOD TIES

A BISHOP/SPECIAL CRIMES UNIT NOVEL

BLOOD TIES

On Sale Spring 2010

PROLOGUE

Six months previously:
October

Listen.

"No."

Listen.

"I don't want to hear." She kept her eyes down, staring at her bare feet. Her toenails were painted pink. Only not here. Here, they were gray, like everything else.

Everything except the blood. The blood was always red.

She had forgotten that.

You have to listen to us.

"No, I don't. Not anymore."

We can help you.

"No one can help me. Not to do *that*, what you're asking me to do. It's impossible." At the edge of her vision, she saw the blood creeping toward her, and immediately took a step backward. Then another. "I can't go back now. I can never go back."

Yes. You can. You have to.

"I was at peace. Why didn't you leave me there?" She felt something solid and hard against her back and pressed herself against it, her gaze still on her toes, so much of her awareness on the blood inching ever closer.

Because it isn't finished.

"It was finished a long time ago."

Not for you. Not for her.

ONE

Case Edgerton ran along the narrow trail, aware of his burning legs but concentrating on his breathing. The last mile was always the hardest, especially on his weekly trail run. Easier to just zone out and run when he was on the track or in his neighborhood park; this kind of running, with its uneven terrain and various hazards, required real concentration.

That was why he liked it.

He jumped over a rotted fallen log, and almost immediately had to duck a low-hanging branch. After that, it was all downhill—which wasn't as easy as it sounded, since the trail snaked back and forth in hairpin curves all along the middle quarter of this last mile. Good training for his upcoming race. He planned to win that one, as he had won so many his entire senior year.

And then Kayla Vassey, who had a thing for runners and who was remarkably flexible, would happily reward him. Maybe for the whole summer. But there'd be no clinging to him afterward; she'd be too busy sizing up next year's crop of runners to do more than wave good-bye when he left for college in the fall.

Sex without strings. The kind he preferred.

Case nearly tripped over a root exposed by recent spring rains, and swore at his wandering thoughts.

Concentrate, idiot. Do you want to lose that race?

He really didn't.

His legs were on fire now and his lungs felt raw, but he kept pushing himself, as he always did, even picking up a little speed as he rounded the last of the wicked hairpin curves.

This time, when he tripped, he went sprawling.

He tried to land on his shoulder and roll, to do as little damage as possible, but the trail was so uneven that instead of rolling he slammed into the hard ground with a grunt, the wind knocked out of him, and a jolt of pain told him he'd probably jammed or torn something.

It took him a few minutes of panting and holding his shoulder gingerly before he felt able to sit up. And it was only then that he saw what had tripped him.

An arm.

Incredulous, he stared at a hand that appeared to belong to a man, a hand that was surprisingly clean and unmarked, long fingers seemingly relaxed. His gaze tracked across a forearm that was likewise uninjured, and then—

And then Case Edgerton began to scream like a little girl.

"You can see why I called you in." Sheriff Desmond Duncan's voice was not—quite—defensive. "Since this is outside the town limits of Serenade, it falls into my jurisdiction. And I'm not ashamed to admit it's beyond anything the Pageant County Sheriff's Department has ever handled." He paused, then repeated, "*Ever.*"

"I'm not surprised," she replied somewhat absently.

His training and experience told Des Duncan to shut up and let her concentrate on the scene, but his curiosity was stronger. He hadn't known what to expect when he had contacted the FBI, never having done so before; maybe any agent would have surprised him. This one definitely did.

She was drop-dead gorgeous, for one thing, with a centerfold body and the face of an exotic angel. And she possessed the most vivid blue eyes Duncan had ever seen in his life. With all that, she appeared remarkably casual and unaware of the effect she was having on just about every man within eyesight of her. She was in faded jeans and a loose pullover sweater, and her boots were both serviceable and worn. Her long gleaming black hair was pulled back into a low ponytail at the nape of her neck.

She had done everything short of take a mud bath to downplay her looks, and Des still had to fight a tendency to stutter a bit when speaking to her. He wasn't even sure she had shown him a badge.

And he was nearly sixty, for Christ's sake.

Wary of asking the wrong question or asking one the wrong way, he said tentatively, "I'm grateful to turn this over to more experienced hands, believe me. I naturally called the State Bureau of Investigation first, but . . . Well, once they heard me out, they suggested I call in your office. Yours specifically, not just the FBI. Sort of surprised me, to be honest. That they suggested right off the bat I should call you folks. But it sounded like a good idea to me, so I did. Didn't really expect so many feds to respond, and I sure as hell didn't expect it to be so fast. I sent in the request less than five hours ago."

"We were in the area," she said. "Near enough. Just over the mountains in North Carolina."

"Another case?"

"Ongoing, though at the moment mostly inactive."

Duncan nodded even though she wasn't looking at him. She was on one knee a couple of feet from the body—what was left of the body—her gaze fixed unwaveringly on it.

He wondered what she saw. Because, word had it, the agents of the FBI's elite Special Crimes Unit saw a lot more than most cops.

What Duncan saw was plain enough, if incredibly bizarre, and he had to force himself to look again.

The body lay sprawled beside what was, among the high-school track team and some of the hardier souls in town, a popular hiking and running trail. It was a wickedly difficult path to walk at a brisk pace, let alone run, which made it an excellent training course if you knew what you were doing—and potentially deadly if you didn't.

There were numerous cases of sprains, strains, and broken bones in this area all year round, but especially after the spring rains.

Still, Duncan didn't have to be an M.E. or even a doctor to know that a fall while running or walking hadn't done this. Not this.

The dense undergrowth of this part of the forest had done a fair job of concealing most of the body; Duncan's deputies had been forced hours before to carefully clear away bushes and vines just to have access to the remains.

Which made it a damned good thing that this was obviously a dump site rather than a murder scene; Duncan might not have been familiar with grisly murders, but he certainly knew enough to be sure the feds would not have been happy to find their evidence disturbed.

Evidence. He wondered if there was any to speak of. His own people certainly hadn't found much. Prints were being run through IAFIS now, and if that avenue of identification turned up no name, Duncan supposed the next step would be dental records.

Because there wasn't a whole lot else to identify the poor bastard with.

His left arm lay across part of the trail, and it was eerily undamaged, even unmarked by so much as a bruise. Eerily because from the elbow on the damage was . . . extreme. Most of the flesh and muscle had been somehow stripped from the bones, leaving behind only bloody tags of sinew attached here and there. Most if not all of the internal organs were gone, including the eyes, and the scalp had been ripped from the skull.

Ripped. Jesus, what could have ripped it? What could have done this?

"Any ideas what could have done this?" Duncan asked.

"No sane ones," she replied in a matter-of-fact tone.

"So I'm not the only one imagining nightmare impossibilities?" He could hear the relief in his own voice.

She turned her head and looked at him, then rose easily from her kneeling position and stepped away from the remains to join him. "We learned a long time ago not to throw around words like 'impossible.'"

"And 'nightmare'?"

"That one too. 'There are stranger things in heaven and earth, Horatio...'" Special Agent Miranda Bishop shrugged. "The SCU was created to deal with those stranger things. We've seen a lot of them."

"So I've heard, Agent Bishop."

She smiled, and he was aware yet again of an entirely unprofessional and entirely masculine response to truly breathtaking beauty.

"Miranda, please. Otherwise it'll get confusing."

"Oh? Why is that?"

"Because," a new voice chimed in, "you're likely to hear all of us referring to Bishop, and when we do we're talking about Noah Bishop, the chief of the Special Crimes Unit."

"My husband," Miranda Bishop clarified. "Everybody calls him Bishop. So please do call me Miranda."

She waited for his nod, then turned her electric-blue-eyed gaze to the other agent. "Quentin, anything?"

"Not so you'd notice." Special Agent Quentin Hayes shook his head, then frowned and pulled a twig from his rather shaggy blond hair. "Though I've seldom searched an area with undergrowth this dense, so I can't say I couldn't have missed something."

Duncan spoke up to say, "Our county medical examiner has only had to deal with accidental deaths since he got the job, but he said he was sure this man wasn't killed here."

Miranda Bishop nodded. "Your M.E. is right. If the victim had been killed here, the ground would be soaked with blood—at the very least. This man was probably alive twenty-four hours ago, and dumped here sometime around dawn today."

Duncan didn't ask how she'd arrived at that conclusion; his M.E. had made the same guesstimate.

"No signs of a struggle," Quentin added. "And unless this guy was drugged or otherwise unconscious or dead, I would imagine he struggled."

With a grimace, Duncan said, "Personally, I'm hoping he was already dead when...that...was done to him."

"We're all hoping the same thing," Quentin assured him. "In the meantime, knowing who the victim was would at least give us a place to start. Any word on the prints your people took?"

"When I checked in an hour ago, no. I'll go back to my Jeep and check again; like I told you, cell service is lousy up here, and our portable radios are next to useless. We have to use a specially designed booster antenna on our police vehicles to get any kind of signal at all, and even that tends to be spotty."

"Appreciate it, Sheriff." Quentin watched the older man cautiously make his way down the steep trail toward the road and their cars, then turned his head and looked at Miranda with lifted brows.

"I don't know," she said.

Quentin lowered his voice even though the nearest sheriff's deputies were yards away. "The M.O. is close. Torture on the inhuman side of brutal."

She slid her hands into the front pockets of her jeans and frowned. "Yeah, but this...this is beyond anything we've seen so far."

"From this killer, at least," Quentin muttered.

Miranda nodded. "I'm not seeing a purpose for what was done here. Whether he was dead at the beginning is still arguable, but this man was most definitely dead a long time before his killer was finished with him, so why keep going if it was torture?"

"For the fun of it?"

"Christ, I hope not."

"You and me both. Am I the only one having a very bad feeling about this one?"

"I wish you were. But I think we've all picked up on something unnatural here, and at the other dump sites. For one thing, I have no idea what means this killer used to strip the body literally to the bone."

Quentin glanced toward the remains. "I didn't spot any obvious tool marks on the bones. Or claw or tooth marks, for that matter. You?"

"No. Or any visible signs that chemicals were used, though forensics will tell us that for certain."

"We ship the body—or what's left of it—to the state medical examiner?"

"We do. Duncan already okayed it; he's been very frank about the state of technology in this area."

"As in the fact that there *is* no technology? I mean, we've been to some pretty out-of-the-way places, but this is what I'd call seriously remote. How many people you figure the town of Serenade can boast? A few hundred at best?"

"Nearly three thousand, if you count those living outside the town limits but still using Serenade as their mailing address." She saw Quentin's brows go up again, and explained, "I checked when we were flying in."

"Uh-huh. And did you happen to notice that the one motel we passed looks an awful lot like the sort that would have Norman Bates behind the desk?"

"I noticed. Though I thought of it as your typical No-Tell Motel." Miranda shrugged. "And we both know it may not matter. If this victim fits the pattern, then where he was found is only a small piece of the puzzle. In which case we won't be staying here long."

"I wouldn't be too sure about that."

She looked at him, her own brows rising.

"Hunch," he explained. "We're only about thirty miles away from The Lodge, as the crow flies, and there was a lot of unnatural going on there for a very long time."

"You and Diana put that to rest," Miranda reminded him.

"Well, we—she, mostly—put part of it to rest. Hopefully the worst part. But that doesn't mean we got it all."

"It's been a year," she reminded him.

"Yeah, to the month. Hell, almost to the day. Which I'm finding more than a bit unsettling."

Miranda Bishop was not in the habit of discounting either a hunch or an uneasy feeling expressed by someone around her, especially a fellow team member, and she didn't start now. "Okay. But, so far, nothing leads us in the direction of The Lodge. No connection to the place, or to anyone there, not that we've found."

"I know. Wish I could say that reassured me, but it doesn't."

"Do you want to drive over to The Lodge, take a look around?"

"If anybody goes, it should be someone with a fresh eye and no baggage," Quentin answered, so promptly that she knew the question had been on his mind for a while. "And probably a medium, given the age and... nature of the place."

"You know very well we only have two available. Diana shouldn't go because of all the baggage, and I'd rather keep Hollis close."

Quentin eyed her. "Why?"

Miranda's frown had returned, but this time she appeared to be gazing into the distance at nothing. Or at something only she could see. And it was a long moment before she replied. "Because her abilities are... evolving. Because every case seems to bring a new ability and ramp up the power on an existing one. And that's faster than we've *ever* known psychic abilities to evolve. It's unprecedented."

"She's been in some unusually intense situations these last months," Quentin said slowly. "From the beginning, really. Hell, the trigger that made her go active was about as extreme and intense as anything *I've* ever heard of."

"Yes, she's clearly a survivor," Miranda said.

"But?"

"I don't know that there is a but. Except that the tolerances of the human brain are likely to be higher than those of the human mind."

Quentin worked that out. "You mean she may not be adjusting to all this quite as easily as she appears to be. Emotionally. Psychologically."

"That's exactly what I mean. So I'd rather keep her close for now. So far, every one of these dump sites has been just that, with no evidence that the killer remained behind in the area. At every site so far, we've collected evidence, asked a few questions and explored a few dead ends, then moved on."

"So... less intensity to trigger something new in Hollis?"

"That," Miranda said, "would be the theory. It isn't something we can keep up indefinitely, for obvious reasons. But short of ordering her to take a sabbatical, which would not go over well at all, it's the best temporary solution we've been able to come up with."

"You and Bishop?"

Miranda nodded. "It doesn't fix the problem—assuming the pace of Hollis's development as a psychic *is* a problem—but we're hoping it'll at least offer her a little breathing space. More time to adjust to what's been happening to her, to work on her investigative skills rather than her psychic ones."

"Okay." Quentin looked around, suddenly and obviously uneasy. "Great theory. But I'm beginning to think this creepy but calm investigation of ours might be turning into something else. Like one of the more intense ones. Because they should be back by now, shouldn't they?"